PUFFIN

THE S👁UL HUNTERS

Praise for the Young Samurai series:

Great Britain Sasakawa Award 2008 – Winner
Fighting Spirit Awards 2008 – Winner
Red House Children's Book Award 2009 – Shortlist

'Fierce fiction . . . captivating for young readers'
Daily Telegraph

'An adventure novel to rank among the genre's best.
This book earns the literary equivalent of a black belt'
Publishers Weekly

Praise for the Bodyguard series:

Brilliant Book Award 2014 – Winner
Hampshire Book Award 2014 – Winner

'Bone-crunching action adventure'
Financial Times

'Bradford has combined Jack Bauer, James Bond, and
Alex Rider to bring us the action-packed thriller'

THE SOUL HUNTERS

CHRIS **BRADFORD**

PUFFIN

PUFFIN BOOKS

UK | USA | Canada | Ireland | Australia
India | New Zealand | South Africa

Puffin Books is part of the Penguin Random House group of companies
whose addresses can be found at global.penguinrandomhouse.com.

www.penguin.co.uk   www.puffin.co.uk   www.ladybird.co.uk

First published 2021

001

Text copyright © Chris Bradford, 2021

Cover illustration by Paul Young, 2021
Cover images © Shutterstock, 2021

The moral right of the author and illustrator has been asserted

Set in 10.5/15.5 pt Sabon LT Std
Typeset by Jouve (UK), Milton Keynes
Printed and bound in Great Britain by Clays Ltd, Elcograf S.p.A.

The authorized representative in the EEA is Penguin Random House Ireland,
Morrison Chambers, 32 Nassau Street, Dublin D02 YH68

A CIP catalogue record for this book is available from the British Library

ISBN: 978–0–241–32670–1

All correspondence to:
Puffin Books
Penguin Random House Children's
One Embassy Gardens, 8 Viaduct Gardens
London SW11 7BW

For Mary –
A dear friend and old soul.
Thank you for your healing.

O

Mesoamerica (Guatemala), 2500 BC

'In honour of Ra-Ka, Lord of the Underworld, Fire of the Earth,' bellowed the High Priest, 'we make this sacrifice!'

Clenched in the High Priest's fist the human heart pulsed, its dying throbs seeming to beat in time with the ceremonial drums that thundered atop the stone pyramid. Rising above this temple, a huge volcano rumbled and spat lava. Streaks of molten red rock ran like veins down its blackened slopes and into the steaming jungle below.

As the High Priest offered up the heart to the fiery peak, a huge cheer erupted from the people gathered in the plaza at the foot of the pyramid. The volcano answered with another ominous rumble. Then the drums ceased and the crowd fell silent.

With great care, he laid the heart in a wooden bowl and set it down before an immense statue of a godhead with cat-like eyes and a snarling fanged mouth. The High Priest himself wore the skull and mottled pelt of a jaguar. His red-painted face protruded through the skull's open jaws, framing his sharp features with even sharper teeth: a nose bladed like a battleaxe, high jutting cheekbones and narrow eyes as hard and black as obsidian rock. In the flickering light of the fires, the High Priest appeared as fearsome as the gods the Tletl people honoured.

The Priest approached the stone altar where the victim's body still lay: a young boy, no more than fourteen, his sightless eyes wide with a terror and pain he no longer suffered. With a curt nod, the High Priest commanded his acolytes to complete the sacrificial ceremony.

Two bare-chested men, their muscles oiled and bulging, drew back a stone slab in the temple's uppermost platform and wreaths of sulphurous steam billowed into the darkening sky. Four jaguar-masked acolytes lifted the boy's limp body from the altar and carried it over to the opening. Once more the drummers struck up a heavy beat and the people in the plaza began dancing frenetically to the pounding rhythm.

'Ra-Ka!' called the High Priest. 'To you we offer this boy's heart, body and soul in sacrifice! Consume them with your fire!'

To another almighty cheer from the crowd, the body was tossed into the pool of lava bubbling far below. Flesh and bone were incinerated in an instant. The High Priest raised his blood-soaked hands in tribute, while the drumming rose to a crescendo before suddenly ceasing –

All was deathly silent. Then the earth began to tremble. Barely noticeable at first, it grew from a tremor into a shuddering quake.

The trees shook . . .

The birds took flight . . .

Huts began to collapse . . .

Stone walls caved in . . .

And down in the plaza the ground *cracked* open like a dry riverbed, fissures snaking their way between the feet of the panicking worshippers.

Growling deep in its throat, the volcano exploded, spewing forth balls of flaming magma and hot clouds of black ash. Shocked by the wrath of their god, the people in the plaza wailed in terror. But the High Priest was unmoved. He stood before them, fearless and formidable.

'Now for the *main* sacrifice!' he declared as the earthquake receded. 'This pure offering will appease our Fire god and bring about a new dawn.'

With a scythe-like smile, the High Priest turned to a young girl. Barely into womanhood, she possessed long curling locks of jet-black hair, an unblemished golden-brown face, and large round eyes that shone like stars. Held firmly by four acolytes, whose skulls were gruesomely elongated, the girl struggled to escape their grip as they dragged her, kicking and screaming, towards the altar. The drums had resumed their thundering rhythm and the crowd took up a ritual chant.

'*RA – KA! RA – KA! RA – KA!*'

The girl, having been lifted on to the altar, felt the cold hard stone press against her bare back. She felt too the slick warm wetness of the previous victim's blood. Terror now silenced her screams and her strength sapped away as each limb was pinned down by the four masked men.

The dark, seemingly soulless eyes of the High Priest fixed upon her, his gaze harbouring such hatred and evil that any last vestiges of hope she might have held were extinguished. Grinning cruelly, he stood over her, brandishing an ornate jade knife in his hand, its hilt carved with the icon of a were-jaguar. Only moments before, the girl had seen that very blade butcher her friend. She'd been forced to watch in sickened horror as the High Priest had reached inside the victim's body and ripped the still-beating heart from his chest.

Now, with her own heart hammering hard, the girl knew she had to fight with all her might. She struggled in a final frantic bid to break free, but it was futile, and she felt all resistance strangely draining away as the High Priest uttered an incantation in a tongue so ancient it sounded like dark magic . . .

'Rura, rkumaa, raar ard ruhrd,
Qmourar ruq rouhk ur darchraqq,
Ghraruq urq kugr rour ararrurd . . .'

The drums pounded in her ears and the chanting from the crowd grew louder and ever more frenzied.

'RA – KA! RA – KA! RA – KA!'

Falling under the High Priest's spell, the girl became lost in a trance. Her soul seemed to separate from her body and float upwards, so she watched, as if from above, the jaguar-masked Priest raise the jade knife, still dripping with her friend's blood, up over his head.

With the blade poised to strike, the High Priest glanced towards the horizon, waiting for the exact moment when the sun set and the last rays of light on earth would be extinguished . . . *forever.*

1

London, present day

As I approach the museum, a group of teenagers gathered in the darkness stop their whispered conversation and watch me climb the steps to the front entrance. I ring the doorbell and wait. A distant pounding of drums sounds in my ears . . . *or maybe it's my heartbeat* . . .

I can sense their eyes upon me. The gang's silence is unsettling, but I daren't turn around in case I provoke them. Then the museum's doors swing open, light spills out on to the street and, showing my invitation card, I'm ushered inside.

The gang left behind and quickly forgotten, I hang up my coat and head through to a noisy foyer thronging with smartly dressed guests.

'Genna! You're here!' Mei cries. She embraces me in a hug and whispers into my ear, 'Thanks for coming. This evening was going to be such a *bore* without you!'

I blink in puzzlement. 'A *bore*?'

My gaze sweeps round the foyer, taking in the astounding array of artefacts on display: a carved Lulua tribal mask from the Congo; a shimmering bronze Greek shield embossed with the face of Medusa; a gleaming gold statue of the Buddha; a pair of samurai swords with ivory-white handles. The room is abuzz with breathless chatter as guests, reporters and photographers all crowd round the various exhibits. In one corner a DJ discreetly plays an eclectic mix of Latin, African and Asian music, adding to the lively atmosphere.

'How could this be a bore? I mean, this is just – it's truly *amazing*!' I gasp. 'Thank you *so* much for inviting me!'

Mei rolls her eyes at me and laughs. 'Jeez, no wonder my parents like you so much. If you go on like this, they'll want to swap us!'

I throw her a quizzical look. 'Aren't you interested in their exhibition *at all*?'

She shrugs indifferently. 'We've got tons of old stuff lying around the house. I see it every day. Honestly, I don't understand why everyone gets so excited about it.'

'Mei, your parents are a real-life Indiana Jones and Lara Croft!' I exclaim. 'They travel the world discovering lost treasures, and tonight they're showing their *private* collection. It's no wonder people are excited.'

'Well, *you* clearly are!' Mei remarks. 'But it's not much fun when they're away all the time.'

I wince. 'Sorry . . . I forgot how hard it is on you and your brother.'

'Don't worry,' Mei replies, putting on a smile. 'Me and Lee know we take second place to their globe-trotting. We've accepted it –'

'Genna! How wonderful to see you,' calls Mei's mother, gliding over in an elegant purple dress, a champagne glass in hand. 'So glad you could make it.'

Mei straightens at her mother's approach. Despite her lack of interest in antiquities, she's like her mother in every other way: long arrow-straight black hair, piercing tiger-brown eyes, high cheekbones and a flawless complexion.

'I wouldn't miss it for the world, Mrs Harrington,' I reply, greeting her with a smile.

'Lin, I think we've discovered our long-lost daughter!' says Mei's father, chuckling as he appears at my side, a twinkle in his eye. Tall with a broad chest and a boxer's jaw, and dressed in a smart khaki suit, he looks like the quintessential English explorer from the movies.

'See? Told you!' Mei mutters, rolling her eyes. 'Swap us in a heartbeat!'

'*Bǎobèi*, you'll *always* be our greatest treasure,' her mother says soothingly to Mei. 'Now I'm sure Genna's dying to see our latest discoveries. Do give her the *full* tour. Oh, and tell your brother that his friends don't have to wait outside.'

Answering her mother with an obedient nod, Mei leads me through to the first room where there's an astonishing collection of Middle Eastern treasures. While Mei messages her brother, I turn to the first exhibit: a four-thousand-year-old Persian vase.

'Were you just being polite to my parents?' asks Mei, glancing up from her phone. 'Or do you *really* find this stuff interesting?'

'Of course I do.' I nod sincerely, examining the delicate pattern painted in blue upon the vase's surface. 'You know I love history.'

Mei cocks her head to one side, looks at the vase and fails to be impressed. 'But it's so deadly dull. It's all in the past!'

'Doesn't feel that way to me,' I reply as I head over to a display cabinet containing an Egyptian stone tablet.

'Whatever floats your boat, I suppose,' says Mei. 'You hungry?'

I lift my gaze from the tablet's intricate hieroglyphs. 'Not really.'

'Well, *I* need something to relieve the boredom,' Mei says with a sigh, pocketing her phone. 'You knock yourself out here, while I'll get us some food from the buffet.'

Mei heads for the hospitality area just as Lee's friends enter the foyer. They make straight for the buffet too, clearly more interested in the food than the exhibition. I turn my attention back to the stone tablet and, as I lean my head against the glass of the cabinet, I once more become aware of the distant pounding of drums. The rhythm is hypnotic. At first I think it must be the DJ, then realize the sound is coming from down a hallway. Intrigued and strangely compelled at the same time, I follow the beat to a room at the far end. As soon as I enter, the drumming stops.

That's weird, I think, peering round for the source of the sound. The space is dimly lit, only the display cabinets spotlighted. Being the furthest from the foyer, the room is still empty of guests. But it's full of treasures from South

America. Curious, I peer at the first artefact, a small clay figurine of a pregnant woman. Next to this is an Aztec death mask inlaid with turquoise and mother-of-pearl, and beside that – I grimace at the sight – a shrunken mummified head! Then I notice, in a glass cabinet all of its own, a knife of pure jade. The six-inch blade is so green it almost glows.

For some reason I can't take my eyes off the knife. The hilt is carved with a bizarre icon of what looks like . . . a jaguar crossed with a man. Unbidden, my fingers reach out for the latch to the cabinet and, surprised to find it unlocked, I pull it open. At once there's a thrumming in my ears. I think it must be the noise from the foyer but, no, it's distorted, as if it's playing through a damaged speaker. I hear what sounds like a girl screaming, then the heavy beat of drums again, followed by the rumble of distant . . . *thunder?*

Still my fingers stretch out towards the knife, its curved blade like a tongue of green fire. The room around me turns hazy, unreal; the thrumming in my ears grows more intense. A sharp acrid smell like . . . *singed hair* . . . fills my nostrils. I'm about to clasp the hilt when –

'I wouldn't touch that if I were you.'

I spin round, startled. The room comes sharply back into focus and the noise from the foyer suddenly grows louder. A boy in a dark-grey Adidas hoodie and slack jeans is standing in the open doorway, watching me.

I feel guilty, like I've been caught in the act of stealing.

He sees the anxious look on my face and grins. 'Oh, don't worry. I won't tell anyone,' he says, quietly closing the door behind him and striding over to me. 'But best not to play with knives, especially ones that are priceless.'

'Priceless?'

He nods. 'That's a ceremonial knife from Guatemala. Over four thousand years old.'

I stare in amazement at the knife. It's so well preserved that it looks as if it was carved yesterday. 'What sort of ceremony was it used for?' I ask.

'Human sacrifice.'

My eyes widen in shock and a chill runs through me, as if someone's just walked across my grave. Then I look at the boy and wonder if he's teasing me. 'I don't believe you.'

He shrugs. 'Believe what you want. But it's what it says there.' He points to a small information panel beside the cabinet. Then he takes a step closer. 'What's your name?'

'Genna,' I mumble and glance shyly up at him. My pulse races a little. With a flop of black hair over his hazel eyes and pale skin, he has a rough, just-got-out-of-bed look. But it's an appealing look nonetheless – and while it appears he doesn't see much sun, he clearly goes to the gym, judging by his well-toned physique.

He flashes me a smile. 'Well, Genna, I'm Damien. Best we close this display case before anyone finds out we've been having a sneaky peek, eh?'

As he reaches across to flip the latch, our bodies touch and a spark of static electricity passes between us. The air suddenly seems hot and tingling with energy. For a moment we just stare at one another, our eyes locked.

I shift on my feet, feeling awkward and slightly uncomfortable at our closeness.

'I *know* you,' he breathes.

I brush aside a loose strand of hair from my face. 'I-I don't think so,' I stammer. The room suddenly feels overly warm and thin on air.

He clasps my wrist and looks deeper into my eyes. His pupils now seem unnaturally large and ever-expanding. Like spilled ink. *Contact lenses?* Strange I didn't notice them before.

I try to pull my hand away, but his grip tightens. His voice deepens too, into a dog-like growl. 'I've been seeking you!'

'*What?*' Now I'm confused and a little frightened. The pressure on my wrist increases. '*Ow!*' I cry. 'That's hurting!'

But Damien takes no notice. He starts dragging me towards the door.

'LET ME GO!' I shout, trying to wrench myself free of his iron-like grip.

And then the door opens and Mei walks in, a plate of buffet food in her hand.

'There you are, Genna!' she says with a relieved smile. 'Honestly, I've been looking all over for you.'

The panicked expression on my face stops her in her tracks, however. She glances between me and the boy, and her smile is replaced by a scowl. 'Everything all right?'

'Yeah, of course,' says Damien, releasing my wrist. 'Was just giving Genna here a guided tour.'

Mei glares at him. 'Well, she's seen enough, thank you . . . as have I!'

'Suit yourself,' says Damien with a shrug, and he brushes past her and stalks out of the room.

I let out a shuddering sigh. My body is trembling and my mouth bone-dry.

Mei narrows her eyes at me. 'Genna? Are you –?'

'I'm fine,' I say, avoiding her curious gaze. Then, steadying myself on rubbery legs, I make my way back to the foyer, collect my coat and head for the door.

Mei runs after me, a mix of confusion and concern on her face. 'Genna! Where are you going?'

'Sorry, but . . . I-I-I don't feel well,' I say, pushing past a group of newly arriving guests and out through the main doors.

I hear Mei calling after me but I don't stop. I don't even reply. As I hurry down the road to the tube station, I risk a glance back. Damien is standing in the front window of the museum. Just staring at me.

I quicken my pace and daren't look back again.

2

On reaching the entrance to the Underground, I discover to my dismay the station is closed following an incident. A sign redirects me to a bus stop on the other side of the park. I could go round, but that would take ages and, according to the timetable, I'd miss the next ride home anyway. And all I want to be is *home*. Safe in my room.

My wrist still aches. In fact, a dark ring of a bruise is already forming. *What was up with that boy?* The way he . . . *turned*.

There's no other way to describe it. One moment he was friendly and charming. The next savage, like a wild animal. Then there was that strange experience with the jade knife – the thrumming rumble in my ears, the girl's screams and that horrible stench of burning hair. *What on earth could explain that?*

All of a sudden I've the unsettling feeling that I'm being watched. I glance nervously around, half expecting to see the boy from the museum again. The street is busy though. A group of men tumble out of a pub, shouting and swearing. A loved-up couple stroll along arm-in-arm towards a restaurant. High-pitched laughter alerts me to a party of women in cocktail dresses, trailing silver birthday balloons behind them. There's an office worker waving his arm frantically in my direction . . . but I quickly realize he's just flagging down a taxi. Nobody is taking the slightest bit of notice of me –

Then I spot a figure loitering in a darkened doorway. More shadow than anything else. But, even though I can't see their face, they seem to be staring straight at me.

My heart pounds faster. *Has Damien followed me?*

A lorry drives by, blocking my line of sight. I crane my neck to try to keep the figure in view. However, once the lorry has passed, the shadow in the doorway is gone. Now I question if I even saw the figure. Maybe it was just someone letting themselves into their flat . . .

Shrugging off the shiver running down my spine, I check the timetable once again. If I miss my bus, there won't be another for a whole hour. Against my better judgement, I turn and head into the park, following the temporary signs from the Underground. It's a lot quieter in here than on the street. But I tell myself the quicker I reach the bus stop, the quicker I get home.

The route cuts diagonally across the gloomy park. Half the lamps have been vandalized, so I'm forced into darkness between the intermittent pools of yellow light. With every step, I feel eyes upon me. My paranoia is getting out of control. Even as a young child I was aware of people watching me, and I still am. My parents tell me it's natural to be cautious of strangers, but it's not that. There are some people who stare at me a little too long, like they're trying to recall if they know me. Sometimes I believe I've seen a person before. I actually *recognize* them, even though it may be the first time I've ever met them in my life. It's a very weird kind of déjà vu.

In fact, I often experience déjà vu. The sensation is so strong at times. I remember when my parents took me to a National Trust property, a seventeenth-century country house in Berkshire. I was about eight years old at the time. We were on a guided tour and had reached the drawing room when I desperately needed to go to the toilet. My parents asked the guide, a rather prim old lady, who sniffily replied that I should have gone before the tour started since the only public toilet was back at the entrance. But I knew – on my life, I *knew* – there was a toilet behind the bookcase in the corner. The guide scowled at me through her mother-of-pearl spectacles and told me not to be so ridiculous. But I was adamant about it. Then the head curator at the house came over and explained that a long time ago there *had* been a toilet, but it had been bricked in. About a hundred and twenty years ago! My parents had both stared at me, open-mouthed and dumbstruck. I had no answer for them. Somehow I'd just *known*.

My phone pings in my pocket. I stop to glance at the screen. A message from Mei.

> G, u ok? Worried about u.
> Txt me when u get home. x

As I go to reply, I catch a flicker of movement out of the corner of my eye. My pulse quickens and I peer into the night. The glow from my phone screen has momentarily dulled my vision but I'm certain I can make out a figure standing stock-still in the middle of the park. The absolute *stillness* of it is so unnatural and disturbing that the hairs rise on the back of my neck and I let out a shuddering breath, trying to calm myself.

Pocketing my phone, I set off again down the path. It's worryingly deserted of people. *Where is everyone? Why's no one else taking the diversion?* For once I wish I was among a busy crowd. I can see the bus stop in the distance, on the far side of the children's play area, like a beacon of hope. I hurry towards it, each island of lamplight offering me a brief safe haven from the treacherous dark.

Another figure slips through the park on my left. Then I spot three more shadows. All converging on me.

Stupid, stupid, stupid, Genna! How many times have Mum and Dad warned me about taking risks? Why the hell did I take this shortcut?

Now the bus stop appears further away than ever. I begin to run. My breathing is loud and rapid, the blood pounding in my ears. As I pass the play area, a gang of hoodies materialize out of the dark and block my path. They surround and trap me in a circle.

'Where you going in such a hurry?' one of them asks, her face hidden.

'H-home,' I reply, my voice quavering.

'Not tonight, you aren't.'

Swallowing back my panic, I reach into my jacket and pull out my purse. 'Here, take it,' I say, holding it out to them. My father told me that if I was ever mugged to just give them what they want. After all, he said, money could be replaced – my life couldn't. But none of them react. They just stand there, hands in pockets, faces in shadow.

I now reach for my phone and hold that out. 'This is all I have. *Please*, just take it and leave me alone.'

'We don't want your money . . . or your phone,' says a boy.

My stomach tightens with a horrible emptiness. 'What *do* you want then?'

The boy steps into the light, revealing a pale face with eyes so dilated that they look like black holes bored into his head.

'You, Genna,' says Damien. 'We just want *you*.'

3

Sheer panic grips me as the five hoodies close in on all sides. Limbs frozen in fear, I'm unable to fight or flee. Even my voice seems to have failed me: a desperate attempt at a scream choking like a stone in my throat. My eyes dart around, looking for someone, *anyone*, to help me. But the park is desolate and deserted.

I can see the bus shelter in the near distance, people milling around, absorbed in their phones, oblivious. The noise of passing traffic and the shouts of revellers reach my ears, but they sound distant, indistinct, as if a glass wall has risen between the park and the street. I feel totally cut off.

As the circle tightens round me, a hoodie seizes my right arm, another my left. Only then do I find my voice and scream for help, praying that my cries will carry over the noise of the traffic. But a hand clamps fast across my mouth.

I struggle and kick – *No, no, no!*

More hands grab at my body. My legs are taken from under me and I'm carried into the play area. Out of the light and away from the main path, we are cloaked in darkness and hidden from view. They lay me on a picnic table, pinning me down by each limb. The horror is made worse because the gang works together in complete silence. With their features still shrouded in shadow, they loom over me like a brethren of faceless monks in cowls.

Damien approaches, a demonic grin twisting his handsome features. 'Don't worry, Genna – it'll soon be over.'

He pulls out a knife from his pocket – the jade knife from the museum! Its curved blade gleams like a shard of polished glass. All of a sudden an acrid whiff of burning taints the air and the distant pounding of drums resumes in my ears. Any remaining strength I have leaches from my body and I lie limp on the picnic table, the wood hard against my back, as I begin to weep.

Then . . . just as I'm thinking all hope is lost, one of my attackers is yanked backwards, landing on the kiddies' slide with a deafening *clang*.

The rest of the gang wheel round. Silhouetted against the night, a teenage boy in a leather biker jacket stands tall over their fallen comrade.

Damien's dark, fathomless eyes fix upon him. 'Ah, what do we have here?' he sneers. 'A have-a-go hero?'

'Let her go,' the boy orders. There's a hint of an American accent.

'Ooh, a tough guy.' Damien's tone is condescending. 'Go and be a good Samaritan somewhere else. *Get lost!*'

But the boy stands firm, his fists clenching. 'No can do.'

Damien sighs in irritation. 'You might live to regret that decision. That is, *if* you live.' And, with a jerk of his head, he sends two of his gang to take on the boy.

My arms no longer pinned, I push myself up from the picnic table.

'Uh uh,' says Damien, pointing the tip of the knife at me. 'You're going nowhere.'

The girl who's still holding me now releases her grip on my left leg and seizes me by the hair instead. She wrenches my head back and I wince in pain. With the jade knife to my throat, I can only watch as the other two advance on my would-be rescuer. The one by the slide has also now recovered and is back on his feet, itching for revenge.

With the boy outnumbered three to one, I realize he stands no chance. But, as they approach him, he shifts into what looks like a martial arts stance – feet slightly apart, hands raised – and a tiny spark of hope re-ignites in me.

The three hoodies attack simultaneously. The boy ducks the first punch thrown at him and counters with a strike so fast I barely see it. His fist connects with the chin of the nearest assailant and sends him reeling like a concussed boxer.

The next hoodie lashes out with a brutal kick to the leg, but the boy blocks it with his shin, then drives forward, grabbing his attacker by the arm and throwing her over his shoulder. She lands with a bone-shattering *thud* on the tarmac, all the breath knocked out of her.

The third thug – the stockiest of the lot – charges into the boy like a battering ram. My rescuer is thrown backwards and the two of them crash on to a graffiti-daubed roundabout, sending it spinning. The roundabout creaks and groans as the hoodie thumps the boy with hammer-like fists and the boy fends off the blows the best he can. A spray of blood splatters the roundabout's metal decking.

'Stop! STOP!' I cry but I know my pleas are in vain. The brute just hits him harder until I hear a sickening *crunch* and there's more blood. I wince at the sight ... before realizing this isn't the *boy's* blood.

It's the thug's nose that's been broken by a power strike with the palm to his face. With a muffled howl, he tumbles off the roundabout, the spinning bars colliding with his head and knocking him out cold.

Damien spits in disgust at his gang's failure. He glares at the tall girl still holding me. 'End it!' he orders as my rescuer rises back to his feet.

While Damien keeps the knife to my throat, she strides over to join the fight. The first two casualties, now back in the fray, are lunging at my rescuer like a pair of attack dogs. The boy is so focused on fending them off that he doesn't see the girl coming up behind – nor the weapon in her hand.

'Watch out!' I shout. But I'm too late.

She hits him across the back of the head with a length of steel pipe, and the boy crumples to his knees. The other two begin kicking him like he's a football.

Damien laughs cruelly. 'Oh yes, from hero to zero!'

His sadistic glee at my rescuer's downfall sends a surge of anger through me. With Damien's attention on the fight, I lash out with my foot and catch him hard in the groin. He doubles over, clutching himself in agony. I roll off the picnic table and scramble away. Disorientated and my legs weak from shock, I stagger across the playground, seeking a way out.

Damien roars in fury and gives chase.

I weave between the bars of a huge climbing frame in an attempt to lose him in the dark. I realize I'll never be able to outrun my tormentor so, as I pass a playhouse, I duck inside. Traumatized and scared out of my wits, I crouch in the corner, drawing my legs up and wrapping my arms round them, trying to make myself as small as possible.

Outside a blade scrapes eerily along the metalwork of the climbing frame.

'No use hiding, Genna,' Damien snarls. 'Now I've seen into your soul, you can't hide from me any longer.'

Seen into my soul? *He's demented!* His ravings terrify me even more.

The sound of the knife draws closer and closer, now screeching like a tortured cat. It passes right by the door to the playhouse . . . and moves on, heading further and further away from me.

I huddle, trembling in the darkness, not daring to breathe. The furious scuffle of the fight is still going on. I want to cry. I *should've* helped the boy. Instead I ran and hid. Shame burns in me. The boy tried to save me and now –

Damien's face appears suddenly through the window like a horrifying black-eyed jack-in-the-box.

'Found you!' he trills in a sing-song voice as if we're playing a fun game of hide-and-seek.

I let out a scream and shrink away from his clawing hands. He catches hold of my jacket. I wriggle and squirm.

My jacket rips as I manage to yank myself free and bolt from the playhouse. But in my panic and confusion I run straight into the netting of the climbing frame. For a moment I'm entangled, trapped like a fly in a spider's web. I turn to run the other way . . . only to discover Damien blocking my escape.

'Oh, Genna, you're not making this easy for me,' he snaps, striding over with the jade knife in his hand.

I'm out of options. My back is against the netting, I've nowhere left to run. *Except up.* I turn to climb the net when a flash of black leather flies past. Damien is slammed against the playhouse. My mystery rescuer elbows him in the face and wrestles him for control of the knife. As they battle one another, the vicious shard of jade stone gleams in the darkness. The blade cuts across my rescuer's left forearm, slicing straight through his leather sleeve. Blood runs freely from the wound, but he refuses to let go of Damien.

'Run, Genna! RUN!' yells the boy.

Without a second thought, I flee the play area. Passing the prone bodies of the gang, I'm too panicked to question how the boy managed to defeat them all . . . *or even how he knows my name!*

Sprinting across the grass and back on to the path, I reach the first lamp that works. Only then do I stop and look back. Against the climbing frame two silhouettes are still locked in hand-to-hand combat, the lethal jade knife flicking like a serpent's tongue between them.

Spotting me lingering under the lamp, the boy cries out again, 'Run, Genna! *Run for your life!*'

In the playground one of the hoodies is slowly rising back to their feet and heading my way. I don't hang about any longer. Dashing down the path, I reach the park gate and burst out on to the busy street. The number 37 bus is pulling up at the stop. *My* bus. I fling myself across the road. There's a screech of tyres, the angry blare of a car horn. But I daren't stop. The doors to the bus are closing as I leap on board. The driver glowers at me. I must look a right state – jacket torn, hair in a mess, eyes wild. But no doubt he's used to seeing far worse on the night shift so he doesn't ask, just mutters, 'Ticket?'

Dismayed by his lack of concern, I fumble for my bus pass, fingers shaking so badly I can hardly hold the darn thing. The driver waves me irritably on board, seemingly more worried about his schedule than whatever trouble I'm in. Likewise, the other passengers are keen to keep their distance, either ignoring me or suddenly transfixed by their phones. Finding an empty seat at the back, I slump against the worn springs and peer nervously through the rear window. Seen from the bright interior of the bus, the park outside is an impenetrable curtain of night.

I can't see the play area. I can't see the hoodies. And I can't see the boy who saved me.

4

'Have you reported it to the police?' asks Mei, as we sit together on a bench during school break with our friends Anna and Prisha. Around us our classmates are chatting freely, playing football on the field, snacking on crisps and fizzy drinks, or generally just being happy to be out of lessons. I feel oddly disconnected from it all – everyone else's carefree behaviour and untroubled laughter today seem alien to me.

I shake my head. 'No. I haven't even told my parents,' I admit. All weekend I struggled over whether or not to tell them. Apart from not wanting to worry them, I felt ashamed by the incident, that I'd been foolish enough to take a shortcut in the dark, and I was still fearful and confused about the gang leader saying he knew me.

'But you were *assaulted*!' Anna exclaims, her freckled cheeks reddening in outrage to the colour of her auburn hair. 'That's a crime! You've got to tell someone.'

'What good would it do?' I say. 'There weren't any witnesses. Who'd believe me?'

'*We* believe you, and that's enough,' says Prisha. Her slim eyebrows crease either side of her bindi. 'And what about the boy?'

I suddenly experience a crushing guilt and bury my nails into the back of my hand, almost drawing blood. The whole weekend I've been torturing myself about his fate. The boy had been badly beaten, his arm cut. Yet his only concern had been for *my* safety. And all I did was . . . *run*.

'I-I don't know if he's even alive,' I stammer.

Seeing tears well up in my eyes, Mei takes my hand and gives it a reassuring squeeze. 'I'm sure he's fine. You said yourself, there was nothing in the news or on the internet, so he can't have been too seriously hurt.'

'And it sounds like he could handle himself,' adds Anna.

I nod, recalling how the boy had taken on three attackers at once. He was either incredibly brave or utterly reckless.

Prisha offers me a tentative smile. 'It's kinda cool to have your own guardian angel, don't you think?'

Wiping away the tears, I sniff. 'Yeah,' I say, 'it is. If it wasn't for him . . . well . . . I'd hate to think what would've happened.' I choke back a sob. 'I just want to know he's all right. Get a chance to thank him for saving me.'

'Well, perhaps we can find him so that you can,' Mei suggests, handing me a tissue. 'What did he look like, this guardian angel of yours?'

I frown. 'I-I don't know,' I say, trying hard to remember.

'What do you mean, you don't know?' says Anna.

'It was dark . . . I was in a panic . . . I didn't get a good look at his face,' I explain, scrunching up the tissue in my trembling fingers. Suddenly a bloodstained roundabout flashes across my mind, cruel laughter echoes in my head, and a boy with black sockets for eyes leers at me. I shudder at the memory. 'But I'll *never* forget the gang leader's face,' I whisper, more to myself than to my friends.

'Any idea who *he* was?' Mei demands.

I look at her, half scared, half livid. 'Yeah, as it happens. The boy from the museum . . . Damien.'

Instantly Mei's soft features harden into granite. 'That creepy guy who grabbed your arm? That's it! I'm calling my brother.'

'*What?*' I cry. 'Don't do that!'

But Mei ignores my plea. She jumps up from the bench and pulls her phone from her pocket. 'My brother will know where this *Damien* lives,' she says, almost spitting out the boy's name. 'We can put the police on to him.'

'But what if they come after me first?' I say. 'Damien and his gang.' I'm scared they'll hound me. Hurt me. *Kill* me even.

'No, Genna,' Mei says firmly. 'We've got to report this.' And she continues to walk away, fierce and determined, and starts talking rapidly into her phone.

Prisha puts her arm round my shoulders. 'It's the right thing to do, Gen,' she assures me quietly. 'If we don't report this boy, he'll attack someone else. And they might not be so lucky as you to have a guardian angel.'

I nod numbly, seeing the sense in it, but still worried about the potential fallout. I know my friends are only looking out for me, but there is something deeply disturbing about the black-eyed boy. Something *evil*. Unrelenting. I mean, who steals a four-thousand-year-old jade knife just to mug someone? Who in their right mind pins you by all four limbs to a table and tortures you? I've no idea what he wants with me, but I've a feeling he'd stop at nothing to –

Mei is back beside the bench, a deep frown etching her brow.

'What is it?' I ask hesitantly.

'Lee says he doesn't know anyone called Damien.'

After school, I find Mei and Prisha waiting for me at the gates.

'You're going to miss your bus,' I say, noticing the last students boarding.

Mei studies me with concern. 'Are you sure you're OK to walk home alone? Shall we walk with you?'

'I'm not in kindergarten any more!' I reply. My tone is a little sharper than intended and Mei looks injured.

Prisha reaches out and gently touches my arm. 'You know that's not what we mean.'

'Sorry,' I mumble, offering Mei an apologetic smile. 'I'm still a bit tense, that's all. But I'll be fine. There's lots of people around, it's daylight and I haven't got that far to go.'

'Well . . . if you're absolutely certain,' says Mei, giving me a hug and reluctantly letting me go.

Mei and Prisha wave goodbye and step on to their bus. I watch it depart, then immediately wish I'd taken them up on their offer. As I walk along the main road in the opposite direction, my bravado soon gives way to unease and I can't help but glance over my shoulder every few paces.

Cars whizz by, the road heavy with traffic. The pavements are crowded with pedestrians, school students and shoppers. But no one appears to be following me, or even watching me. I shake my head, laughing at my own paranoia. The fact that Lee doesn't know who Damien is suggests that the boy just wandered in off the street and gatecrashed the exhibition. This means the attack was random, so the likelihood of it happening again is low. At least that's what I tell myself. The alternative – that I was targeted – doesn't bear thinking about.

Carrying on down the road, I try to put the attack to the back of my mind. I focus instead on the history test I've got coming up.

It's only when I turn on to the high street that I become aware of a figure keeping pace with me on the opposite side of the road. A deep instinct warns me not to stare directly at them – not to give it away that I *know* I'm being followed. So I stop outside a boutique and pretend to browse the clothes on display when really I'm focusing on the reflection in the shop window. Pedestrians flow by in either direction, streaming past like fish in a river. At first no one particularly stands out. Then I glimpse a tall boy loitering beside a bus stop, a blue baseball cap pulled low over his face. A bus turns up but he doesn't get on board.

My heart begins to pound. *Is it Damien? Or one of his gang?*

Forcing myself not to run, I head down the road then turn right into a busy street market. My plan is first to find out if I really am being followed, then, if I am, to lose my stalker among the crowd.

29

'Two punnets a pound!' a trader bellows as I pass close to his fruit stall. Another yells, 'Jeans for a tenner! Only a tenner a pair!'

Pushing through the throng of shoppers, I try to keep low and out of sight. Once I'm in the thick of the crowd, I glance back and catch a glimpse of a blue baseball cap bobbing in my direction.

I was right! I *am* being followed. My mouth goes dry, my breathing rapid, my heart pounds even harder, and I feel the sharp edge of panic rise up in me.

Quickly I dart into a narrow gap between two market stalls and crouch low. From behind the blue-and-white striped tarpaulin I watch the shifting crowd and wait.

After a few seconds the boy in the baseball cap dashes past, clearly agitated. He fails to spot me and carries on down the road. I soon lose sight of his cap amid the throng. Letting out a sigh of relief, I decide to wait another minute or so before doubling back on myself and heading home along a different route.

As I linger in the shadow of the stall, I feel a small tug on my elbow and almost jump out of my skin. Whirling round, I'm confronted by a greasy bearded man wearing a bobble hat and an old duffel coat. His breath stinks of stale cigarettes and his bony fingers constantly scratch at his scabbed neck.

'Spare some change, luv?' he mutters in a heavy south London accent.

When I don't respond – only stare back at him mutely in shock – he adds for clarification, 'For a cuppa tea, luv.'

And he gives me what I assume is his most ingratiating smile: a gap-toothed, red-gummed, tobacco-stained leer.

Pulling myself together, I search hurriedly in my coat pocket for some change. I'm anxious to get rid of him so he doesn't draw attention to me. As I drop the coins into his open palm, he clasps my hand in gratitude and gives me a wink.

'Ah, bless ya, darlin' –'

Then his face goes slack and his eyes seem to lose focus. His hands begin to tremble and, for a moment, I think he's about to have a seizure. But then a sharp clarity re-enters his darkening gaze and his bony fingers clamp round my wrist like talons.

'*C'est elle! C'est elle!*' he shouts in a high, raspy voice, raising up my arm for everyone to see. '*Elle doit être tuée, au nom de la Révolution! Liberté, égalité, fraternité! Vive la Nation! Vive la République! À la guillotine! À la guillotine!*'

His ravings go on and people begin to stare at us. He's waving my arm around, blabbering loudly in a cascade of fluent French. More people turn in our direction. If this continues much longer, my stalker is bound to notice the scene and discover me.

Twisting my arm free from the man's steely grasp, I dash back through the market. In my haste I knock over a box of apples and the fruit tumbles across the ground. I stumble, regain my balance and keep running, even as the stall owner shouts abuse after me.

Behind me, the tramp raves on, his fist in the air. '*À la guillotine! À la guillotine!*'

5

'Everything all right at school?' my mum asks as I push my food round my dinner plate. She sits opposite me at the dining table, sipping from a glass of water, her pale-blue eyes upon me, her Nordic blond hair done up in a bun.

'Yeah ... fine,' I murmur, lost in my thoughts. The strange tramp in the market freaked me out even more than the boy in the baseball cap. The way he ... *turned*. Not just in his manner, but his voice as well. He'd sounded like a totally different person. Acted like one too. And his French seemed so fluent and natural. I suppose it's possible he might be French or have lived in France at some point. You can't judge by appearances, but his accent at first was most definitely south London. Whatever his situation, the poor man seemed to be struggling with some sort of mental health problem in order to switch personalities like that ... Either that or he was a very good actor!

'You've been awfully quiet since seeing Mei on Saturday,' my mum says, pressing the matter. She puts down her glass and rests her hand gently on top of mine. 'You two haven't had a falling out, have you?'

'No, we're good,' I reply, but I still can't meet her eye. I don't want her to see how upset and shaken I am. As lovely as my parents are, I'm not quite ready to open up to them about what's happened. They'll only overreact and have more questions than I have answers for. To be honest, I've no idea what's going on myself. I'm confused and scared – to the point that I'm starting to doubt my own judgement. I now question if the boy in the baseball cap was following me at all. As for the tramp, perhaps it was *me* that was having a panic attack? A post-traumatic episode caused by the gang assault. Yet that still doesn't explain my strange experience with the jade knife . . . I'm beginning to wonder if I'm actually losing it.

'Is someone bullying you?' asks my dad, always direct and to the point. His nostrils flare and a concerned frown wrinkles his otherwise smooth brown brow. He stabs at a piece of chicken, but waits for my answer before putting it in his mouth.

I shake my head and nudge another pea to the edge of the plate.

'Boy trouble then?'

'No, Dad!' I exclaim, my fork clattering on to the plate. I realize he means 'romance' but his phrasing is too close to the bone. With no appetite, I push my plate away. 'Can I be excused?'

Mum's jaw drops. 'But, darling, you've hardly eaten anything!' Then, putting a hand to my forehead, she asks, 'Are you coming down with something?'

My chair scrapes on the wooden floor as I stand. 'I'm fine. I've a lot of studying to do, that's all. History test next week.'

'Of course,' says Dad, waving softly to my mum to ease off. 'You must be under a lot of pressure at school. You go up. Just let us know if you need anything.'

Forcing out a cheery smile for Mum's benefit and kissing Dad on the cheek, I head out of the dining room and into the hall. As I climb the stairs, I can hear them talking.

'Something's *definitely* wrong,' she's saying. 'She's so withdrawn. It's not like her at all.'

'It's probably just teenage hormones,' my dad replies with a sigh. 'You know what kids are like at this age.'

I hear my mum snort. 'Steve, she looks almost grey! And her eyes are bloodshot. I can't help worrying –'

'We're her parents. That's what we're supposed to do: worry. Listen, let's see how she is in the morning, after she's had a good night's sleep. It might only be a twenty-four-hour virus. But if there's a bigger problem, we'll sort it out. Together.'

A bittersweet smile crosses my lips. Dad is always the problem-solver in our family. Ever willing to listen and try to make things better. But I question whether my particular problem has an easy solution.

I cross the landing to my bedroom, close the door and slump down at my desk. My room is my sanctuary. My white metal-framed bed is tucked into one corner, piled high with cushions propping up Coco, my old fluffy bunny I can't bear to throw out. Above the bedhead, my corkboard displays postcards from various family holidays as well as posters and magazine cut-outs of my current favourite boy band, The Rushes. On the opposite wall is my bookcase, one whole shelf devoted to historical novels, and above that a handful of school certificates for academic achievement and, pride of place in the centre, a gold trophy for gymnastics. To the left of the bookcase, the large sash window overlooks a row of gardens backing on to more houses, the suburban view framed by fairy lights and my fuchsia-coloured curtains.

Safe in my haven, my encounter with the tramp fades like a bad dream. Even the gang assault begins to feel more distant, as if it happened to someone else. But my underlying sense of unease doesn't diminish. To keep my mind occupied, I pull out my schoolbooks from my bag. Maths homework can wait. So too can geography. Selecting my history textbook, I flip to the bookmarked page. By a strange coincidence, the forthcoming test covers the French Revolution. Powering up my laptop so that I can make notes, I begin reading:

The Reign of Terror (5 September 1793–28 July 1794), also known as *La Terreur*, was a period of violence that occurred after the onset of the French Revolution. It was sparked by the conflict between two rival political factions – the Girondins and the Jacobins . . .

I tap in the dates and the two political groups. History isn't a chore for me. In fact, I rather enjoy it. Unlike some in my class who find the subject dull and boring, history is very much alive for me. Some periods in particular feel fresh, like the Tudor period or the Second World War. I'm able to remember the facts almost as if they were yesterday. And, if I concentrate hard, I can almost transport myself back to those times, envisaging the period vividly in my mind's eye.

La Terreur was notable for its mass executions of 'enemies of the revolution'. The death toll exceeded 40,000, with 16,594 people executed by –

Thunk . . .

– guillotine, and more than 25,000 killed in summary executions across France. Virtually the whole of the French aristocracy was . . .

Thunk . . .

I glance up as yet another dull heavy *thunk* disturbs my study. Peering out of the window, I spot our neighbour Mr Jenkins in his garden, his portly frame stretching the seams of a green parka jacket that's seen better days. He's chopping a pile of wood with an axe under his apple tree. It's still only September but he likes to keep his log-store well stocked for his wood-burning stove. I return to my book; his chopping carries on its irregular but insistent rhythm in the background. *Thunk . . . thunk . . . thunk . . .*

The guillotine, nicknamed the 'National Razor', became the symbol of the revolutionary cause, and was made infamous by a string of high-profile executions: King Louis XVI and Marie Antoinette among the most notable.

Beneath the text is a reproduction of an oil painting of Marie Antoinette's execution in the Place de la Révolution on 16 October 1793. I can clearly picture the scene in my mind, as if I'm in the crowd: the former queen is in her white gown, a white shawl covering her shoulders, and a white cap with a black ribbon fastened round her temples. I sense her regal dignity as she is manhandled off the open cart to the jeers and insults of the people gathered in the square. The guards are dressed in tunics of red, white and blue, and they sneer and spit their disgust at her. As she ascends the scaffold, Marie accidentally treads on the executioner's foot and offers a courteous *'Pardonnez-moi'*. The executioner – the infamous Charles-Henri Sanson – shears off Marie's long locks of hair to ensure a quick, clean cut of his guillotine blade. The former queen kneels for an instant, utters a half-audible prayer, and is then strapped to the guillotine's wooden plank. With workmanlike efficiency, Sanson lowers the plank, slides Marie forward and secures her head in the stocks.

The crowd falls silent. The eyes of every man, woman and child are fixed upon the imminent beheading.

With a quick, sharp tug, Sanson releases the guillotine's blade . . . *Thunk!*

Marie Antoinette's head tumbles into the basket and the people cheer in joyous celebration, *'Vive la Nation! Vive la République!'*

Reaching into the basket, Sanson displays the decapitated head on a spike for the crowd to roar their approval. It's at that very moment that my wrist is grabbed. I turn in shock to be confronted by a gap-toothed leer. It's the face of the tramp! Only now he is clean-shaven and in the uniform of a guard.

'*C'est elle! C'est elle!*' he cries, raising up my arm for Sanson to see.

The executioner rounds on me, his coal-black eyes widening in a mix of disbelief and delight. Thrusting Marie's spiked head in my direction, Sanson declares, in French, 'She must be put to death, in the name of the Revolution! Liberty, equality, fraternity!'

As I'm dragged up the steps of the scaffold, the crowd take up the chant of 'To the guillotine!' *À la guillotine! À la guillotine!*

Against my will, I'm bound to the wooden plank, the leather strap cutting deep into my back. There's a clatter as the plank is lowered into place and my head is forced into the stocks. With the neck-brace secured, I can only stare into the blood-drenched wicker basket. A piercing scream rises up from my lungs but is cut short as the steel blade drops –

I wake with a jerk. The scream passing my lips turns to a whimper. A sheen of cold sweat plasters my brow. My hand instinctively goes to my throat. The nightmare was so vivid that I can almost feel the razor-sharp blade slicing through my neck.

I glance at the clock on my desk. It's gone eleven. The moon casts a silvery glow across my room and on to my bed. Coco is slumped at an odd angle, his long threadbare ears flopping to one side, giving the impression that his neck is broken.

My gaze returns to the picture of Marie Antoinette's execution. In the painting I now notice a woman in the crowd, her face unnervingly familiar. A cold shiver runs down my spine and I slam shut the textbook.

It's only my imagination, I tell myself, *just my imagination.*

Making my way unsteadily to bed, I switch off the fairy lights by my window and draw the curtains. As I do so, I glimpse a ghostly figure beneath the apple tree in my neighbour's garden. The shadow stands stock-still beside the axe, its blade buried in a large log as if it were an executioner's block.

Stifling a cry, I tug the curtains closed and dive under my bedcovers. With my eyes clamped shut and my hands clasped together, I begin to pray. I know someone is out there in the darkness. Watching my window. Watching me.

6

The next morning, in the cold light of day, the figure beneath the tree turns out to be Mr Jenkins' parka jacket left hanging from a branch. Still, in the middle of the night the sinister apparition had appeared scarily real. I now realize that my mind was playing tricks on me . . . but I can't shake the nagging doubt that there *had* been someone in the garden.

I put on my best game face for my parents – all smiles and lightness. I bound down the stairs and cheerily tuck into a hearty breakfast. This seems to allay their fears, although mine still simmer away. So I text Mei and she agrees to meet me at my house to walk to school, even though it's well out of her way.

'Thanks for coming,' I say as we head down the road together.

'Hey, that's what friends are for,' she replies, taking my arm. 'Now, what's this all about?'

I tell her everything. Well, *almost* everything. About the boy in the blue baseball cap. The tramp and his French outburst. The ghost in the garden. But I keep the guillotine nightmare to myself. I don't want Mei to think I'm going totally crazy.

Deadly serious through most of it, Mei can't help but laugh at the parka incident. 'You were spooked by a coat!'

'Yeah,' I say flatly.

She must see the terror in my eyes, because her laughter immediately dies and her grin drops away. 'That Damien and his gang really did a job on you!' She looks carefully around, checking up and down the road on both sides. Her expression becomes cold and hard. 'Well, if I see anyone in the least dodgy approaching you, they'll have *me* to deal with.'

'My own personal bodyguard,' I say, attempting a smile. But it falters on my lips and turns to an anxious tremble. I look at my friend in earnest. 'You don't think I'm imagining it all, do you?'

Mei shakes her head, but there's a slight shrug to her shoulders too. 'After what happened last weekend, I'm not surprised you're feeling jumpy. I suppose there's a chance one of the gang *could* be following you, although I think it's unlikely. How about I meet you each morning to go to school? I know it isn't on my way but I hate seeing you shaken up like this.'

'You *can't* babysit me every day,' I protest, although I'm touched by her offer and already feel better at the thought of her by my side.

'I'm sure Anna and Prisha will come along too.' She flashes me a bright reassuring smile and takes my arm. 'Us

41

girls have got to stick together in this world. Come on, otherwise we'll be late.'

We carry on down the road. At a pedestrian crossing, I glance back over my shoulder, my eyes darting nervously around, searching for the boy in the blue cap, the tramp or anyone else who might look suspicious.

'Hey, relax! That's my job!' says Mei, pulling out a pair of sunglasses from her bag and slipping them on. '*I'm* the bodyguard, remember?'

I laugh as she makes a show of securing the way ahead, then clearing a path through the people crossing the road as if I'm some major celebrity. Mei might not be the most subtle bodyguard, but she's definitely my best friend.

Over the course of the following week, Mei, Anna and Prisha take it in turns to walk with me to and from school. At first I'm constantly checking behind me. Jumping at shadows. Positive that people are staring at me. Convinced that I'm being followed. We even vary the route, just to be sure.

However, after a few uneventful days and no sightings of any potential stalkers, I settle down. I start to think I'm being silly and paranoid. But my friends assure me that it's all right. That it's better to be safe than sorry. Still I can't help but wonder if it was all in my mind. After all, I haven't had any more strange experiences, odd dreams or hallucinations. Perhaps my dad was right when he said it was just teenage hormones.

By the end of the week, it's clear no one's following me. So I suggest my bodyguard squad stand down. My friends object, but I know they've had to get up extra early just to escort me to school. I tell them I'll be perfectly OK. Mei though insists she'll meet me on Monday morning to ensure I make it to the history test. *One last mission*, as she puts it.

I'm waiting outside my front door, school bag packed, when I get a text from Mei.

> Hi G. Really sorry. Sick as a dog. Won't be in school today.
> U all right to go in on your own? x

With a wry smile curling my lips, I wonder if she's pulling a sickie to avoid the test. But I know my bestie wouldn't let me down, so she must be actually ill, for once. I text her back to say it's fine and hope she gets better soon.

Putting my phone in my bag and opening the front gate, I step out on to the pavement and immediately feel uneasy.

You're being stupid, I tell myself. Nothing has happened since my run-in with the tramp over a week ago and no one has been tailing me . . . *as far as you're aware*, pipes up a little voice in my head. I ignore it and hurry on down the road.

I keep to the busiest route. Always looking around, never letting my awareness drop. Everyone's going about their own business; a student on their way to school the least of their concerns. As I approach the high street, I snatch another quick glance over my shoulder, just to be sure, and bump straight into an elderly gentleman with a moustache and pinstriped suit.

'Oi, look where you're going, girl!' he snaps.

'Sorry,' I mumble, catching the look of disdain in his rheumy, grey-specked eyes.

As I walk off, the old man continues to glare at me. Whether out of annoyance or vague recognition, I don't know, but his gaze remains oddly fixed and I don't like it. Keeping my head down, I try to blend in with the rest of the morning commuters. At a pedestrian crossing, I look left and right to check the traffic. Then, as I go to cross the road, I spot a teenage boy in a blue baseball cap and black leather biker jacket standing directly opposite me on the other side. For a long moment we simply stare at one another.

It's *not* Damien, that's for sure. This boy's eyes are as blue as sapphires. They are striking against his olive-tan face and long waves of chestnut-brown hair. Faded bruises colour his high cheekbones and there are grazes on his knuckles from a recent fight. *One of the gang? Or perhaps –*

A white delivery van pulls up at the kerbside and blocks my view. Two men jump out of the driver's front cab. Without warning, they seize me by the arms, then the van's side door slides open and I'm flung into the cargo hold. Before I can gather my wits, the door is slammed shut and I'm plunged into darkness.

A sudden and grim horror hits me: *I'm being abducted!*

My chest tightens in panic and I claw my way blindly over to the door. Outside the muffled sound of the traffic rumbles by and I can hear people walking past. Desperately I search for the handle.

There isn't one.

I pound my fists against the sides of the van, only to find they've been lined with padding. My blows are dulled to little more than a soft thud. I cry out for help. *Someone* must have seen me being grabbed, surely? But it happened so quickly, and so many Londoners are often in too much of a hurry to notice – or even care – what's going on around them. My parents won't have a clue what's happened to me!

I fumble in the dark for my bag, looking for my phone. But there's no signal. That makes no sense – *I'm in the middle of London, for goodness' sake!* Then it dawns on me that the van's padding must be blocking my phone's reception. Realizing the lengths my abductors have gone to, I panic even more.

Outside on the street there's shouting, a scuffle, then a deafening *clang* reverberates through the cargo hold, as if something or somebody has been thrown against the van's side. More angry shouts, followed by a pained scream.

For a moment all goes quiet. Only the coursing of blood in my ears and the rasp of my fretful breathing. Then the door bursts open. Sunlight dazzles me momentarily. I blink it away. Framed by the door is the boy in the blue baseball cap. He reaches a hand out to me.

I hesitate, afraid.

'Trust me,' he says, his American accent smooth and reassuring. 'Your life with mine, *as always*.'

I'm confused by his words, but recognizing I have little other choice I clasp his outstretched hand . . .

7

I watch as if from above as the High Priest stands over my inert body, spread-eagled upon the sacrificial altar. His ceremonial jade knife held high, he waits for the sun's dying rays to finally fade from the sky. But, before he can plunge the knife into my chest, one of the masked acolytes at my side pulls an obsidian blade hidden within his robes – and thrusts its barbed tip straight into the heart of the High Priest himself.

My trance instantly broken, my soul returns to my body, and I draw a sharp intake of breath. The bitter stench of sulphurous smoke invades my nostrils and the roar of the erupting volcano once more thunders in my ears. Stung by fear and panic, I flinch away as the masked man reaches out his hand to me.

'Trust me,' he insists. 'Your life with mine, as always.'

I hesitate, confused and afraid. Although my trance may be broken, I'm still wary of this mysterious saviour. His voice is muffled by the mask yet he speaks in the tongue of the Omitl people, my clan.

'TRAITOR!' the High Priest howls as he collapses against the godhead statue. He claws at the black blade

embedded in his chest, his red-painted face contorting, not in pain but in fury.

The masked imposter locks eyes with the fearsome Priest. 'I was never one of your followers to begin with, Tanas.'

This use of his true soul name triggers a flash of recognition in the High Priest's coal-black sockets. 'YOU!' he snarls. 'I thought I'd banished you forever!'

'No, not quite "forever",' my saviour replies. He kicks out at one of the masked acolytes still holding me and sends the man tumbling down the stone steps of the pyramid. Then he rips off his own jaguar mask and once more reaches out his hand to me. 'Zianya, it's me!' he says.

My eyes widen. I instantly recognize his dark striking face with its black swirls of tribal tattoos. 'Necalli!' I gasp. Kicking my legs free of the other two captors, I embrace the young warrior who's been my friend since before I can remember.

Around us chaos reigns. The mighty volcano roars with fire and brimstone, the eruption spewing flaming balls of magma like a meteor shower into the hellish black sky. In the plaza below, the Tletl tribe are at once terrified and enraged. Fearing the wrath of their fire god, and furious that an imposter could have stolen their sacrifice, an angry mob has quickly gathered and is already storming up the pyramid.

Necalli urgently seeks a way for us to escape, but slumped against the statue Tanas now appears to defy death. Empowered by the spirit of the were-jaguar, he pulls the obsidian blade from his heart; blood as black as tar seeps from the wound. Then rising slowly back to his feet, he bellows, 'KILL THE TRAITOR!'

The two muscled guards draw their swords – the wooden shafts edged with splinters of obsidian rock, but Necalli grabs one of the torches burning around the statue of the god and drives them back with fire. As he fends off the guards, however, one of the sinister-looking acolytes with an elongated skull seizes me from behind; another snatches up the jade knife from the temple floor and, with a wide-eyed look of zealous rage, he raises the knife to strike at my heart.

'I'll complete the ritual for you, master!' he shouts, and resumes the strange incantation: 'Rura, rkumaa, raar ard ruhrd –'

I struggle, scream and spit like a wild cat. Before he can finish the chant and bury the blade in me, a lump of molten rock drops from the sky and strikes his head, the super-heated magma burning a hole straight through his deformed skull. The man shrieks and writhes at my feet as the acrid stench of singed hair fills my nostrils. The remaining acolyte, shocked at his fellow's fate, briefly loosens his grip on me – long enough for me to throw back my head and smash him in the nose. Then I turn and shove him away with all my might. He teeters on the edge of the lava pit before tumbling over the side with a high-pitched screech.

'That's for Meztli!' I cry, recalling my young friend's fate as the acolyte's scream is drowned out by the bubbling lava.

I turn to look for Necalli. The young warrior has managed to burn a guard on his sword arm, forcing him to drop his weapon. With a second well-aimed thrust of the torch, he sets the guard's loincloth alight. The muscled man squeals like a stuck pig as he tears at his flaming clothes and flees.

But the other guard is faster, and more skilled with his sword. He cuts the torch in half, leaving Necalli unarmed and defenceless. Then with a succession of vicious swings, he drives the young warrior back. Forced to the very lip of the lava pit, Necalli can retreat no further. He whirls his arms, desperately trying to keep his balance. The guard's next swipe of the sword will be sure to either take his head or send him spiralling into the pit.

Young as I am, I've been raised among a clan of Omitl warriors. I won't stand by and let my friend die. Prising the jade knife from the hand of the dead acolyte at my feet, I rush over and plunge the blade into the guard's back. He grunts in pain and drops to his knees. I kick the sword from his grasp, then grab Necalli just as he's about to lose his balance entirely.

'And I thought I was the one who was supposed to be saving you!' Necalli says, laughing in relief.

With the guard down but not out, Necalli takes my hand and we make a dash for the southern staircase . . . only to be met by the mob surging up towards us.

I stop. 'What now?' I ask.

Glancing around, Necalli's gaze falls upon a large ceremonial shield among the numerous offerings to the fire god Ra-Ka. He drags it over to the staircase and lays it down on a smooth plane of masonry, which runs either side of the steps, all the way to the plaza below.

'Climb on!' he orders.

I shoot him a look of utter disbelief at his perilous idea. But now Tanas is lurching towards us, snarling and snapping like a wounded beast. As he passes the fallen guard, he wrenches the jade knife from the man's back and charges at me. I have no choice. I leap aboard the shield, and Necalli jumps on behind me.

'Hang on tight,' he says, kicking off, as Tanas takes a swipe at us, the jade blade passing within a hair's breadth of my neck.

Using the shield as a sledge, we slide down the outer slope of the pyramid's staircase. Anyone attempting to stop our descent is knocked aside, setting off an avalanche of people on the steps. We reach the bottom at breakneck speed, crash into the plaza and are flung head over heels as the shield shatters into a hundred pieces.

'DON'T LET THEM ESCAPE!' thunders Tanas from atop the pyramid. 'She MUST be sacrificed!'

The mob turns and swarms after us. Necalli pulls me to my feet and we make for the jungle. But he is limping badly, the impact of our landing having injured his leg. The frenzied whoops and angry shouts of the worshippers chase us all the way. Arrows and blowdarts fired by the Tletl warriors zip past like whistling demonic birds, while deadly lumps of molten rock continue to shower down as if the sky itself were on fire.

Entering the dense jungle, we gain some cover but there is little light by which to see the path, the only illumination coming from the volcano's rain of fireballs. Trees are set ablaze and howler monkeys screech in terror. A thunderous boom signals the mountain itself splitting apart, and the very earth begins to shake with a fury only a god can possess.

'Is this my fault?' I cry with a fearful glance back at the raging volcano.

'It's what Tanas would want his people to believe, but no –' Necalli gasps, stumbling. He urges me on, always keeping close, a human shield.

Behind, the Tletl warriors are gaining on us. All around, the zip of their blowdarts and thud of their arrows striking tree trunks impel us onwards. Leaves and ferns whip at our faces as we dash through the dense undergrowth. By some miracle, we manage to reach the jungle's river where a dugout canoe is waiting for us.

Necalli helps me aboard. At the stern, holding the paddle, is a young girl about my age.

'Keep her safe. Keep her hidden,' Necalli tells her, pushing the vessel out into the fast-flowing waters.

'But what about you?' I ask, my heart fearful and full of anguish. 'Aren't you coming with us? To protect me?'

The jungle is now alive with Tletl warriors. Necalli responds with a bittersweet smile that is edged with pain. The river's current snatches the canoe away, but he makes no attempt to swim after us.

'In the next life,' he replies before collapsing in the water, an arrow embedded in his back.

8

A wave of nausea washes over me as the vision passes. It seemed to last eons, but can only have been seconds. My hand is still in his, the hand of the boy whose blue eyes are sparkling bright like stars. Then the light fades, and I question if I even saw the supernatural gleam.

'Come on,' he says, as he helps me out of the van.

I sway unsteadily as my feet touch the pavement. A crowd of onlookers have gathered, some filming the scene on their smartphones, others merely gawping, but none come forward to help. The two men who'd grabbed me earlier are now lying on the floor, groaning in pain; one of the men's arms is twisted at an unnatural angle.

'*You* did that?' I ask in shock. The American boy, tough as he looks, is surely no match for two fully grown men.

'We have to go,' he insists, pulling me away through the crowd as a siren sounds in the distance.

'No!' I protest, and shake myself free of his grip. 'The police are on their way.'

'Exactly. And you're not safe.'

I frown, confused. 'How can I not be safe with the police?'

At that moment the van's front cab opens and a boy in a dark grey hoodie jumps out. Raven-haired, vampire-pale and possessed with eyes as black as pitch, there's no mistaking him.

Damien.

A horrible sinking sensation swamps me. All my limbs seem to fail me and I lose the will to move. To run. To do anything but stare at my tormentor.

Damien reaches into the front pocket of his hoodie and pulls out a handgun. As he takes aim and fires, I'm yanked sideways into the shelter of a postbox and the bullet hits an office worker instead. She crumples to the ground, her take-away coffee spilling across the pavement. Screams erupt from the crowd and people scatter in panic. I stare, open-mouthed and dumbstruck, horrified at the bright burst of blood staining the woman's blouse.

'Move!' orders the boy, and he hauls me away from the mayhem. Too shocked to resist, I numbly let him push me through the crush of people. We step off the pavement and sprint down the street. Behind us, there's a *screech* of tyres, and I glance back to see the van doing a sharp U-turn. It weaves through the traffic, its driver clearly determined to catch up with us.

In my haste I bump into somebody, stumble and drop my schoolbag in the road.

'Leave it!' the boy orders as I turn back to retrieve it.

'But it has my phone in,' I protest. 'I only just got it. My parents will kill me.'

'You'll be dead anyway if you don't move,' the boy snaps, dragging me away by the arm.

Abandoning the bag, I race after him, my feet pounding on the tarmac, my breath ragged in my throat, my heart thudding in my chest. The roar of the van's engine is growing louder. The boy cuts left into the street market and we duck under a yellow-and-black NO ENTRY barrier. But the restricted access doesn't stop the van. It careers straight through, shattering the barrier to pieces.

Still the boy urges me on, zigzagging a path through the stalls and shoving people out of our way. Behind us, the van ploughs through a fish stall, sending ice and fish flying through the air in an explosion of silver and scales. Damien – or whoever is driving the van – appears intent on mowing us down, whatever the cost.

Just as we near the end of the market, a loose kerbstone trips me up and I fall to my knees. The boy helps me back on my feet . . . but it's too late: the van is almost on top of us. He wraps his arms round my head and shoulders in an attempt to protect me, and screwing my eyes shut, I brace myself for the impact. There's an ear-splitting *crunch* and I press my eyes even tighter closed . . . then I hear the smash of glass, followed by a loud thud.

Cautiously I open my eyes. The van has come to a sudden and violent stop. The windscreen has shattered where the driver has been flung through it on to the road ahead, and she is lying in a broken bloody heap on the tarmac. I see steam billowing from the van's crumpled radiator, having crashed into a solid concrete bollard.

For a moment all is eerily calm. The boy relaxes his grip on me and I gaze around at the devastation. The market looks like a bomb has hit it. Stalls are overturned or else smashed to smithereens, their goods scattered everywhere. Some people huddle in fearful groups, others wander aimlessly, or simply stand still in shock. The pained cries of the injured fill the air.

The cause of all this destruction is no more than a metre from me. The van is a complete wreck, its engine dead, radiator wheezing, the windscreen now a gaping hole . . . and its mangled white bonnet is smeared with blood.

There's a metallic *squeal* as the passenger door opens, and Damien steps out, dazed but apparently unhurt.

I let out a soft cry of anguish. Quietly but urgently, the American boy pulls me to my feet. Masked by the clouds of steam spewing from the van's radiator, he bundles me over to a nearby stall, and we duck down among the other shoppers who are sheltering behind it.

A young woman in a tank top and jogging bottoms clasps my arm and gasps, *'He's got a gun!'*

Her gaze flicks from Damien to me. Utter terror is etched on her face, her bright pink lipstick and thick purple mascara accentuating her fear. Then her expression morphs into one of real horror. Her eyes take on a wild look, savage and dark. Her lips twist into a sneer. And her grip on my arm tightens, her false nails digging deep into my flesh.

'The girl is here!' she screeches, and her voice has changed too. She suddenly sounds older as she cackles, *'Here! Here –'*

But her cries are cut short as the American boy strikes the side of her neck with his hand. Her eyes roll back in her head and she slumps to the ground, out cold. Indifferent to the other shoppers' protests, he mutters, 'Just our luck. A Watcher.'

'W-What's a watcher?' I stammer, eyeing the comatose woman fearfully.

But there's no time for him to explain. Damien has spotted us. Raising his gun, he fires off a round. The bullet zips past my head and ricochets off the stall's metal frame. Before he can take another shot, my saviour grabs my hand and drags me down a nearby alley. Damien sprints after us, silent yet swift in his pursuit.

Coming out on a main road, we dart between the traffic and dive down another lane. My lungs begin to burn and my legs stumble under me as we try to lose our pursuer among the warren of back streets.

'Keep going!' urges the boy, seeing me struggling to maintain his pace.

We switch left down a busy street and pass a bus stop just as a clutch of commuters disembark. Damien is held up, tangled in the crowd, and we leave him behind. Hanging a right at the next junction, then left, then right again I begin to think the boy's changes in direction are completely random, until we stop beside a sleek electric-blue motorbike. He pulls out a set of keys from his jeans pocket.

'What ... the hell's ... going on?' I pant, in between rapid intakes of breath.

But the boy ignores me and shoves a crash helmet into my hands. He mounts the bike and guns the engine. 'Get on,' he orders.

'You can ride this thing?' I exclaim, giving him a doubtful look. *He can't be old enough to have a licence, can he?*

'Sure I can!' he replies impatiently. 'I was a Hells Angel in the Sixties. Now, get on!'

'No!' I say, ignoring his strange answer. 'First tell me what's happening. Who are you? Why am I being followed . . . kidnapped, even? *Shot at!*'

The boy glances back down the road. 'Come on! We don't have time for this now.'

I stand my ground. I feel caught in a tornado: terrified, confused and battered. But I can't let myself be carried away. I've no idea who this boy is or where he'll take me.

He curses. 'OK, fine – I'll tell you as we ride!'

Still I hesitate, just a moment longer, then I spot Damien rounding the corner, gun in hand, racing towards us. Quickly slipping on the helmet, I jump on the bike and wrap my arms round the boy's waist.

'Hang on tight,' he says, before rocketing us away to the staccato blast of gunfire.

9

The motorbike engine roars as we weave through the traffic. I've never been on a bike before and the speed at which we're going is terrifying. Several police cars and an ambulance whip by in the opposite direction, their sirens blaring and their lights flashing. Shock now overwhelms me and I think I'm going to be sick. My mind is in turmoil. So many questions, fears and doubts. I'm distraught at the thought of those poor people knocked down by the van, and the woman shot by Damien and his accomplices. My emotions are torn between panic, guilt, fury and confusion.

The boy catches my eye in the bike's wing mirror. 'Are you hurt?' he shouts over the engine's rumbling drone.

I shake my head, and he throws me a relieved grin. 'Good. The name's Phoenix, by the way.'

'H-hi, I-I'm Genna,' I manage to reply.

'Genna Adams. I know,' he says as we zoom past a street I recognize.

'My house is just round the corner,' I yell into his ear.

'I know,' Phoenix replies again, riding on.

'We should go there. My parents –'

'Not safe.'

He leans into a corner, zipping past a road sign for central London. The boy seems to know a lot about me, while I know nothing about him.

'You promised to tell me what's going on!' I shout.

'You're being hunted,' he says bluntly.

'Hunted? What do you mean, *hunted*?'

'It's my fault . . . I found you too late . . . the Incarnates know who you are . . . they'll stop at nothing . . . your soul . . .'

What with the wind whipping past, the noise of the traffic and the fact that my ears are muffled by the helmet, I find it hard to catch everything he's saying. And what he's saying isn't making any sense. 'Sorry, the *Incarnates*?' I ask.

Phoenix eases back on the throttle, the traffic becoming heavier as we approach the junction at Elephant and Castle.

'Soul Hunters,' he explains. 'An ancient religious sect whose purpose is to find First Ascendants and extinguish their souls forever.'

Still he makes no sense. 'First *what*?' I ask. 'But what do they want with *me*?'

Raising an eyebrow, Phoenix throws me an incredulous look. 'Your soul, of course.'

'What d'you mean, my *soul*? Why?'

'Because –' Phoenix glances in his wing mirror and curses. Twisting the throttle hard, we surge forward and I almost lose my grip on him. Clasping my hands tighter, I cling on for dear life as we shoot off up the road, whizzing past the snarled traffic.

'Slow down!' I cry.

'Can't!' Phoenix replies. 'He's found us.'

Risking a glance over my shoulder, I see Damien on our tail. He's riding a bright yellow motorbike emblazoned with XP DELIVERY in red letters – a bike no doubt stolen at gunpoint from some hapless courier. Flanking him are two other bikers in black helmets with dark-tinted visors. My blood runs cold at Damien's ruthless determination.

The trinity of bikers race after us, weaving between the traffic like sharks amid a shoal of fish. There's a blare of car horns as we jump a red light and skim the roundabout, taking the third exit towards the City. My legs tighten and my heart's in my mouth each time Phoenix darts through gaps in the traffic we can barely fit through.

'Lean with me!' Phoenix yells as we approach another junction at breakneck speed.

I do my best, but banking over at forty-five degrees is almost too much for me. The tarmac races past inches from my face. Somehow we make the corner and right ourselves – only to almost run straight into the back of a lorry. Phoenix brakes hard, swerves on to the other side of the road. I'm now almost too scared to breathe. My pulse racing out of control, I risk a glimpse in the rear-view mirror, which reveals Damien and his riders closing the gap –

Phoenix veers left, then right, then left again, taking a side road under London Bridge railway tracks. 'I can't shake them off!' he yells as we zoom into the tunnel, the thunder of motorbike engines echoing off the brick walls. The tunnel spits us out the other end and we just miss a car coming the other way.

But the first biker on our tail doesn't have as much luck. He hits the car's bonnet at full speed and is flung over the handlebars before slamming at full force into the steel fence beside the tunnel exit. I wince in horror and tug on Phoenix's arm. But we don't stop . . .

Nor does Damien and his remaining biker.

As I cling on even tighter to Phoenix, he accelerates away, then cuts right, the flash of a red NO ENTRY sign catching the corner of my eye.

'NO!' I shout. 'It's a one-way street!' But this seems to be his plan.

We career up the road, against the flow of traffic, slaloming between the vehicles. Behind us, an angry driver honks his horn . . . takes evasive action . . . crashes into a parked van – and ends up blocking the road. At the last second, the black-helmeted biker brakes hard. But Damien just mounts the kerb and races along the pavement, scattering pedestrians like startled pigeons. He puts on a burst of speed and comes up alongside us.

'You can't escape!' he snarls, making a lunge for me. I cry out as he seizes the collar of my jacket and tries to pull me from my seat. Phoenix retaliates by kicking Damien's motorbike into the path of an oncoming bus. Swerving to avoid a fatal collision, Damien is forced to release his grip on me.

At the end of the one-way street, we hang a sharp left and take the main road towards the River Thames. Phoenix accelerates hard, trying to extend our lead over Damien and the other biker. Ahead of us is the fort-like gateway to Tower Bridge and beyond, on the far bank, the Tower of

London with its four stone turrets piercing the city's skyline.

As we approach the bridge, a klaxon sounds, the traffic lights flash red and a pair of gates start to close across the road. Looking upriver I see a tall-masted ship waiting to pass through.

Panicking, I shout into Phoenix's ear, '*The bridge! It's opening!*'

'I can see that!' he snaps back. Nonetheless he rides determinedly on. We zip through the red lights and under the closing barriers. The road ahead is already splitting in half and the bridge beginning to rise – *fast*.

Behind us, the black-helmeted biker looks to have given up the chase, but Damien is still powering on, hell-bent on pursuing his quarry to the bitter end.

I hear Phoenix telling me to 'Hold on!' as he accelerates up the ever-increasing slope. As if I'd think about letting go now! The end of the bridge draws nearer and nearer and Phoenix's intention becomes all too clear.

'*This is insane!*' I cry, even as I wrap my arms tighter round his chest.

The gap across the river is widening with each and every passing second, going from one metre . . . to two . . . to five . . . The bike's engine is straining against the steepening incline, and I realize. . . *We're never going to make it!* But it's too late to turn back now –

We shoot off the end of the bridge. My whole body feels weightless and my stomach lurches. For a brief second we're suspended in mid-air: I have a bird's-eye view of the Tower of London, while directly below, like an abyss, lie the dark, slate-grey waters of the River Thames, waiting to drown us. The moment seems at once terrifying and surreal to me, as if I'm caught in an action movie. But then I'm snapped back to reality when we land with a bone-jarring *thump* on the other side of the bridge. The bike careers down the slope, Phoenix wrestling to control the handlebars. He brakes hard, and skids sideways, to a stop just before the closed barriers on the north side of the river.

Breathless from shock, and relief, I glance back in time to see Damien attempt the jump too. His yellow motorbike soars through the air . . . I get the grim feeling that the chase isn't yet over . . . But no – in the seconds between our jumps, the gap between the two halves of the road has widened and proves too great for him to clear. Missing the lip of the bridge by a whisker, Damien and his bike plunge like a diving bell into the river below.

Phoenix rides across to the balustrade and peers over. 'Can you see him?' he says.

I look down at the murky waters of the Thames. There's an expanding circle of ripples but no sign of Damien or his bike. I shake my head.

'Keep looking,' Phoenix orders, his eyes still scanning the river. 'We have to be sure –' He glances up as the wail of sirens heralds the arrival of the police on the southern bank, and the bridge begins to lower back into place. Bike engine revving and back wheel spinning, Phoenix doesn't wait around for the police to greet us, or to see if Damien eventually surfaces. Instead we race off through the opening barrier and down the road, before anyone can stop us.

I numbly hold on to my rescuer, dazed and exhausted by our daredevil escape. I can't quite believe that we've *jumped* Tower Bridge! After several turns, Phoenix slows to the legal speed limit and rides on through London. I'm no longer aware of our direction or the turns he makes until we enter some back streets and, finally, an alleyway. Cutting the engine, Phoenix flips out the kickstand and we both dismount.

After I've taken off my helmet, I lean against a crumbling brick wall for support. My whole body is trembling like a leaf and I feel sick, the after-effects of all that adrenaline coursing through me. I have to try hard not to vomit.

Phoenix goes over to a rusted iron gate in the side of a building, unlocks the padlock and pulls the gate open with a harsh *screech*. He gestures me inside. Cautiously I enter what looks like the foyer of a disused London Underground station. Gloomy and dusty, with a cracked glass-fronted ticket booth and a rickety old turnstile, the place doesn't appear to have been touched in decades.

Phoenix wheels in his bike, hurriedly covers it under an oil-stained tarpaulin, then closes the gate behind us. He guides me over to a concrete spiral staircase that descends into the darkness. Switching on a pocket torch, he shows the way ahead and beckons me to follow. The sound of dripping water gets louder and the cold dank smell grows stronger with each step we take further down into the stairwell's depths. Above, the weak daylight recedes. Below, there's only blackness.

Finally we reach the bottom. Phoenix hands me the torch and, by its trembling beam, unlocks a heavy steel door. He turns on a switch and a strip of overhead fluorescent tubes flickers into life.

'We're safe here,' he says. 'For the time being at least.'

In the light's harsh glare a low narrow tunnel is revealed, with row upon row of old metal bunk beds.

'Where are we?' I ask.

Phoenix turns to me, a peculiar grin on his young yet worldly-wise face.

'You should know, Genna. You've been here before.'

10

I gaze up and down the seemingly endless tunnel, white iron girders arcing across the ceiling like the ribs of a long-dead whale. The bunk beds stretch on and on, disappearing round the bend in the distance. I have no recollection of the place at all.

'This is an air-raid shelter from the Second World War,' says Phoenix. 'We took cover here during the Blitz, you and me.'

My brow knots in confusion. 'But . . . that war was in the last century! I wasn't even born then.'

Giving me a knowing smile, Phoenix slips off his biker jacket and hangs it on the corner of a bunk bed. He tosses his baseball cap on to a crumpled sleeping bag and runs his hands wearily through his locks of chestnut-brown hair. His left forearm is bandaged, a dark patch of dried blood visible. And at once everything falls into place. The leather jacket. The baseball cap. His American accent. The faded bruises on his face –

'*You're* the boy from the park! The one who saved me.'

Phoenix nods.

I narrow my eyes at him. 'And the one who's been following me all this time.'

A roguish grin graces his lips. 'Guilty as charged. But it was for your own protection.'

'Yeah? So why are you protecting me?'

Phoenix shrugs. 'Because that's what I do. What I've always done.' From a cardboard box he pulls out a bottle of fizzy drink and a cereal bar and offers them to me.

Too astonished by his answer, I shake my head. Eating is the last thing I can think about right now.

'You should,' he says, twisting off the bottle cap and almost draining its contents, 'while you have the chance.'

Fishing in the box again, he finds a bottle of water and hands that to me. This time I accept, unscrew the cap and take a long sip. The water cools and clears my head. Looking around, I notice a backpack propped up against the bed frame. A small camping stove, pans and a plate, along with some dirty cutlery – there's also a pocket Swiss Army knife, its three-inch blade locked out. On the opposite bunk bed is a portable lamp, a well-thumbed paperback, a small pile of clothes, and a box of supplies – breakfast cereal, bread, baked beans, soups and various other tins.

'You live down here?' I ask, incredulous.

'It's a secure hideout,' says Phoenix, unwrapping the cereal bar and biting off a chunk. 'Places with a strong connection to our shared past have an element of protection. They *cloak* our presence somewhat from the Soul Hunters and any Watchers nearby. It's not a hundred per cent effective, though. More like a fog than a force field.'

I take another sip of water. 'What *are* you talking about?'

Wiping the dust from the edge of his bunk bed, he gestures for me to sit. I warily take my place, and he plumps down beside me, the bedsprings creaking under his weight. His expression is solemn and serious.

'Genna,' he says, turning to me, 'you're one of the First Ascendants, a reincarnating soul originating from the dawn of humankind. You and I have lived countless lives together. As Omitl warriors in the jungles of Central America. As samurai in Japan. As sailors aboard a Spanish galleon. As Cheyenne on the Great Plains of North America. Our lives are many and entwined. But you're in grave danger. Always have been, always will be. The Incarnates are set upon seeking out First Ascendants like you, and destroying your souls – and, by doing so, they hope to extinguish the Light of Humanity. But these Soul Hunters are very hard to spot. They look like anyone else. In fact, they *could* be anyone else. You need to see their eyes, up close.'

'Black, like the night,' I murmur, thinking of Damien's fathomless holes for eyes.

Phoenix nods. 'They go like that when the Hunters *turn* and become aware of their true nature. That's why I had to wait until they made their move. Had to stay hidden, otherwise I'd lose my only advantage – the element of surprise.'

I shake my head in denial. 'This can't be true – I don't believe it. Why me? There's nothing special about *me* –' My voice catches in my throat and tears blur my vision. 'T-tell me the truth: why did Damien *really* try to shoot me?'

A scowl passes across Phoenix's face. '*Damien?* Is that the name he's going by now?' He snorts, then emits a hollow laugh. 'Well, he wasn't trying to shoot *you*. He was trying to kill *me*.'

I blink in shock. '*You!* Why?'

'Because I'm your Soul Protector.'

I stare at Phoenix, open-mouthed and uncomprehending.

'Don't get me wrong: Damien wants you dead. But not by a bullet.' Phoenix takes another bite out of his cereal bar. 'That won't solve anything. It'll just delay the ritual sacrifice for another life.'

I take a sip of water to moisten my dry mouth. 'I don't understand.'

Phoenix finishes eating, then turns to me. 'The Incarnates can't just kill you,' he explains. 'They have to perform a sacrificial ceremony, an ancient and gruesome ritual designed to extinguish your soul *forever*.'

'A ritual sacrifice?' I whisper. I think of the ominous jade knife and Damien's attack on me in the park, and begin to cry.

Phoenix lays his hand on mine and gazes at me with his sapphire-blue eyes. The starlit sparkle is back in them. 'Don't worry, Genna. As your Soul Protector, it's my mission to keep you safe and hidden from the Soul Hunters.'

For a moment I want to believe him. Even feel a glimmer of hope. I imagine being wrapped in his arms, safe and secure from all danger. Then I pull my hand away. Of course I'm terrified of Damien and his so-called Hunters, but I should be equally afraid of this boy and his fantastical tales of reincarnating souls and past lives. He may *act* thoughtful, strong and brave – but what do I really know about him? He's obviously homeless, and possibly mentally unstable.

Putting down my water bottle, I rise from the bed. 'If you don't mind me saying, this is all a little . . . *crazy*. I think it's best if I go home now.'

Phoenix stands up too, blocking my way to the door. 'I realize it sounds unbelievable. I often have trouble convincing you. You rarely recall your past lives . . . to begin with at least. I think it's a way of keeping you safe. More hidden. If you're not aware, then the Incarnates are less likely to be aware of you too.'

'I want to leave *now*!' I insist, his babbling only seeming to become more implausible.

'Hear me out,' Phoenix urges, holding up his hands to prevent my escape. 'Have you ever experienced dreams so vivid it seems like you have lived them? Or had déjà vu so strong you're convinced you must have been there before?'

I keep my expression neutral, but the strange episode during my French Revolution homework immediately springs to mind. Phoenix notices me hesitate and seizes upon it. 'Do you possess knowledge or skills, Genna, that no one has ever taught you?'

I swallow as if there's a pebble stuck in my throat. At school, I often seem to know facts before my history teacher has said anything, and I've even corrected her on some points. Then there was that time I tried archery – I'd never so much as held a bow before in my life, yet every arrow I shot hit its target dead centre. The instructor said I was a natural; my friends and I thought it was simply luck. But *a skill from a past life*? Come on, that's ludicrous!

Phoenix shifts closer, resting his hands on my shoulders and looking deep into my eyes. 'And do you recognize the faces of strangers? Feel an ancient bond like old friends reuniting?'

There's a sincere and longing affection in his gaze that is at once familiar yet frightening in its familiarity.

'These are all echoes of your previous lives,' he explains. 'Reincarnations of your soul. Glimmers, as the First Ascendants call them.'

I recall the bizarre vision I had when he took my hand for the first time. My world seems to be crumbling around me, even as I deny the truth of what he's saying, the truth that I know is planted in my heart. In my soul.

'*Let me pass!*' I cry.

'Look, I'll prove it to you.' Phoenix pulls out an old, battered metal box from beneath his bunk bed. 'Lay your hands on this.'

'What is it?' I ask warily.

'A medical box. The first-aid kit you used on me during the Blitz. A *Touchstone*.'

Against my better judgement, I kneel down beside the box. I'm determined to prove that everything he's told me is a lie – for both his and my own sanity. I place my hands on the lid and –

The lights flicker overhead. A heavy boom *resounds. Dust dislodges from the ceiling. Another deep rumble and the lights go out completely. Screams and whimpers echo up and down the tunnel. A siren whines in the darkness. The acrid stench of burning taints the air. Gas lamps flicker on, to reveal rows of pale fearful faces, women and children staring at the ceiling in dread.*

'The shrapnel cut deep. Got any bandages left?' asks a young soldier in an east London accent. His lean face is pale with shock but his blue eyes are bright as he grits his teeth against the pain.

I glance down at the metal box in my hands, now new and undented, then back at the young man stretched out on the bunk bed. I recognize him immediately, although his face and accent are different and his name is now ... Harry. There's a large bloody gash in his right leg. Next to him, on the adjacent bunk, is another poor soldier, groaning and clutching his arm.

Nodding to Harry, I put down the first-aid box, open the lid and pull out a fresh dressing. Another bomb explodes overhead. The bunker shudders from the blast, bricks and mortar fall upon me, and I cry out –

'What have you done to me?' I cry, taking my hands off the box as if it were on fire. Disorientated and nauseous, I stare accusingly at Phoenix. The tunnel lights are back on, their glare harsh and bright. The explosions and screams are gone too. We're alone in the tunnel, the bunk beds bare and empty.

Phoenix grins triumphantly. 'You felt a connection, saw a past life, didn't you?'

I shake my head vehemently, denying everything, even to myself.

72

'No . . . I don't know . . . what I saw –' My eye catches the water bottle at the foot of the bunk bed. 'You put something in my drink, didn't you?'

'NO!' Phoenix protests, seizing me by the arm. 'You *have* to believe me. Your *soul* depends upon it.'

I struggle to break his grip, but he won't let go and I fear for my life. Snatching up a tin of beans from the supply box, I swing it at his head with all my strength. Its hard metal edge strikes his temple and he collapses to the floor, stunned. Leaping to my feet, I bolt for the open door, slam it behind me, and launch myself up the spiral staircase.

As I flee, I hear Phoenix shouting after me. 'Genna, come back! The Incarnates know who you are!'

But I don't stop. I daren't stop.

His desperate voice chases me up the stairwell. 'They won't stop hunting you, Genna. Not now. *Not ever!*'

11

'*Four people were killed and many more injured when a van was driven into pedestrians at Clapham Market earlier this morning,*' a solemn voice announces, as I open the front door to my house and quietly step into the hallway. From the lounge I can hear the newsreader on the TV. '*A woman in her mid-twenties remains in a critical condition following a gunshot wound to her chest. Police believe both incidents are linked, and are treating it as a suspected terrorist attack, although no organization has yet come forward to claim responsibility. Three arrests have been made so far, and at least three further suspects are being sought in connection with the attacks . . .*'

As I enter the lounge, the TV is showing mugshots of three people. I recognize the two men as the brutes who tried to kidnap me. The woman I presume is the van driver. Damien isn't among them. Upon seeing me in the doorway my mum leaps up from the sofa; her mascara has run and a pile of crumpled tissues sits on the coffee table.

'*Genna!*' she cries, rushing over and kissing me on the forehead and cheeks with an almost desperate fury. Then she breaks off and studies me with teared-up eyes. 'We've been worried sick about you. School called to say you hadn't turned up for your test this morning. Then we saw news of the attacks and feared the worst –' Mum breaks down in sobs.

Behind her stands my dad, staring at me, a mix of anger, relief and joy battling it out on his face, which now appears as creased and worn as old leather. It's like he's aged twenty years since breakfast. 'Where have you been all this time?' he says.

'I . . .' But words fail me. For some reason, I don't want to – *I can't!* – tell my parents about Phoenix. I'm inexplicably protective of him and his existence. Nor do I want to mention the attempted abduction. Not yet anyway. They're both stressed out enough, and I figure they don't need anything more to worry about. 'I was hiding,' I reply, sticking to the truth as far as possible. 'After the attacks, I was so scared. I didn't know what else to do. I lost track of time . . .'

'Why didn't you *call*?' Dad demands. 'That's why we gave you your own phone! I've left you countless messages!'

I shrug weakly. 'I dropped my bag when I ran . . . I'm sorry I lost the phone . . . I didn't mean to upset you –'

Mum pulls me into an embrace, holding me so tight I fear she might never let go. 'We're not angry with you, Genna . . . We were just so, so worried . . . We thought you were –' Her voice catches and she lets out another sob.

On the TV the news switches to another story: *'At Tower Bridge, police are investigating a second incident also believed to be connected to this morning's attack involving the van in Clapham,'* the newsreader is saying.

Behind her there's a shot of a floating crane fishing out a yellow XP delivery bike from the river. '*Following what appears to be a high-speed pursuit involving four motorbikes, a motorcyclist with passenger jumped Tower Bridge as it was opening –*' The newsreader raises an incredulous eyebrow and the screen switches to a shaky mobile-phone clip of a bike flying between the two sections of open bridge.

I stare dumbstruck at the death-defying stunt. Witnessed from the riverbank – the bike and its two riders leaping across that ever-growing gap, the chill waters of the Thames some hundred feet below – it's clear that what Phoenix did was nothing short of a miracle!

'*A second bike attempted to follow,*' the newsreader goes on, '*but failed to make the jump and plunged into the River Thames. Despite fears the rider may have drowned, a young man was later spotted emerging from the river near Butler's Wharf and last seen fleeing the scene on foot –*'

I stiffen, my blood turning cold at the news –

'*A third suspect was surrounded by police and arrested, while a fourth is under police guard at Guy's Hospital, where they are in a critical condition following an earlier crash. Meanwhile, the daredevil rider and their unidentified passenger were witnessed travelling east, at speed, into the City. Police are seeking any information that may lead to . . .*'

The rest of the report is lost amid my rising panic.

'Are you all right?' Mum asks, feeling the tension in my body.

'I need to lie down,' I murmur, withdrawing from her arms and retreating into the hallway.

Mum makes as if to follow me, but Dad lays a hand on her shoulder, gently dissuading her. 'That's a good idea, Genna,' he says with a careworn smile, by now his anger having given way to his usual tenderness. 'This morning must have been a traumatic experience for you.'

On shaky legs I make my way upstairs to my room. 'I'll check on you later,' Mum calls after me. Then I hear them close the lounge door and engage in a tense, whispered discussion.

In my room I collapse on my bed and hug Coco, my floppy-eared bunny, to my chest. I feel shattered, almost hollow with shock. The news that Phoenix and I were spotted fleeing the scene doesn't overly concern me. We're innocent, after all. It's the fact that Damien survived the leap, *and escaped* . . . My tormentor is still on the loose.

I grab my laptop off my desk and boot it up. Without my phone, I video call Mei using my browser. After a couple of rings, it connects and my best friend's face, drained and somewhat grey, appears on the screen. She's propped up in bed, a bowl perched next to her on the bedside table.

'Genna!' Mei exclaims in surprise, peering into the camera. 'What are you doing home already?'

'Hey – you OK?' I ask.

Mei nods. 'Of course. Just a stomach upset. But what about you? How was the test?'

I bite my lower lip. 'I didn't make it.'

'*What?*' Mei exclaims, her eyes going wide. 'The Wonder Brain misses a test! How come?'

'Have you seen the news?' I ask.

'Sure, it's awful,' Mei replies with a disapproving pout. 'Those terrorists are sick. I mean, how could they run people over in the name of –'

'It *wasn't* a terrorist attack,' I interrupt. Mei blinks in shock and falls silent. 'They were after *me*.'

Mei's jaw drops. '*You?* What are you talking about?'

'Damien tried to kidnap me,' I explain.

Mei's mouth continues to open wider and wider as I tell her about the white van and my abduction, about Phoenix's rescue, and the disturbing hallucination of the ritual sacrifice. She listens aghast as I relate the shocking details of Damien shooting someone, then trying to run Phoenix and me over; about our perilous escape on a motorbike, followed by Phoenix's remarkable revelation about Soul Hunters and his claim to be my Soul Protector. And finally I divulge to her my surreal flashback to a past life during the Blitz in the Second World War. Even as I tell her my story I realize how absurd it all sounds.

By the end, Mei's expression is a mix of wonderment, disbelief, horror and mirth. 'You're having me on, aren't you?' she says. 'It's a joke to get me back for bunking off the history test!'

'It's *no* joke,' I reply, my tone deadly serious. 'What do you think I should do?'

Mei sits up straighter in bed. 'Well, you *have* to tell the police.'

I baulk at the idea. 'You think they'll believe me?'

'Probably not,' says Mei, shaking her head. 'At least not all of it. I'd maybe keep the past-life stuff to yourself.'

'Do *you* believe me?' I ask, feeling a pang of desperation enter my heart. The idea I might be losing my grip on reality terrifies me.

Mei purses her lips, considering her reply, then says, 'I believe Damien is really after you, and that Phoenix stepped in to save you – at the park and again this morning. But I'm not so sure about those stories of past lives. You've been mugged and now kidnapped. That would put anyone under serious mental strain. D'you think you could have *imagined* these flashbacks?'

'No. They felt like *memories*,' I insist. 'Whole and complete. I could see, taste, smell – even feel the emotion of the moment. There's no way I could imagine such things – and they weren't dreams, either. They were as real as you and me talking now!'

'But you said Phoenix might have put something in your drink. Could it be that?' Mei reminds me.

I sigh and shrug. 'I honestly don't know . . . Even if he did, that doesn't explain *all* the flashbacks I've had.'

Mei falls silent again, apparently lost in thought. Eventually she says, 'Don't some religions believe in reincarnation? I'm sure Prisha's talked about it at some point. I suppose there must be *something* in it.'

'I'm not mad then?' I ask hesitantly.

Mei smiles kindly at me. 'No, I'm sure you're not. But your guardian angel might be. With all his talk of "Incarnates" and "protecting your soul", he definitely sounds a bit bonkers . . . however brave or good-looking you think he is!'

She laughs, and so do I, and I feel more reassured now that my instincts in the bunker have been confirmed. But my heart skips a beat at the very thought of Phoenix; and deep down there's a longing to see him again. I try to suppress the impulse.

'So what should I do if Phoenix finds me again?' I ask.

'Do you feel threatened by him?' asks Mei carefully.

'Quite the opposite,' I admit. 'I feel *safe*. That's what freaks me out. I barely know him, so why should I feel this way?'

'It's natural. He protected you,' Mei explains, then her expression darkens. 'To be honest, I'd be more worried about Damien finding you again. He's the *real* threat –'

We're interrupted by a knock on my door, and Mum pokes her head in. I'm about to tell her I'm on a call with Mei when I notice the grave look on her face.

'The police are here to see you.'

12

'Is this your schoolbag and phone?' asks the detective inspector, holding up a clear plastic bag containing a floral-print satchel and a smartphone in a glitter case. Her expression is stern but not overtly hostile, her grey eyes sharp and watchful behind her tinted glasses, and her charcoal-black hair is pulled back into a tight bun. She has introduced herself as DI Katherine Shaw of the Metropolitan Police, but she's wearing a tailored navy-blue suit and chalk-white blouse rather than the standard police uniform.

'Yes,' I reply, and I reach out to claim my possessions. But she doesn't hand them over. Instead she passes them to her colleague, a middle-aged police constable, in full uniform. He's heavyset, with a neatly trimmed beard, and looks more like a bodyguard than a policeman.

'We'd like to keep these for evidence, if you don't mind,' DI Shaw explains, her terse tone indicating this was a statement rather than a request.

'Evidence?' questions my dad sharply. He gives the detective inspector a hard look. 'You don't suspect our daughter has anything to do with this terrorist attack, do you?'

DI Shaw pulls out a notebook from her jacket pocket and clicks the top of her ballpoint pen. 'That's what we're here to find out, sir. We simply wish to ask Genna a few questions. Clarify some matters.'

My parents exchange uneasy looks as the detective takes a seat opposite me at the dining-room table and stares me directly in the eye. I squirm a little in my chair. All of a sudden the dining room feels hot and airless. My mouth goes bone dry.

Mum sits down at the end of the table, cradling a mug of tea but without showing any desire to drink it. Dad stands next to her, his arms crossed, his thick brow knotted, looking decidedly uncomfortable about the whole situation.

DI Shaw smiles coolly at me. If she intends to set me at ease, her put-upon smile only serves to make me even more unsettled. 'Genna,' she begins, 'can you confirm your whereabouts this morning?'

'I . . . was walking to school,' I reply, a noticeable tremor in my voice.

'Oaklands School?' she queries, and I nod and she jots this down. 'Were you anywhere in the vicinity of Clapham Market?'

I nod again, and she makes another note.

'And did you witness any of the attacks?'

Again I nod. I don't know how much I should tell this woman. I'm scared that I might say something that will incriminate me. At the same time Mei advised me to speak to the police and here they are. But the detective inspector's officious manner is off-putting, making me feel more like a criminal than a victim.

'If required, could you identify any of the attackers again?' she asks.

'I think so,' I reply.

DI Shaw holds up a grainy CCTV photo of Clapham Market. 'Do you recognize the boy in this picture?'

I peer at the black-haired, pale-skinned youth standing amid the destruction of the market stalls. His face is out of focus, but I recognize him instantly. A shudder runs through me. Even in a photo, the boy's sinister presence makes my skin crawl. 'Yes . . .' I say. 'His name is Damien.'

The detective inspector glances over at the constable and raises an eyebrow; this piece of intelligence has clearly piqued her interest. 'What else do you know about him, Genna?' she asks.

Not wishing to divulge anything about the Soul Hunter fantasy that Phoenix has fed me, I shrug and say, 'Nothing really.'

Leaning forward in her chair and resting her elbows on the table, DI Shaw fixes me with her piercing gaze. 'Nothing? Several witnesses claim they saw *you* exiting the white van that was involved in the attack –'

'Hang on!' interrupts Dad, uncrossing his arms. 'This is more than just "clarifying matters". Who are these so-called witnesses? Shouldn't we have a lawyer present for such questions?'

'I don't think that will be necessary,' says DI Shaw. 'Will it, Genna?' Again it is implicit in her firm tone that this is a statement, not a question.

I mutely shake my head, both relieved and somewhat afraid at the prospect of finally telling someone in authority about my tormentor and stalker. I take a deep breath. 'I believe Damien was trying to kidnap me –'

'*Kidnap?*' cries Mum, almost spilling her tea. I avoid her horrified gaze and continue.

'He and the others threw me into the back of the van . . . but I managed to escape, and that's when he tried to shoot me . . .'

'*Damien* tried to shoot you?' DI Shaw clarifies.

I nod. 'He missed and hit that poor woman instead.' Tears sting my eyes and my chin starts to tremble as I recall the tragic incident. 'A week ago, Damien and his gang mugged me in a park near the museum –'

Dad lurches forward and plants his hands on the dining table. He stares at me in utter shock. 'Genna, why didn't you tell us any of this?' he demands, visibly shaken. 'We could have done something. Called the police. Had him arrested!'

Seeing the look of dismay and betrayal on my father's face, I feel I've let him down, and begin to cry. 'I . . . I was scared . . . I didn't know what to do . . . I was worried no one would believe me . . .'

Mum draws closer and puts an arm round my shoulders. 'It's OK, honey,' she soothes, handing me a tissue. 'You're home now. You're safe. You don't have to be scared.'

Once I calm down, DI Shaw asks, 'Why do you think Damien would want to kidnap you?'

Wiping my eyes, I hesitate before replying, 'I . . . don't know.'

She maintains her stony stare, clearly waiting for another answer – the truth.

In the ensuing silence the atmosphere in the room turns heavy. The pressure on me to say something grows like an increasing weight upon my chest. Yet I know that the truth, or at least the reason I've been given, is so far-fetched and unbelievable that everyone will think I've lost it or, at the very least, that I'm lying.

Just at the point when the silence becomes unbearable for me, DI Shaw asks, 'Who was the other boy you were with?'

'What . . .' I swallow hard. Again I'm conscious of an inexplicable urge to guard Phoenix's identity. 'What other boy?'

The detective taps her pen impatiently on her notebook. 'The one you were seen running away with,' she says.

I lower my gaze to the table, purposefully avoiding hers. 'I don't know who he is,' I mumble. 'Never met him before.'

DI Shaw's lips stretch thin: she's clearly unconvinced. After making a note in her book, she holds her hand out towards the police officer, who passes her a slim manila file. She flips it open. Clipped to the document inside is a passport photo of a boy with high cheekbones, olive complexion and chestnut-brown hair. His eyes appear darker in the photo, and I wonder if only *I* can see the star-like blue hue in them.

'Well,' she says, 'our preliminary investigations have uncovered a few basic facts about him. His name is Phoenix Rivers. He's an American citizen, born in Flagstaff, Arizona, according to his passport. Father is unknown. Mother is Ángela Silva, originally from Córdoba, Mexico; she died in a car crash when he was three, after which he was raised in a series of foster homes. It seems he was something of a "problem child" and, according to his medical records, he has undergone numerous psychotherapy treatments. He landed at Heathrow thirty-two days ago from Los Angeles International Airport. Location thereafter unknown. What I want to know, Genna, is *your* connection with him.'

I wring my hands under the table, my palms clammy, my pulse rapid. 'There is no connection.'

DI Shaw's eyes narrow behind her tinted glasses. 'Then why did he risk his life for you?'

I shrug. 'Because he's a good person, I suppose.'

'Where is he now?'

'I-I-I don't know,' I half lie. There is every chance he's still in the underground bunker, but again my instincts prevent me from revealing this.

Sitting back in her chair, DI Shaw draws in a long, measured breath. 'I'm not convinced you're telling me the whole truth, Genna,' she declares. My father opens his mouth to protest, but she holds up a hand, cutting him off. From the file she produces a CCTV image of Tower Bridge, showing two riders on a sleek electric-blue motorbike: Phoenix's face is clearly visible beneath his baseball cap, but his passenger's is obscured by their helmet.

'Phoenix Rivers has been positively identified as one of the motorcyclists in the Tower Bridge incident.' She looks me up and down, taking in my jeans, white blouse and green jacket. 'Since your clothing matches the CCTV footage, I'm presuming *you* were his passenger.'

Suddenly there doesn't seem to be enough air in the room and I desperately want someone to open a window.

Both my parents are scrutinizing me as if they no longer know me, their faces screwed up in shock and disbelief. The police constable positions himself solidly by the door, apparently half expecting me to bolt, while DI Shaw continues to impale me with her steadfast glare.

Under the weight of everyone's hostile gaze, my defences crumble. In a flood of sobs and tears, I divulge the whole story: Phoenix's improbable tale of past lives and First Ascendants, Incarnates and Soul Hunters, and Damien's intention to kill me in a ritual sacrifice. I don't admit to my own past-life flashbacks for fear the police and my parents will question my state of mind. But when I've finished they all look at me with a deep and almost humiliating pity.

DI Shaw's icy demeanour thaws. She reaches out and touches my hand. 'Genna, you've done the right thing by telling us. It's understandable that you're confused and scared after what you've experienced. This Phoenix boy may have saved you, but, in my professional opinion, he's taking advantage of you in your vulnerable state.'

I look at her and frown. 'Why would he do that?'

'Taking into account his upbringing, his medical history and the fact that he's an orphan, the boy likely has attachment issues,' she explains. 'He's created this fantasy world of Soul Protectors and Soul Hunters as a way to draw his victims in and convince them to be solely reliant on him. So I wouldn't set a lot of store by what he says. I'm no psychologist but he sounds as if he could be a paranoid schizophrenic.'

'A what?' I ask.

'Someone with a chronic mental health problem in which they lose touch with reality. Such individuals are generally harmless in themselves, but they often believe they're being chased or plotted against. It's also common for them to have delusions of grandeur, believing they're someone important or famous; this fits in with Phoenix's past-life narrative. Most paranoid delusions are complex, but this boy's seem exceptional. His backstory doesn't require a shred of proof, and that's why it's so effective.'

The detective inspector's assessment leaves me both reassured and dismayed. 'So Phoenix is delusional?' I ask.

DI Shaw nods. 'In fact, I'd go so far as to say dangerously so. Considering his daredevil exploits, he's as serious a threat to you as that other boy Damien . . . if not more.'

13

'We'll need to take Genna in to make an official statement,' Detective Inspector Shaw announces, standing up and ending the interview. She issues an order to the police constable, who rounds the dining table towards me.

But Dad intervenes. 'Is our daughter being taken as a witness or a suspect?'

'This is merely standard police procedure, Mr Adams,' DI Shaw replies. 'We're not arresting her. She's just helping us with our enquiries. But if it makes you feel more comfortable, then by all means arrange for a lawyer to be present.'

The constable indicates for my father to step aside. For a moment Dad refuses to move. Then with great reluctance he allows the officer past. 'Yes, I will call a lawyer,' he says.

Suddenly I feel nervous, as I'm taken by the arm and escorted out of the dining room.

'Does it have to be *right* now?' asks Mum, chasing us down the hallway.

'Time is of the essence in terror-related investigations, Mrs Adams,' DI Shaw replies, opening the front door and ushering me out into the bright, cold sunshine.

'But Genna said it was a kidnapping, not a terrorist attack,' Mum reminds her.

'That is for *us* to assess,' DI Shaw replies, as I'm marched down the path towards the blue-and-white police car parked outside our house. She opens the rear passenger door and the constable helps me into the back seat.

'Shouldn't *we* take Genna to the station?' says my dad firmly.

'For your daughter's own safety, it's best that we do,' says DI Shaw. 'Genna's a key witness to these suspected terrorist attacks and therefore a potential target. If Phoenix is as unbalanced as he seems, and this Damien as determined and ruthless as he's proven so far, then the safest place for her is at the police station. The quicker we get her there, the better. You can follow along in your own car, though. We'll wait for you.'

For a brief moment it looks as if my father might leap into the back of the police car with me, but then the detective slams the passenger door shut and all of a sudden I'm alone, cocooned inside the vehicle.

My father scrambles for his coat and car keys, while Mum hurriedly puts on her shoes. Outside, the detective inspector and the constable appear to have a short, heated debate about who's driving, then the man hands his superior the keys to the vehicle and rushes round to the passenger side. I fumble with my seat belt as my hands begin to tremble and my anxiety spikes. The danger posed by Damien becomes sharp and all too real. If the police are acting so spooked, then I have every reason to be worried.

Even more so when presented by the double threat of Phoenix's unstable state of mind.

Through the window I watch my parents hastily lock up the house and dash for the garage. Despite her promise to wait for them, DI Shaw climbs into the driver's seat, presses the ignition and puts the police car into gear. As we head off down the road, I glance back through the rear windscreen. My parent's silver Volvo has only just turned out of the driveway. At the end of our street DI Shaw bears right and accelerates away through the traffic, the vehicle's blue lights on but the siren silent. My parents struggle to keep up.

'Er . . . can we slow down?' I ask. But both the officers ignore me.

The high street passes by in a blur, heads turning as the flashing police vehicle shoots down the road. Distinctly uneasy now, I dig my fingernails into my palms. Everything is happening so fast and I feel totally out of control, like a feather caught in a hurricane.

We approach a crossroads and DI Shaw jumps the red light, leaving my parents held up behind it.

'Stop!' I cry. 'My parents got caught at the lights.'

'They know the way,' DI Shaw replies curtly. She speeds down the road, my parents' silver Volvo rapidly receding into the distance.

'But do *you*, ma'am?' questions the constable with a touch of hesitancy. He points to a left-hand turn we've just flown by. 'The station's down there.'

'I know,' she says, but drives on regardless. 'We're being followed.'

I stiffen in horror. My eyes dart this way and that as I scan the traffic around me like a startled rabbit. *Has Damien tracked me down* already?

'Which is the suspect vehicle?' asks the constable.

'Four cars back. Right-hand side,' replies the detective.

As the constable turns in his seat to look behind him, DI Shaw suddenly lashes out at him with a brutal knifehand strike to his throat. There's a sickening *crunch*. The attack is so swift and devastating that the man, despite his size and strength, collapses face-first against the dashboard.

'What the – !' I gasp, staring in open-mouthed shock.

DI Shaw discards her glasses and glances in the rear-view mirror. Her eyes – previously grey through the tinted lenses – have melted into inky pools. A Soul Hunter's eyes. For a full second I gaze into those pits of darkness, then the horror of my predicament hits me: either I'm going totally insane . . . or Phoenix is telling the truth.

I scream and yank at the passenger-door handle. But it's locked. Hammering with my bare fists against the window, I yell for help. But no one in the other vehicles or on the street seems to take any notice – and even if they did, I'd only look like any other criminal ranting in the back of a police car.

'Shut up!' DI Shaw snaps. 'Or I'll crush your windpipe too.'

I shrink back into my seat, furtively looking around for anything I can defend myself with. But the rear compartment is spartan and functional. A purpose-built mobile prison cell.

As I try to figure out how to escape, DI Shaw dials a number on her phone, waits for someone to pick up, then says simply, 'Soul captured.'

The starkness of her statement sends an icy chill through my body, her call surely proving there *is* a network of Incarnates on the hunt for me. Then again . . . *am I the one suffering a paranoid delusion?*

As I'm contemplating my own fragile sanity, a helmeted rider on a blue motorbike draws up alongside the police car. The leather-jacketed biker looks into the car then flips up his visor. His sapphire eyes lock with mine.

'*Phoenix!*' I whisper in astonishment.

He gestures for me to tighten my seatbelt. All of a sudden I lurch to the side as the police car swerves, trying to knock him off his bike. He veers away and into the oncoming traffic. With a deft zigzag, he dodges a white van, mounts the kerb and powers ahead of the police car. Then he switches back across lanes. From the pocket of his leather jacket I see him toss a handful of nails on to the road. Hurriedly I tug my seatbelt tighter as DI Shaw runs straight over the iron spikes. There's a deafening *BANG*. One of our front tyres bursts and the vehicle pulls hard left, but DI Shaw fights the steering wheel, keeping the car on the road. Then she floors the accelerator, determined to ram Phoenix off his bike.

The fender of the police car is almost grazing his back wheel when he cuts sharply to one side and launches a brick through the front windscreen. DI Shaw shields her face as the glass implodes and she loses control of the vehicle. We hit the kerb hard, and the police car flips over.

I'm flung around, the seatbelt locking out, my limbs flailing – a shrill screech of metal, and more glass shatters as we strike the tarmac and skid along upside down. Colliding with a concrete pillar, the vehicle spins and my head hits the window and –

My life flashes before my eyes. But not just one life. Many.

Me as a child making daisy-chains with my father in a country meadow . . . me as a handmaiden walking through a heavily scented garden in Babylon . . . as a fisherman battling the waves aboard a Chinese junk boat . . . as a cook baking bread in the steaming and stifling kitchen of a castle . . . as a Berber crossing a searingly hot desert . . . as a German countess inside a rickety stage-coach, hurtling out of control before flipping over, the horses whinnying in pain and terror, the broken coach coming to a rest at the edge of a cliff, the cruel laugh of my nemesis mocking me as I watch a pair of black leather boots approach the shattered window –

'Genna? Are you all right?' asks Phoenix in a panicked voice.

Disorientated and dazed, it takes me a moment to figure out where I am . . . *when* I am . . . and even *who* I am. The police car has finally skidded to a stop, its engine hissing. I'm hanging upside down, my arms limp, my hair in my face, the blood rushing to my head. Phoenix kicks away the glass fragments from the passenger window, then reaches in and carefully cuts the seatbelt with his penknife. I slump awkwardly to the upturned roof of the car. Then, wrenching open the door, he helps me clamber out of the wreck.

'Are you hurt?' he asks, frantically examining me all over.

Apart from a few cuts and bruises, I seem to be in one piece. 'I don't think so . . .' I gasp. 'Just a bit battered.'

From the front seat comes a groan of pain. DI Shaw is caught in the twisted wreckage. Blood streams from a gash to her forehead, but she's alive. Next to her, in a crumpled heap, lies the body of the police constable, now looking like the tragic casualty in a car crash rather than the murder victim I know he really is.

In the distance, police sirens can be heard approaching fast.

'Come on!' Phoenix urges, taking my arm and leading me over to his bike. I limp alongside him. He passes me a spare helmet and we hurriedly mount the motorcycle as DI Shaw reaches for the police radio on the dashboard.

'Officer down . . .' she gasps. 'Witness abducted . . . Suspect armed and dangerous . . . Blue Honda motorbike . . .'

She drops the handset then gropes for her mobile phone amid the glass chips of windscreen. Her black eyes fix on me as she presses speed dial. *Summon all Hunters . . . Soul lost!*

14

The motorbike engine's heavy thrum is a numbing roar in my ears as we race along the highway out of London. Cars and lorries flash by, Phoenix riding like a demon possessed. I cling on, gripping him like a lifebuoy in a storm, afraid that if I let go I might be lost forever. But my grip on reality is tenuous by comparison. I'm still in shock at the detective inspector's *turning* – though I realize now she was probably a Hunter from the start. The interrogation a sham to get me away from my parents.

My paranoia grows ... If a police officer can be an Incarnate, that means I'm not safe *anywhere* or with *anyone*!

Unless I'm with Phoenix.

I desperately want to talk to him, to have him convince me that these so-called Incarnates are real and that I'm not losing my mind. But right now I can only hold on and hope.

As we leave London behind, the traffic thins out and Phoenix opens up the throttle. I daren't look back, for fear of falling off and of what I might see: a trail of pursuing police cars or a pack of Hunters on motorbikes. But, even above the engine's noise, I can't hear any wail of sirens or the angry buzz of bikes closing on us. So maybe, just maybe, we've managed to escape.

But for how long?

Detective Inspector Shaw has ensured that both the police and Hunters are on the lookout for us. Against such a powerful combined force the odds of evading capture seem desperately low. I pray that Phoenix has a plan, since I've no choice but to put my life into his hands.

The sun is low in the sky as Phoenix pulls off the road and we wend our way down a long dirt track. We stop beside an old, timber-framed barn, the roof in disrepair, the walls mossy and mottled. The yard area, a hard-packed square of dirt and weeds, overlooks grassy meadows and rolling hills. The only habitation in sight is a farmhouse in the far distance. Two horses grazing in the nearest field look up at our approach, their steadfast gaze studying us with wary curiosity.

Phoenix drops the kickstand and cuts the engine. After what seems like hours on a roaring bike, the silence is a blessed relief. Removing my helmet, I'm greeted by birdsong and the rustle of the breeze in the nearby trees. The peace of the countryside – in sharp contrast to the bustle of the city and the chaos of our escape – calms my heart and settles my soul. The place immediately feels like a safe haven ... *almost* as if I've been here before.

Dismounting, I stretch my weary, aching limbs. 'Where are we?' I ask.

'Near Winchester,' Phoenix replies, taking off his own helmet and scanning the yard. 'This place still looks secure enough. We'll stay here tonight.'

I shoot him a questioning look. 'Where will we sleep?'

'In the barn,' he replies matter-of-factly.

Glancing through the gaps in the rickety barn door, I spy a couple of stalls and a pile of musty old hay. I grimace at the sight. The prospect of spending the night here isn't appealing – nor is it wise, given that Phoenix is still practically a stranger. By agreeing to his plan I'm putting an awful lot of trust in my new-found friend.

'Do you have a phone?' I ask. 'I need to call my parents. Let them know I'm OK.'

Phoenix shakes his head. 'Sorry, I don't,' he says, wheeling the bike inside the barn.

I stand alone in the yard, wondering how I can contact Mum and Dad. They must be beside themselves with worry. They'll think I've been kidnapped again. 'How about we find a public phone, then?' I suggest.

'It'll be dark soon,' Phoenix calls from the barn, 'and with Hunters on the prowl, best not to take the risk.'

I bite my lower lip, reluctant to agree. But I'm not sure what else I can do . . . at least for the time being. 'I guess you're right,' I reply as he comes back out with a small backpack in his hand.

'Hey, sorry for the literal car crash of a rescue,' he says, a rueful look on his face. 'I had no option but to pull you out on the move. Since you'd kindly *locked* me into my bunker, I got to your house too late!'

I wince guiltily, recalling my quick-thinking action when I fled the foyer of the Underground station. At the time I believed I was being clever. Now I realize I'd just put my life in greater danger.

'I arrived as the police were taking you away,' he continues. 'I didn't know what had happened – whether your parents had called them or you'd been arrested – so I followed the car . . . until I saw that officer get killed. Then I realized a Hunter had you. Sorry for taking such a risk, but I couldn't wait for –'

'No, stop. It's *me* who should be apologizing to you,' I say. 'I'm sorry for locking you in and –' I offer him a regretful look – 'for hitting you with that tin of baked beans.'

His hand goes to the ridge of purple bruising across his left brow. 'You've done a lot worse.'

I raise an eyebrow. 'In previous "lives", you mean?'

Phoenix nods and grins archly. 'You once whipped me in Pompeii, not long before Mount Vesuvius erupted. Another time, in a Rajasthan palace, you had your servants beat me. And as a Zulu warrior, I recall, you set your lion upon me!'

I can't help but laugh. '*Seriously!* You expect me to believe that?'

Phoenix shrugs. 'I can only open the door; you must enter by yourself.'

He strolls over to a bale of hay beside the barn and sits down. Opening his backpack, he takes out a sports drink, some energy bars and a couple of apples. 'I'm afraid it's not much of a dinner, but I didn't get time to go to the store!' he quips.

Tearing the wrapper off one of the bars, he tucks in and gazes at the idyllic view: a sheen of golden sunlight dusting the meadows and haloing the hills. My hunger overcomes my doubts, and I sit down next to him, pick up an apple and munch on it in silence. So many thoughts, questions and concerns whirl in my head that I don't know where to start ... *Can I really trust this boy? Should I believe his fantastical stories? Am I the one who's delusional, or is he? And if it's all real, what am I supposed to do then? How will we survive?* Over and over these questions and others like them consume my mind ...

'I've always loved this spot,' Phoenix murmurs with a contented sigh. 'It's so peaceful.'

Finishing off the energy bar, he pops the lid of the sports drink and takes a long draught before offering the rest to me. 'Often so much changes over the years. But *this* place, it's barely altered since I was last here.'

'And when was that?' I ask, taking a cautious sip from the bottle.

He purses his lips thoughtfully. 'Around the time of the English Civil War. You were here too ... remember?'

As soon as he says this I get a flash of a memory. A *Glimmer* ...

A young man with long flowing hair in ringlets, wearing a burgundy leather doublet and a wide-brimmed plumed hat. Upon his hip is a slim sword, a rapier of steel. A tender smile graces his fair face, though I can see pain in his blue eyes. He's injured ...

The vision fades as quickly as it appeared.

I stare into Phoenix's crystal-blue eyes. Scared to ask the question but needing to know the answer. 'Tell me, honestly, am I going mad?'

Phoenix gently shakes his head. 'No, Genna, you're not. You're simply seeing the truth for the first time.'

15

'*Reincarnation . . .*' I whisper to myself. Its implication is almost too incredible to comprehend, let alone believe. Phoenix's so-called 'truth' seems more ridiculous than if I was actually experiencing delusions!

But then I think back over my childhood and all those weird déjà vu moments I've had; the times when I was sure I recognized a stranger or they seemed to know me; and more recently that dream of the French Revolution, the vision of escaping that sacrificial ceremony, the experience in that Second World War bunker and that cascade of flashbacks when the car crashed. *Were they all to do with my past lives?*

I look questioningly at Phoenix. 'So have I *really* lived before?'

He casually unwraps another energy bar and nods. 'Yup. Many times.'

I shake my head in denial. 'No, no, that can't be possible.'

'Why not?' he challenges. 'Is it any more surprising or miraculous to be born twice than once? Three times, ten times, a million times? Everything in nature is an example of death and rebirth. It's the circle of life – just look at the seasons. Death is only the beginning – no more the end than birth.'

I sit, wringing my hands and staring off into the distance, trying to get my head round the concept. 'So if I am reincarnated,' I persist, 'why am I only remembering my past lives *now*?'

Phoenix chews slowly on his bar. 'From what I understand, the vast majority of reborn souls forget upon birth, or at least within the first few years of their new life,' he explains. 'They're here to learn something from this life, and they can't do that with foreknowledge of previous incarnations. For you it's different. You're a First Ascendant. You carry the Light of Humanity in you – and the Incarnates want to destroy that. Therefore, forgetting your past lives is a means of self-protection.'

I study Phoenix, trying to read the expression on his boyish yet worldly-wise face, seeking any signs he might be lying. But he appears as earnest as a priest. 'So how come *you* remember your previous lives?'

He smiles tenderly. 'I remember in order to protect you.'

My heart now pounds to a different beat. One that makes the blood rush to my face and my cheeks flush hot.

'OK,' I say, doing my utmost to remain both unflustered and sceptical. 'If we've met before, why didn't I recognize you?'

'We're reborn into different bodies,' he replies matter-of-factly.

I frown deeply. 'So I'm a different person every time?'

Phoenix nods – and at that moment I believe I've uncovered a crucial flaw in his story. 'Then how do you ever find me?' I question.

'With difficulty,' he replies, laughing. 'It's a combination of luck, deduction and fate. A bit like water divining. I don't have a GPS or tracker. Rather, it's more a feeling, a sensation. Like two magnets, we're drawn to each other. The closer we get, the stronger the attraction.'

He turns to me on the hay bale. There's a frisson in the air and I feel an undeniable gravitational pull towards him. The soft golden light of the evening sun settles like an aura round him and I'm drawn even closer.

'But that magnetism equally applies to the Incarnates, especially after your Wakening,' explains Phoenix.

'My *Wakening*?'

Phoenix nods. 'Yes, your first true Glimmer.'

'The jade knife,' I murmur. I think back to the way I'd been drawn to it; how I'd heard drum beats, screams, thunder, and smelt acrid smoke; how Damien had suddenly appeared at my side, his eyes inky and dark, a Hunter as soon as he saw me at the museum. '*That* must have been my Wakening.'

'Then it's always a race,' Phoenix goes on. 'Between me and the Soul Hunters.'

'But –' I begin to smile – 'you found me in time.'

He shakes his head, clearly angry with himself. 'This time I was almost too late!' he says bitterly. Then taking my hands in his, as if to seek my forgiveness, he whispers, 'But know this, Genna, whoever I am, whatever my name, however I appear in each life, I will *always* be there for you. All you need do is look into my eyes and you'll recognize me . . . recognize my soul.'

Now no more than a heartbeat away from Phoenix, I'm mesmerized by his gaze. His eyes lock with mine and suddenly they expand into a galaxy of stars. His face ripples out as if in a hall of mirrors, the seemingly infinite reflections of a different person from a different time . . . *warrior . . . sailor . . . soldier . . . slave . . . monk . . . samurai . . . healer . . . gladiator . . .* yet each and every one of them in some way Phoenix, my Soul Protector.

The kaleidoscope of memories sends me dizzy and I flinch away. Lurching to my feet, I stagger off across the yard, the world pitching and heaving like the deck of a boat. It's all too much for me to take in. I grab on to the wooden fence enclosing the field and for a moment I feel as if I might vomit . . . but gradually the disorientation passes and the sickness fades.

Still overwhelmed by the heady rush of images, I gaze in numb silence at the rose-red sun, now dipping below the hills. Like its dying rays, any remaining doubts I had about reincarnation are extinguished and I finally embrace the truth for what it is.

And that truth terrifies me.

While I try to regain my composure, the two horses in the field amble over. One is a well-groomed, muscular, chestnut gelding, the other a beautiful, dapple-grey mare. Absent-mindedly I feed the gelding my apple core and pat his neck. He snorts softly in gratitude.

Phoenix comes up behind me and feeds the mare the remains of his apple. 'You should go for a ride,' he suggests. 'That always makes you feel better.'

I glance sideways at him. 'I can't! I've never ridden a horse before.'

The corner of his mouth curls into that all-too-familiar knowing grin. 'Of course you have. Countless times, in countless lives.'

He opens the gate and leads me into the field. The two horses remain calm and docile at our approach. Phoenix strokes the flank of the mare. As I stand anxiously by, the gelding turns his head and nuzzles into me with a soft nickering.

'He likes you,' says Phoenix, cupping his hands to give me a leg up.

'But there's no saddle,' I protest.

'You don't need a saddle,' he replies. 'You just need to remember.'

Ignoring my objections, he helps me climb on to the back of the horse. I cling on to its mane, my thighs tense as I try not to slip off its smooth flanks. By contrast, Phoenix mounts the mare with impressive ease, using the fence to boost himself up. The gelding seems to sense my nervousness. He snorts and shakes his head as if to say, *Chill out!* But I'm so high up off the ground, and have so little to grip on to, that I'm terrified of falling.

'Sit straighter and a little more forward on his back,' Phoenix advises.

As I adjust my position, my horse suddenly starts walking forward. 'How do I steer without reins?' I ask in panic.

'With your legs,' Phoenix replies, trotting alongside. 'Don't worry, it'll all come back to you. It's like riding a bike.'

'*But I don't have a bike either!*' I cry, as the gelding takes off. As I clench my legs in fear, he accelerates from a trot, to a canter, to a full gallop in a matter of yards, and I have to hang on for dear life. We race across the field, his hooves thudding in the soft earth. At any second I expect to tumble to the ground and break my neck. Terror grips me as tightly as I grip his mane, but the gelding gallops on, heading straight for the opposite fence. In my pounding, panicking heart I know the horse intends to jump – and I know that without a saddle I'll be flung from his back.

In desperation, instinct tells me to lean forward and apply pressure with my left leg and relax my right one. Immediately the gelding starts to turn left, veering away from the fence and back out into the open field. Astonished, I switch over, squeezing now with my right leg. My horse takes his cue and wheels back towards the fence.

In spite of my nerve-shredding fear, I smile to myself. With both my thighs, I press against the horse's flanks and he slows at my command. Then I relax and tap him gently with my heels and he's off again. Galloping at full pelt! But I'm no longer scared and out of control . . . I'm *exhilarated*!

My whole body loosens up and I start to flow with the gelding's graceful stride.

'*Woo! Woo! Woo!*' I yell, feeling the cool wind whip against my face, my brown ringlets of hair streaming out behind me.

Phoenix rides up alongside on his grey mare. 'I told you!' he shouts. 'You ride like the wind!'

The smile on my face widens to a grin. The field appears to roll on forever, the grass giving way to red earth, the green hills to rugged mountains, the sun now bloodshot and bold on the shimmering horizon . . .

'Ride like the wind!' shouts Phoenix. But he's no longer in his leather biker jacket – he's wearing a fringed and beaded tunic of buffalo hide, and his deep-ochre skin is embellished with red paint. A tightly woven band of beads encircles his upper arm and an eagle feather sprouts from his shoulder-length dark hair. And his Cheyenne name isn't Phoenix, it's . . . Hiamovi.

A crack of a gunshot reverberates across the prairie. I glance back over my shoulder. A US marshal in a wide-brimmed white hat and wielding a revolver is thundering after us on his steed. His coal-black eyes stare fixedly at me. A posse of bounty hunters rides with him, armed with rifles and six-shooters.

I urge my horse on, my long black plaited hair flowing out behind me, the wind whipping at the beads hanging from my deer-skin dress. As we flee across the Great Plains, Hiamovi strings an arrow to his bow, turns and lets loose. The arrow pierces a Hunter, who tumbles from his saddle. The marshal and his men retaliate with a hail of bullets, the deadly rounds zinging past us like angry hornets. But one strikes Hiamovi in the side. Blood oozes out of the gash in his tunic. He slumps against his horse and drops the bow.

'NO!' I scream, watching his horse veer off. I turn to follow, galloping up close to his side.

Hiamovi is slipping from his mount yet he waves me away. 'No, Waynoka, ride on!'

But I won't leave him behind to die. As I reach across to grab him, another volley of gunfire assails us and –

I hit the ground hard, rolling over and over. But the red earth of the Great Plains is gone, replaced by lush, green grass that cushions my fall. Eventually I roll to a stop and lie there, winded.

As my gelding canters off to the far end of the field, Phoenix gallops over to me and hurriedly dismounts. 'Are you all right?' he asks.

I groan, 'You . . . were . . . *shot*!'

Phoenix helps me sit up, checking for broken bones.

'What happened?' I demand, brushing him off. 'I had a Glimmer – we were Cheyenne, and a US marshal was chasing us across the Plains.'

'I . . .' Phoenix looks to the setting sun as if seeking a long-lost memory – 'I don't remember all our past lives in detail,' he admits, his face troubled. Then he puts on a cheery smile and pulls me to my feet. 'But now you've experienced that Glimmer of riding across the Great Plains, you will always be able to ride in this life.'

With a gentle pat, he bids farewell to his mare and sets off back towards the barn on foot.

Sensing Phoenix remembers more than he's letting on, I call after him, 'Who was the marshal?'

Phoenix stops mid-stride and turns; a shadow falls across his face. 'He goes by many names, but his soul name is . . . *Tanas*.'

16

When I awake the next morning, the sun is watery in the dawn sky, a low mist hanging over the fields, the hills glistening like islands amid the haze. Emerging sleepy-eyed and yawning from the barn, I find that my trust in Phoenix was well placed – at least in this case. While I slept in one of the stalls, he'd kept a quiet watch beside the barn door.

Despite his apparent all-night vigil, Phoenix is soon up and ready and waiting for me in the yard, sitting astride his motorbike. Shrugging off the morning chill, I climb on to the rear seat and take hold of his waist. The engine roars into life, and we set off.

After a night sleeping rough in the hay, the blast of wind as we ride soon blows the cobwebs away. But the many dreams and nightmares that visited me in the night still linger. It's as if a floodgate has been opened in my mind and a river of memories now flows through. Some are blissful, like the time I led a rural life, farming the paddy fields in Northern Thailand some eight centuries ago. Others are harrowing, like the desperate trek across the dry and cracked plains of Abyssinia, my body withered and weak from starvation. And a few are terrifying – grim flashes of torture racks, cramped cells and burning stakes. But there are two constants in all my past lives: the reassuring presence of Phoenix, in whatever body he has been born into ... and the long, dark shadow of Tanas, the ruthless threat that looms over each and every life of mine like a sinister black thundercloud.

As we ride the back country lanes, I wonder what my present life has in store. *Is it even relevant, now I know I've lived before? What will my parents think about my being reincarnated? Of being a First Ascendant? Will they even believe me?* I can imagine Mei laughing me out of the park! Saying I've read too many historical novels. But the reality is stark: Tanas has found me, yet again – and I've the ominous sense that each time he finds me, the closer he gets to accomplishing his wicked end. *Will this be the life when he finally destroys me? That he completes the ritual sacrifice to extinguish my soul forever? Or will Phoenix be able to protect me ... once more?*

My arms wrapped round his slender waist, I'm acutely aware of how young and mortal my protector is. He's no god or superhero. He's flesh and blood. A mere boy.

And there are only the two of us against an apparent *army* of Soul Hunters. If I'm truly honest with myself, I don't favour our chances.

I fear this life may be our last.

After speeding along a main road light of traffic, we stop at a roadside cafe and petrol station for breakfast and to refuel.

'Don't take your helmet off!' Phoenix warns as he parks beside a pump.

'Why not?' I ask.

Phoenix nods upwards at the corner of the petrol station, where a CCTV camera is aimed at the forecourt. 'We don't want to advertise ourselves,' he says.

Filling the tank of his bike, Phoenix then ducks inside the shop to pay. He comes back out with a couple of pre-packed sandwiches, a spiral-bound pocket roadmap and a collapsible snow shovel.

'What's that for?' I ask as he stows the shovel in his backpack.

'I'll explain later,' he replies. 'First we need a proper breakfast.'

Leaving the bike in a parking bay at the back, we head inside the adjoining cafe. Phoenix quickly scopes out the place before choosing a red plastic booth away from the sightline of the only visible CCTV camera. Finally able to remove our helmets, I shake my hair free and rub my weary face with both hands. It's still early, so the restaurant is empty except for the chef, one bleary-eyed waitress and a bald-headed, heavyset lorry driver plumped on a stool at the counter.

We have a quick look at the menu and soon the young waitress is traipsing over. Phoenix orders a full English breakfast and orange juice. Despite having eaten so little in the past twenty-four hours, I don't have much of an appetite, so I just order a round of toast and a mug of tea.

As we wait for our food, I say, 'Tell me more about Tanas.'

Phoenix picks up the knife from his place setting and examines the blade, as if contemplating its usefulness in a battle. 'Tanas is the *blackest* of souls,' he murmurs. 'Death incarnate.'

The unsettling description forces a lump in my throat and I swallow hard. I think of Damien's fathomless eyes and realize I now know what death truly looks like: cold, callous and cruel. 'Does he reincarnate like us?'

Phoenix nods. 'Tanas has been on this Earth at least as long as the First Ascendants. Maybe longer. Maybe even before the Light. He is the Lord and Master of the Incarnates –'

He stops as the waitress comes back with our drinks. With a flirtatious smile in Phoenix's direction, she dumps the glass of juice and mug of tea on the table, then trudges off.

I lean forward and whisper, 'Who *exactly* are these Incarnates?'

Phoenix takes a gulp of his orange juice. 'Servants and slaves of Tanas,' he explains. 'Blackened souls, tortured souls . . . or souls that have been turned away from the Light. There's a hierarchy of Priests, Soul Hunters, Watchers and the Faithful. The Soul Hunters are our greatest concern.' He waves the tip of the knife at me, his expression grim. 'Like a pack of wild dogs, they will track you, stalk you, and never stop hunting you down . . . until you're dead. They have one mission, and one mission alone – to help Tanas eliminate every First Ascendant and their soul forever, thereby extinguishing the Light of Humanity.'

A shudder passes through me. I recall the Glimmer of the ritual sacrifice atop the ancient pyramid as the volcano erupted and the earth shook. The knife in Phoenix's hand seems to morph into the curved, green tongue of the jade blade, and I see in my mind's eye Tanas's red-painted face, and his black-eyed vengeful leer as he prepares to plunge the blade into my heart –

I shake off the horrifying vision. 'So why does Tanas want to destroy this Light that the First Ascendants supposedly carry?'

'Why does any evil want to destroy?' replies Phoenix, jabbing the knife tip into the Formica tabletop. 'So it can rule in its own dark way. With each First Ascendant soul snuffed out, Tanas's power and strength grow.'

At that very moment a cloud passes across the sun, casting the booth into shadow. I want to ask Phoenix more, but I'm almost too afraid to find out the answers . . .

Then the waitress interrupts us again, bringing our food – hot, steaming and greasy. Once she's gone, Phoenix carves a sausage in half and pops it hungrily into his mouth. I watch him tuck into his breakfast like it might be his last meal ever.

'So what's our plan?' I eventually ask, cradling the mug of tea between my hands and ignoring my toast. All the talk of Tanas has put me off my breakfast. 'Run . . . hide . . . *fight*?'

The last option fills me with dread. I've always hated arguments, or any sort of confrontation, and I've never been any good in a fight. In fact, I've no idea *how* to fight.

'All three,' Phoenix replies, chasing his sausage down with a mouthful of scrambled egg. 'But we need to find Gabriel.'

'Who's Gabriel?'

'A Soul Seer.'

Frowning, I take a sip of tea. 'OK . . . And what's a Soul Seer?'

'Someone who can see the past lives of others and how they're connected,' Phoenix explains. 'A Soul Seer is a sort of spiritual guide on Earth, a conduit between here and the Upper Realms. They can offer temporary protection as well as guidance as to what we should do next and where our best hope of survival may lie. But Soul Seers are few and far between; there are perhaps a handful in any generation, scattered around the world.'

Finally finding my appetite, I take a bite of my buttered toast. 'So where's this Gabriel, then?' I ask.

'Lucky for us, in this country.' Phoenix pulls out the pocket roadmap and lays it on the table. 'According to my sources, he's working as a priest in the village of Havenbury.'

We hunch over the map. The village isn't listed in the index so we begin scouring the place names page by page.

After a few minutes of fruitless searching, I complain, 'I wish I had my phone. Then we could Google it.'

'I don't trust technology,' Phoenix mutters, and turns to the next section of map. 'Besides, a mobile would make you too easy to track.'

I shift uncomfortably in my seat as paranoia creeps back in, and the feeling I'm being watched returns with a vengeance. But a quick glance round the cafe proves my anxiety unfounded. The chef is leaning out of the kitchen's fire exit, smoking a cigarette, while the waitress is engrossed with her phone, and the lorry driver has his head buried in a tabloid newspaper. No one is paying us the slightest bit of attention. And that's the way I wish to keep it. Yet the lack of a phone makes me feel cut off from the world, and over-reliant on Phoenix. I'd feel better if I could talk to Mei, get her opinion on it. In a situation like this I realize how much I value her friendship.

I finish off my toast and tea in silence as we continue to study the map.

'It's like looking for a needle in a haystack!' I say with a sigh after another ten minutes. 'Any idea where this village might be?'

Phoenix furrows his brow. 'Sorry, the information I got from my contact was a bit vague ... "Glockester" or "Glou-something" ...'

'Gloucestershire?' I suggest.

Phoenix clicks his fingers. 'Hey, that's it!'

He flips the map to the county of Gloucestershire and we resume the search. After four more pages of drawing a blank, I'm on the point of giving up, when I spot the word *Havenbury* in tiny script. 'There!' I say, pointing to a village nestled in the heart of the Cotswolds.

Phoenix squints at the map. 'We're about a hundred miles away,' he calculates. 'Two hours ... maybe less. We should get going.'

As Phoenix shovels down the last of his breakfast, I rise from my seat.

'Where you off to?' he asks through a mouthful of food.

'Err . . . the toilet?' I reply, feeling like a dog on a very short leash.

Draining his orange juice, he nods. 'Well, don't be too long – and watch out for the camera.'

17

Mindful to keep my head down, I slip out of the booth and across the restaurant. I pass the counter, where the lorry driver is slurping on a mug of coffee and reading the sports section of his paper. The waitress doesn't even bother to look up from her phone. Heading down a short corridor, I enter the ladies' and, after using one of the cubicles, I wash my hands. Splashing cold water on my face, I wipe away the grime from the motorbike ride, then study my reflection in the mirror.

I barely recognize myself. My brown hair is frizzy and a mess, my complexion waxy and washed out. My cheeks are hollow and my eyes look sunken from stress and lack of sleep. But there's a faint blue-white sparkle to my usually hazel-brown irises . . .

As I peer closer, I'm sure I can see ghosts of other faces. Past-life features where my lips are fuller or my chin broader, my hair shorter or my skin lighter. But the person behind them all is still, in essence, *me*.

Fascinated by the seemingly infinite mirror of lives, I stand transfixed by my reflection.

I have noticeably changed in the past week, since that first fateful encounter with Damien at the museum. The gang attack, the attempted kidnapping and the car-crash escape from Detective Inspector Shaw have, of course, all taken their toll. And, even aside from the physical signs of shock and exhaustion on my present-day face, I look somehow *older* . . . Not that I've aged. It's more that I now appear . . . *wise beyond my years*. As if the knowledge and experience of my past lives are gradually filtering through to this one, each Glimmer leaking more and more fragments of information as to who I *really* am.

But the answers continue to float frustratingly just beneath the surface . . .

What does it mean to be a First Ascendant? How do I exactly 'carry' the Light? And what am I supposed to do with it?

I guess Gabriel, being a Soul Seer, will be able to tell me more, but it seems a huge responsibility has been bestowed on me for someone so young. If what Phoenix says is true, then I partly hold the fate of the world in my hands.

The idea terrifies me. Surely I'm just a girl from south London . . . not a reincarnating soul from the dawn of time!

I stare at myself in the mirror, desperately looking for the girl I once was. But all I see are my countless previous incarnations . . . Then another face – brooding and black-eyed – looms out of a darkened cubicle directly behind me.

Damien!

Terror grips me and the room seems to plunge into an icy chill, my skin prickling with goosebumps and the hairs on the back of my neck rising. I spin round to confront my nemesis – only to discover the cubicle empty.

My imagination is playing tricks on me. The stress of the last few days has clearly pushed me to breaking point, shredded my nerves, so that I'm literally jumping at shadows.

With my heart still racing, I leave the washroom and hurry back along the corridor. As I emerge into the neon-lit brightness of the restaurant, I notice a public phone on the wall. All of a sudden the thought of my parents springs into my head.

I've been missing a whole night. They'll be out of their minds with worry!

Frantically I search my pockets for loose change and find a pound coin stuffed in the back of my jeans. I lift the receiver and go to dial my home number when the phone is roughly snatched from my hand and slammed back into its cradle.

'STOP!' Phoenix hisses, his eyes fierce. 'What do you think you're doing?'

'Calling my parents,' I reply, shocked by his angry reaction.

'You *can't*!' Phoenix says sternly. 'You can't call anyone. You can't trust *anyone.*'

'I can trust my *parents*!' I shoot back, going to pick up the phone again.

Phoenix seizes my wrist and shakes his head. 'No, Genna, you can't. Their line will likely be tapped, either by the police or by Hunters. You can't give our location away or tell anyone our destination. Your life depends upon it . . .'

As Phoenix lectures me, I roll my eyes in frustration. Then I happen to glance over his shoulder and notice the lorry driver staring at us. That's when I spot the lead story on his newspaper, and my jaw drops open. My face is plastered all over the front page, along with Phoenix's passport photo, enlarged and unflattering. The headline screams . . . *TERRORIST KIDNAPPER!*

'Hey!' growls the lorry driver, rising from his stool. 'You let that girl go.'

Phoenix turns round with an easy smile. 'It ain't what you think, man. Go back to your coffee.'

But the man's eyes flick to the front page of his newspaper, then back to Phoenix and me. A grimace descends on his craggy face. The chef and the waitress are now watching us too.

Hitching his belt, the lorry driver strides towards Phoenix, his fists clenched. 'I said, let her go!'

Releasing my wrist, Phoenix sizes up the man, who must be twice his weight and width at least. Before the driver can make his move, Phoenix swings his motorbike helmet and smashes him in the belly. With a pained gasp, he doubles over and collapses against a table. Phoenix hits him again on the back of the head to ensure he stays down, then grabs my hand and drags me towards the exit. As we pass our booth, he tosses a couple of tenners on to the table.

'Keep the change!' he shouts to the waitress, collecting up my crash helmet as we go.

Bursting out of the front door, we dash to the motorbike and leap on. As the chef runs out to give chase, Phoenix guns the engine and we leave a trail of smoking rubber behind on the forecourt. Through the restaurant window, I spot the waitress talking rapidly into her phone; the lorry driver is still laid out on the table.

Over the thundering roar of the bike, I shout into Phoenix's ear. 'Why did you have to hit him so hard?'

Phoenix rides on, head down, determined to put as much distance between ourselves and the petrol station as possible.

'Was he a Hunter? A Watcher?' I cry. My mind racing, I go over the scene again and try to recall the lorry driver's eyes. I'm sure they were normal and I can't help but feel sorry for the man who tried to rescue me – even if I didn't need rescuing.

Phoenix doesn't reply, either not hearing or else ignoring me. I lean forward and shout again into his ear. The bike wobbles with my shift in weight, and Phoenix eases back on the throttle.

'Are you trying to kill us?' he complains.

'No,' I reply, 'but I think you might have killed that man!'

Phoenix gives me a dismissive shake of his head. 'Unlikely, although he might have a nasty headache when he comes to.'

'But why hurt him?' I ask. 'Why hit him *twice*?'

He glances at me in the wing mirror. 'I'll do whatever is needed to protect you.'

'*Whatever*?' I question, the cool unequivocal nature of his reply ringing alarm bells. 'You mean, even *kill* someone?'

Phoenix's eyes fix back upon the road as he replies, '*Whatever*'s necessary.'

He twists the throttle hard and we accelerate away, the noise of the engine ending our conversation. I clasp on to him, streamlining my body with his. Once more putting my life in his hands. But, as much as I'm coming to trust my protector, a small seed of doubt has been planted . . .

Am I riding with a killer?

18

Watcher or not, someone at the restaurant definitely put a call out. The wail of a siren warns us of an approaching cop car, followed by an ambulance, and we have to ride down a litter-strewn bank and hide ourselves as a flash of blue-and-white, then a streak of neon yellow, shoot past on the other side of the dual carriageway. With the police alerted to our whereabouts, not to mention our faces in every national newspaper and on the TV news and internet, it'll only be a matter of time before we're spotted again. The Soul Hunters won't need Watchers to find us – *anybody* at all could identify us and report our location to the authorities.

The idea of being a fugitive fills me with dread. *Where will we stay? What will we do for food?* Phoenix appears to have money . . . but how long will that last? And how are we supposed to stay one step ahead of the police *and* the Soul Hunters? Even if we do make it to Havenbury, will this Gabriel, this Soul Seer, really be able to offer us sanctuary and guidance? I doubt even *he's* above the law.

As we get back on the road, all these worries whirl around my head – especially what my parents and friends must be thinking, and the fact Phoenix says I can't even contact them without risking my life. Yet at the same time I can't deny there's a certain thrill at being on the run with him. An excitement at our escape and a keen awareness that we've done this *before* . . . and somehow survived.

I press myself closer to Phoenix, reassuring myself with the warmth of his body and the tautness of his muscles. He is a fighter. A survivor. My protector. With that role, I'm now realizing, comes a necessary use of force, even violence . . . but also the promise of safety.

For some reason a snippet of Latin enters my mind: *Si vis pacem, para bellum.*

Even though I've never studied the language – well, not in this life, at least – I know exactly what the words mean. *If you want peace, prepare for war.*

Phoenix is my preparation. He's been preparing all his life, and all his lives before. For he is my armour and my shield in the battles to come.

We zoom past a road sign pointing north to Newbury. Recalling the directions from the map, I tap Phoenix on the shoulder. 'I thought we were headed to the Cotswolds?' I shout.

'Need to make a small detour,' he replies.

'Detour?' I question but he doesn't answer; or if he does, I don't hear his reply above the noise of the engine. I bite back on my frustration at being kept in the dark. In the past twenty-four hours my life has spiralled out of my control and I've had to put my trust completely in Phoenix. *Surely he could trust in me a little more?*

A mile or so before the junction to Andover, Phoenix pulls off the carriageway and we snake along a warren of high-hedged country roads, eventually stopping at the base of a low hill. Parking the motorbike in a clump of woods, he shoulders his backpack and leads the way through the trees, over a boundary fence and into a farmer's field.

'So where *are* we going?' I ask, stopping in front of him.

'Up there,' Phoenix replies, pointing to a stone circle at the top of a hill. He gestures for me to go on ahead.

With the sun upon our backs, we walk upslope until we come to the hill's brow. Here the field flattens out. The circle of chest-high sarsen stones stands atop the rise like some prehistoric crown. An eroded bank and shallow ditch surround and enclose the ancient monument, from which unbroken views of the rolling Hampshire countryside stretch out in all directions.

As soon as we step over the ditch and enter the circle, I feel a thrum in my bones.

'What is this place?' I murmur, reaching out to one of the lichen-covered stones. As my fingertips brush across its rough surface, the sky goes . . .

. . . *dark. Stars burst in their millions across the firmament. A crescent moon gleams down upon a group of shrouded figures, their arms raised to the heavens, a soft low chant issuing from unseen lips. A young girl with long, flowing hair stands at the centre of this small and intimate congregation, her white dress shimmering and fluttering in the warm breeze. A divine light seems to shine from within her, as if her very heart was a miniature sun.*

Then her head suddenly turns. She looks directly at me and her radiance becomes blinding –

Phoenix catches me in mid-faint. 'The Glimmers get easier,' he reassures me, settling my trembling body upon the green grass.

'Why was *that* vision so strong?' I ask, still feeling the thrum in my bones.

Phoenix nods at the sarsen stone. 'I suppose because that's literally a Touchstone! The same as with the first-aid box. It mainlined you into a past life.'

'No. This Glimmer was even stronger,' I insist. 'It felt hyper real. I wasn't just remembering a past life; I was *living* it!'

I explain my vision to him, and how the girl looked at me as if aware of my modern-day presence. Phoenix chews his lower lip thoughtfully.

'That's not possible,' he says. He reaches out and touches the same stone but a flicker of a frown tells me he's disappointed. 'That Glimmer may be before my time,' he admits. 'A life before our lives together.'

He stands and shrugs off his backpack. 'I suspect the intensity of your Glimmer is due to this being an ancient temple of the First Ascendants. Ceremonial stone circles, like the pyramids in Egypt and Central America, are used to concentrate the Earth's energy and focus the power of the universe. Sacred and safe, this circle is a place to refuel with the Light.'

As I'm sitting recovering from my Glimmer, I become aware of a tingling energy entering my body, like warm honey seeping into my bones and muscles. A deep sense of calm settles over me and I lie back in the grass, enjoying the sensation.

Leaving me to rest and recharge, Phoenix delves into his backpack and pulls out the collapsible shovel. Then he walks over to the circle's head stone, a rock taller and wider than the rest, before carefully pacing out seven strides. Having selected his spot, he drives the shovel into the ground.

I peer curiously at him. 'What are you digging for?' I ask.

'A Soul Jar,' Phoenix replies, tossing aside a clod of earth. He notices the bemused look on my face. 'A sort of time capsule,' he explains. 'I leave them in one life for use in another.'

'What's in them?' I ask.

He gives a wry smile. 'I can't always remember, to be honest. But the contents are always useful. A talisman, a weapon, sometimes gold or other precious items. Occasionally there's information we've gathered on Tanas, something that might help us stop him.'

I sit up. '*Can* he be stopped?'

Phoenix wipes the sweat from his brow with a soiled hand. 'He can certainly be killed in this life, but whether he can be stopped from ever reincarnating again –' he shrugs – 'that's another matter.' He resumes digging and, after removing several spadefuls of earth, his shovel strikes something hard.

Intrigued, I join him beside the hole. 'What is it? Have you found your Soul Jar?'

Phoenix shakes his head. 'I think it's just a rock.' Kneeling down, he scrapes the dirt away, only to reveal more stones and earth. He sighs. 'That's the problem with Soul Jars. Many are lost or destroyed over time, especially in this era, what with roads being built, cities expanding, archaeological digs and treasure hunters!' He sifts through the earth. 'But there's no evidence this Soul Jar has been disturbed or even found. So I don't know why it's not here –' He suddenly slaps his forehead with his palm. 'Idiot! Of course! I was shorter back then.'

Re-pacing the route from the head stone, this time with smaller strides, Phoenix stops at a different spot and starts digging all over again. As he shovels away, I hear the growl of an engine approaching. A moment later a battered Land Rover crests the brow of the hill and an old farmer in an olive-green wax jacket and flat cap clambers out.

'Oi!' he shouts. 'What d'you think you're doing?'

Phoenix glances up but doesn't stop digging. 'We've . . . er . . . we've lost her ring,' he replies.

The farmer hobbles over towards us. '*Tsk*. Likely story. You don't need a shovel to find a ring. Now get off my land!'

'We won't be much longer,' Phoenix promises, piling up the earth.

'I said –' the farmer stops abruptly at the edge of the circle – 'get off my land! Go on – hop it!'

He squints at me with malice, hovering at the stone boundary, but coming no closer. It's as if he's met an invisible wall. Unnerved by the man's strange behaviour, I turn to Phoenix and whisper, 'Why's he just standing there?'

'Must be a Watcher,' Phoenix replies, and I stiffen in alarm. 'Don't worry,' he adds. 'He can't enter the circle.'

I glance nervously at the old farmer, who's standing stock-still, staring at me. Like a veil descending, his rheumy eyes slowly dissolve into dark pools. 'Phoenix?' I say. 'Are you *certain* about that?'

He nods, but nonetheless begins digging faster. 'Incarnates like him often unconsciously stand watch over places such as this, in the hope of spotting First Ascendants. But Incarnates can't enter a sacred stone circle that is protected by the Light.'

Seeming to lose his patience with us, the farmer limps back to his Land Rover. He picks up a handheld radio from the dashboard and jabbers into the receiver.

'I think he's calling for Hunters,' I warn Phoenix. 'We should go –'

'Not yet!' cries Phoenix, his shovel clanging against what looks to be a clay pot. Getting down on his hands and knees, he starts clawing at the dirt.

Setting aside the CB radio, the farmer now reaches into the rear of his cab and pulls out something else: a shotgun. From the glove compartment he grabs a handful of red cartridges, then breaks the gun's barrel and begins to load the two chambers.

'*Phoenix!*' I plead, backing away towards the far side of the circle.

But he's still too engrossed in retrieving the pot. 'I told you,' he says, 'a Watcher can't get us in here –'

'*He has a gun!*'

Phoenix looks up, startled. As the farmer lurches towards us, Phoenix wrenches the Soul Jar from the earth and shakes the pot furiously. Dirt, stones and a few coins tumble out on to the grass.

'Damn it!' Phoenix swears. 'It's empty!'

The farmer lets out a snort of laughter. 'I could've saved you the hassle, boy,' he declares. 'Your little trinkets have already been taken by treasure hunters.'

Phoenix clutches the dug-up earth in his bare hands in frustration.

'And now I've got you trapped,' the farmer sneers. Halting at the circle's boundary, he snaps shut the shotgun and points it at my chest.

I stand rooted to the spot, the double-barrelled muzzle staring at me as black and baleful as the farmer's eyes.

The farmer grins. 'This'll be like shooting fish in a barrel . . .'

Rising quickly to his feet, Phoenix strides towards the farmer. 'STOP! You can't shoot her. Tanas wouldn't want that!'

A crafty grin cuts across the farmer's stubbled face. 'No, that I can't, not unless she runs . . . But *you* I can shoot.'

He swings the barrel towards Phoenix. At the same time Phoenix flings a handful of earth into the farmer's face. As the gun goes off, Phoenix dives aside and the shot hits a standing stone, scarring it with a strafing of pellets.

'GO, GENNA!' Phoenix shouts, grabbing his backpack and sprinting from the circle.

Like a startled rabbit, I bolt and dash down the slope. From on top of the hill the farmer rants and raves as he claws the dirt from his eyes. Phoenix runs up close behind me, his backpack on. A second blast of the shotgun echoes across the field. I nimbly vault the fence. Shot whizzes past like lethal hail . . . but none appear to hit me. We dive into the cover of the woods as a third blast harmlessly peppers the leaves above our heads.

19

'Well, that was close!' I remark, dismounting and removing my helmet. Phoenix has ridden a good few miles and put in a couple of switchbacks to ensure we aren't followed; now he's pulled over and stopped beside a river. The country lane is quiet and the river meadow deserted of all but wild flowers and long grass.

'Yeah ... too close.' He winces, dropping the bike's kickstand.

As Phoenix removes his backpack, I notice the nylon material is perforated like a cheese grater. His leather jacket is peppered with tiny holes too.

'You've been shot!' I gasp. Only now do I realize that he must have shielded me from the farmer's shotgun blasts.

Easing himself off the bike, Phoenix walks stiffly over to the riverbank and crouches at the water's edge. Without a word, he washes the dirt off his hands, then splashes his face. I go over to him and discover his face is creased up in pain.

'Are you badly hurt?' I ask with concern.

'You tell me,' he groans, and gingerly removes his jacket to reveal a blood-soaked T-shirt. I clamp my hand to my mouth to stifle a cry of shock. For a second I feel sick at the sight of so much blood.

'That bad?' he says, noting my horrified expression.

Doing my best to compose myself, I offer a non-committal shrug. 'Oh, I can't really tell . . . You'll have to take your top off for me to see.'

Gently helping him to peel the T-shirt away, I inspect the gunshot wounds and grimace. His back is bloody and pockmarked. But the backpack and leather jacket appear to have absorbed the worst of the impact. There's more bruising than broken skin.

'It doesn't look like many of the pellets have penetrated that deeply,' I say.

'Still hurts like hell!' he growls through gritted teeth. He gestures towards the damaged backpack. 'There's a first-aid kit in the side pocket.'

I fish out a large dented tin and pass it to him. Miraculously the kit is intact.

'Uh-uh. *You're* going to have to patch me up,' he says, handing it back.

'Me?'

He nods. I hold the first-aid kit in my hand, as if it's some alien artefact, and glance at his bleeding back again.

'Shouldn't we go to a hospital for this?'

Phoenix gives me a look. 'Unfortunately, Genna, we don't have that option . . . unless we want to get arrested.'

I open the tin reluctantly and stare in bewilderment at the assortment of dressings, plasters, tourniquets, antiseptic wipes, syringes and gauzes. 'What am I supposed to do with all this?'

'What you always do,' he replies. 'Fix me.' And he smiles, his apparent confidence in my medical ability both encouraging and, in my mind, misplaced.

'But I've never –' I stop, guessing what Phoenix will say in reply to my protest. I let out a sigh. 'Right. Never mind.'

I sift through the tin's contents, but I'm at a loss as to where to start. I've only ever done basic first aid at school. How to put on a plaster . . . treat wasp and bee stings . . . call 999. Dealing with gunshot wounds is a little beyond my skill set. Then I recall my Glimmer back in the disused tube station. I was too freaked out at the time to notice the details, but I'm certain I was wearing a white uniform. The image stirs up long-forgotten memories of my life as a wartime nurse.

Giving myself over to the Glimmer, I allow my intuition to guide me. First putting on a pair of surgical gloves, I carefully clean Phoenix's back with antiseptic wipes. Next I find a pair of tweezers and sterilize them too. Then, with practised efficiency, I prise out the pellets one by one – Phoenix gritting his teeth as each tiny lead ball is removed. Once they're all out, I clean up his wounds, then dress his back in a patchwork of plasters and bandages. At the end, I stand back and examine my handiwork.

'So what's my prognosis, Nurse Genna?' says Phoenix with a pained grin.

'You look like a badly wrapped present,' I reply, laughing, 'but you'll live.'

Phoenix gently shakes his head. 'Sometimes I wonder who's looking after who in these lives.'

I smile tenderly at him. 'Maybe we're supposed to look after each other,' I say.

He glances at me with those sapphire-blue eyes of his, his sparkling gaze so open and unguarded that once again I experience that strange, irresistible magnetism . . . Before the sensation becomes too intense, I break off and busy myself with tidying up the first-aid kit.

After a moment or so, Phoenix looks away too and delves into his lacerated backpack. He takes out a punctured bottle of water and two obliterated sandwiches. 'Well, there goes our lunch!' he says ruefully.

After the meagre breakfast I chose, a pang of hunger now grips me. 'Perhaps we can salvage some of it?' I suggest.

Phoenix carefully hands me the ruined meal before reaching into the pack again. At the bottom he finds a spare T-shirt, undamaged by the gunshot. But it's wet from the leaking bottle so he lays it out on a bush to dry in the sun. Then we sit down together on the riverbank.

As we wait for the top to dry, we quietly munch on the remains of our sandwiches, picking out the shotgun pellets and listening to the gentle ripple of the water. Every so often I steal a glance at Phoenix. Despite the obvious pain and discomfort he's in, he makes no complaint. Nor has he made a big deal of his self-sacrifice in protecting me. This more than anything – more even than the Glimmers – suggests that he really is my Soul Protector.

He has *literally* taken a bullet for me.

His courage and his selfless heroism stir something deep within my soul –

'What are you thinking?' Phoenix asks.

I blink, suddenly aware that I'm staring at him. 'Um . . . er . . . nothing,' I mumble, diverting my attention to the water bottle in my hand. I plug the leaks before taking a swig. 'Just wondering what we do now?'

Phoenix shrugs. 'We find another Soul Jar, I guess.'

I dab at a spurt of water that's escaped a hole in the bottle and splashed my jeans. 'Why not go straight to Gabriel?' I ask.

'We need an effective weapon against Tanas,' he explains, 'otherwise we're defenceless.'

'What sort of weapon?'

Phoenix purses his lips thoughtfully. 'Depends what's in the jar.'

'So where do we find another of these Soul Jars?'

'Good question,' he replies, his teeth crunching on his sandwich. Grimacing, he spits out a pellet and discards the rest. 'I need to jog my memory.'

Crossing his legs into the lotus position, he shuts his eyes and slows his breathing. A few minutes of silence pass, the peace broken only by the burbling of the river and the soft wisp of the breeze through the long grass. He appears to go into a deep trance. At first still and silent, Phoenix starts to twitch ever so slightly, then he begins to mutter. I lean in closer, but can't make out his words. His voice deepens though, and he seems to lose his American accent. Then, in plain, rough English, he blurts out: *'Take cover!'*

To my alarm, his body starts jerking and his limbs tremble uncontrollably. In an attempt to calm his agitation, I rest my hand upon his arm –

20

'TAKE COVER!' he cries. We duck into the fireside alcove, my hand grasping his arm as the inner gatehouse shudders under the impact. Dust and masonry shower down upon us.

The roar like a pack of fire-breathing dragons, the cannons' bombardment is ceaseless and the castle walls crumble easily under the heavy onslaught.

As the dust settles, William peers out of the shattered window at the legion of Parliamentarian troops besieging the castle. The English Civil War has raged some two years and, despite our early victories, the tide has since turned against the supporters of the King – the Royalists, like us. Even the bleak cold of winter has failed to dull the Roundheads' determination to bring down our Royalist stronghold. Encamped in the fields for the past eighteen days, the Roundheads have not only repulsed Lord Hopton and his men, but they have drained the castle lake and, since the morning, been reinforced with heavy artillery. The grim realization strikes us both that it's only a matter of time before the enemy demolish the battlements and overrun the castle.

'What do we do now?' I ask William.

'We pray for God's intervention,' he replies, then, clasping the hilt of his rapier, adds, 'or else we die by the sword.'

Terrified, I cling to him as the gatehouse trembles from another direct hit. The screams of injured soldiers and the stench of burned gunpowder rise up from the floor below us. The crack of musket shot and the whistle of arrows signal our feeble retaliation to the mighty blasts of enemy cannon fire.

'Anne! What are you doing here?' barks my father, striding into the room. 'You should be safe in the keep.'

A tall, imposing man with a beaked nose and an arrow of a beard, my father is every inch the Royalist Commander of the Castle, and I find it hard to look him in the eye.

'I feel safer with William, Father,' I reply meekly.

My father shoots him a scathing look. 'You should know better, Captain.'

Doffing his plumed hat in deference, William replies, 'Certainly, Commander. I merely thought –'

'You don't think. You do as I order,' my father snaps. 'Now escort Anne to the keep and station yourself on the castle walls!'

'But Father –' I protest before he cuts me off with a wave of his hand.

'Enough! I don't have time to battle my daughter as well as the Roundheads.'

I realize my father will never understand the bond between William and me, or my Protector's duty to live and die by my side. William also appears to see the futility of arguing with his superior, since he ushers me towards the door. But, as we head for the stairwell, a grey-faced and gaunt soldier charges into the room, his tunic torn and bloodied.

'Commander . . .' he pants, 'the Roundheads have breached the walls!'

My father blasphemes in outrage, his words as much of a shock to me as the soldier's news, for I know he is a godly man. Above the rolling thunder of cannon, a blood-curdling battle cry sounds out as ten thousand troops surge towards the castle.

'Order all our men to repel the traitorous intruders,' my father commands.

'But the men are too weak to fight on, sir,' the soldier insists.

My father's face reddens. 'For King and Country, we cannot let this castle fall!'

'But consider, sir, that since the lake was drained, we've not had a drop of water for three days,' argues the soldier, his lips cracked and his eyes sunken. 'I assure you, although the men's spirits may not be broken, their bodies are. Commander, we'll be slaughtered to the last man, woman and child if we fight on.'

My father stares hard at the scrawny soldier before glancing at me, his sharp eyes reflecting a rare paternal love. 'Then we have no choice,' he says, 'but to surrender.' He sighs heavily, lowering his head in defeat.

William turns to me and whispers urgently, 'Your father may be surrendering, but we cannot!' And, taking my hand, he leads me down to the next chamber, which had been my bedroom until it had been commandeered for military operations. From under my mattress, William pulls out a brown leather pouch. He quickly checks the contents.

'We cannot risk losing these,' he says to me. 'Not in this life or the next.'

He takes an empty clay jar from the window sill, puts the pouch inside and seals the lid. Going over to the fireplace, he then unsheathes his dagger and with its steel tip prises out a loose stone from the masonry. Behind it is a small cavity. 'We'll hide the jar here. Remember well, Anne, for you may need this in times to come.'

I look upon his fair face, framed by ringlets of long, flowing hair, and nod. 'I will commit it to memory,' I vow.

As he stashes the jar inside the hole, I happen to glance out of the window. Parliamentarian troops are flooding the lower bailey, but one unit of soldiers breaks away from the main group and heads directly for the inner gatehouse. A chill runs through me, colder than the winter wind blowing outside.

'I think he's coming,' I warn William.

Our real fear has never been the Roundhead army – it has always been Tanas and his Soul Hunters.

William hammers the stone back into place with the pommel of his dagger, just as a young soldier bursts into the room. 'Captain, I've seen the Black Eyes!' he blurts.

'How many?' asks William, leaping to his feet.

'Ten, maybe more,' replies the soldier, who gives me a shy, jerky bow of his head. I recognize the raw-boned lad to be Ralph, though the other soldiers call him Rabbit for his nervous twitch and habit of darting everywhere.

'Then we'll need your sword hand too, Ralph,' says William, drawing his rapier in readiness.

Ralph's round eyes widen to full moons of fear. 'B-b-but I'm no swordsman like you, sir!'

William challenges him with a reproachful look. 'Come now, Ralph. Don't you want to defend our lady's life?'

The lad's pale cheeks flush and with it his courage seems to grow. 'Of course, sir,' he says, puffing out his chest and unsheathing his slender blade with an unsteady hand.

'Good,' states William, 'because we need to fight our way out of this castle.'

Together we rush down the spiral staircase. But the clump of heavy boots rises to greet us. A black-eyed, broad-chested soldier in tan leather, and wearing a round iron helmet, blocks our escape. Seeing me, the Soul Hunter slashes upwards with his sword. The narrow twisting stairwell makes his attack awkward, and William easily deflects the blade before thrusting the tip of his own rapier through the man's throat. The Soul Hunter tumbles backwards down the stairs. But no sooner has he been despatched than more men with the same terrifying eyes surge up to take his place.

Forced to retreat, we race along the corridor to a heavy oak door. William barges it open and we dash on to the battlements that lead to the castle's keep. The biting wind whips my cheeks as we make for the only sanctuary left to us.

But the Soul Hunters are close on our heels. Too close.
At the foot of the keep's stone steps, William and Ralph
stop, and turn to confront our enemies. Two abreast, the
Soul Hunters advance on us, weapons raised. Tanas looms
largest, in a gleaming steel breastplate and wielding a
mighty broadsword. His battle-scarred face leers at me
through the grille of his helmet – not an ounce of mercy in
his fierce gaze.

The cannon bombardment has now ceased, but the
massacre of the Royalist soldiers trapped in the bailey has
only just begun. I catch a glimpse of my father, waving a
white banner, desperately surrendering to the Roundhead
army.

But there'll be no surrender for us, and no quarter
given by Tanas.

'GO!' William urges me. 'We'll hold them back.'

As I flee up the steps, I hear the clash of steel upon steel.
The grunt of brutal combat. The slick slicing of flesh and
the splatter of blood. A scream cuts through the icy air.
Glancing back over my shoulder, I see poor Ralph impaled
on Tanas's immense sword. With contemptuous ease,
Tanas tosses the vanquished lad over the battlements as if
he were no more than a picked bone at a banquet.

Sickened, I now fear for my protector's life. Left to
fend off the Soul Hunters single-handedly, his rapier
flashes like lightning against the rain of sword blows. He
runs one soldier through, then punches another in the face
with his hilt. But as valiant and spirited as his efforts
are, William is outnumbered and outweaponed. A raven-
haired Hunter with a double-ended halberd starts to drive

him back, slashing viciously with the long, spiked axe blade.

If I only had a sword, I would stand by William's side and fight to my last breath. Of course he would say that I shouldn't risk my life for his, that my soul – and the Light that it carries – is too precious. But I can help him by ensuring we have somewhere safe to which we can retreat. I hasten up the steps and, upon reaching the keep's entrance, I beat my fists on the wooden portcullis and shout to the guard of the gate inside.

'Open up!' I cry.

He peers out through the narrow slit of window above. 'Why, m'lady!' he gasps.

'Let us in!' I demand.

At the foot of the steps, a mound of bodies has piled up. Five of the Soul Hunters lie bleeding and defeated, but William has paid a heavy price for these victories. The Hunter with the halberd has pierced his side.

William bounds awkwardly up the steps, clutching his stomach, blood seeping through his fingers.

'OPEN UP!' he barks. 'By order of the Commander!'

Slowly the portcullis begins to rise, too slowly. Tanas and his remaining three Soul Hunters are already clambering over the corpses and mounting the steps after us. Tanas grins, knowing his prey is trapped. He pushes past his Hunters, eager to seize me first.

William heaves on the portcullis in a futile attempt to speed its ascent. The gap between oak beam and stone step is still little more than a narrow slit, but I drop to the floor and squeeze under like a mouse escaping a cat.

As soon as the gap is wide enough, William rolls under after me.

'Close the gate!' he orders, and the portcullis crashes down behind us, a second before Tanas reaches the keep.

'Curse you!' Tanas spits, his hard, pitiless eyes glaring through the grille at us. He examines the gate, reinforced with iron, then looks up at the impregnable stone walls of the keep, and his malicious grin returns. 'Ha! What keeps me out also keeps you in!'

He starts to laugh, deep and harsh. William slams the keep's inner door in Tanas's wicked face and we retreat to the keep's tiny courtyard. I gaze round at the high walls that have now become our prison.

'What now?' I ask.

'We hold out here –' William grimaces in pain as he inspects his bleeding wound – 'for as long as we can.'

'But what good will it do us, Captain?' queries the guard morosely, and he sighs and slumps down on the ground with the handful of other emaciated soldiers who have fled to the keep. 'The white flag is up. The battle is lost.'

I exchange a fearful glance with William. For we both know that if the gate is raised again, the battle for my soul truly will be lost.

21

'Are you *sure* this is the same castle?' I ask as we follow the wide loop of gravel path through the lower gardens and up to the main entrance of Arundel Castle. 'I don't recognize any of this.'

Ahead, a grey-stoned edifice of turrets and tall chimneys commands a steep embankment of green grass. Rows of arched, leaded windows line the outer wall, and the battlements now appear to be more for decoration than defence. At the south-west corner, an immense round tower slit with narrow windows is the most castle-like of the fortifications, but the rest of the rectangular block building looks more like an eighteenth-century stately home.

Phoenix furrows his brow in bemusement. 'I guess much was rebuilt after the Civil War.'

Having left the motorbike in the tourist car park, we continue to make our way uphill, our feet crunching in the soft gravel. A run of old flint wall at the base of the embankment is faintly familiar; otherwise, I still have no real recollection of the place.

'Can Glimmers be wrong?' I ask.

'They're as reliable as any memory,' he replies, then arches an eyebrow. 'Although one's memory can sometimes be wrong, of course.'

I'm starting to think we've wasted our time, that we should have gone straight to Gabriel, when we turn the corner and a pair of square stone towers suddenly come into view. I'm instantly hit by the strongest sense of déjà vu. As if two photos have been laid one on top of the other, I can see both the past and the present. The old and the new. I can spot where the squared towers have been renovated, where the inner gatehouse has been repaired with new flintwork, and, high upon the grassy mound behind, where the battlements of the castle's mighty keep have been rebuilt. Only the keep's well tower has remained intact through the centuries, its construction having weathered both storm and siege.

'*This is it!*' I breathe softly. '*My old home.*'

Phoenix nods. 'Just one of many over your lives . . . though perhaps one of the grandest!'

Our pace quickens in our excitement. As we hurry towards the tourist entrance, we're greeted by a mousey-haired steward at the gate. 'The castle closes in half an hour,' she warns us.

'Thank you,' Phoenix replies, showing our tickets to the woman. 'That'll be more than enough time.'

The steward gives the tickets a cursory glance, but her pale-green eyes linger on me, a little too long for my liking. I smile nervously at her. She doesn't smile back, her thin lips pursing tightly as if sucking on a sour lemon; nonetheless she waves us through.

As we pass under the stone gateway and into a small courtyard, I whisper, 'I think she recognized me.'

Phoenix glances back at the steward, who is observing us from a distance. 'You reckon she's a Watcher?' he asks.

'I don't know . . . she might've just seen my face on the news.'

'Then we'd better be quick in case she calls the police,' Phoenix replies. 'Do you remember the way to your old bedroom?'

'I think so,' I reply, and take the lead.

Mounting some steps, we enter an entrance hall. Apart from a suit of armour, there's little else on show, and the room triggers no memories; the newer stone of the walls suggest the hall was built during the castle's restoration. But I spot a sign pointing up the staircase to the keep. Taking the steep flight of steps to the first floor, we turn left through a large doorway and into a vaulted chamber with animal heads mounted on the walls. Making our way against the flow of visitors heading for the exit, we climb another set of winding stairs, before heading along a narrow corridor and up more steps.

Peering curiously into a couple of the rooms as we pass, Phoenix asks, 'Any of this familiar to you yet?'

I shake my head and continue to follow the signs towards the keep.

Phoenix runs a hand along the smooth, perfectly cut blocks of pale sandstone. 'Let's just hope the inner gatehouse hasn't been entirely rebuilt too!' he mutters. I can tell from his tense tone that he's concerned at the fate of the Soul Jar – and I am too. *Is this going to be another wasted detour?*

The corridor stretches on until the sandstone walls eventually give way to older brick and flintwork. A cool, musty smell hangs in the air and a sense of age descends upon the surroundings. As if stepping back in time, I recall walking this very same corridor in a bright blue bodice and petticoat, my blond hair tied up in a bun, my lily-white hands clasping a bunch of wild lavender. Briefly closing my eyes, I can almost smell the heady fragrance now, and the ghosts of the Civil War return. Just beyond my hearing is the portentous –

– boom of cannon and the agonized cries of injured soldiers. Panicked footsteps are mounting the stairwell and the sweet smell of lavender is replaced by the acrid stench of scorched gunpowder . . .

I open my eyes, half expecting to see my Royalist father bellowing for me to get to the keep, and I gasp when I'm stopped in my tracks by a bearded man as tall and imposing as my long-dead father. But he's just a tourist with a camera, more interested in taking snapshots of the castle than in me.

'Are you OK?' Phoenix asks.

'A flashback, that's all,' I explain, and carry on. Entering the apartments of the castle's inner gatehouse, I instinctively turn right up the spiral staircase to my old bedroom. It is at once familiar and strange. The place has been mocked up for tourists. The timber-beamed ceiling has been carefully restored and the dark oak floorboards re-laid and polished. A red and gold tapestry hangs from an iron pole against a wall of flint and brick. As for furniture, a simple, wood-framed bed occupies the far side of the room, and in the corner near the fireplace sits a high-backed wooden chair. Two candles flicker in their holders and a bunch of dried lavender sprouts from a clay jug on a roughly hewn table.

I can't help but laugh out loud. 'My room was *never* like this!'

An elderly couple stare at me, taken aback by my bizarre exclamation. They shuffle towards the door as I continue to inspect the room and make disparaging comments about the gaudy tapestry and point out where my things were *actually* placed.

Once the couple depart and we're left alone, Phoenix asks me, 'Do you remember which stone the jar is behind?'

I grin at him. 'Of course! You made me vow I'd commit it to memory.' And I point to the third stone up on the right-hand side of the fireplace.

Stepping over the rope barrier, Phoenix shrugs off his backpack and takes out his Swiss Army knife. 'Someone's repointed these walls,' he comments. He selects the chisel tool and begins to chip away at the mortar surrounding the stone. 'Let's pray that's all they've done.'

As Phoenix gouges out the mortar, I wander round my old bedroom, trying to glean more memories. My former life wasn't always consumed by war. There were happier times too – sewing by the fireside with my aunt, learning to play the lute and singing sweet airs. Then there was reading by candlelight the snippets of poems William used to write for me – my heart warms at this memory and I glance across at Phoenix who is jimmying out the stone –

oh, and curling up in my bed as the snow fell upon the fields beyond the castle walls while Father read me stories from the Bible . . .

An information panel by the window attempts to explain what life was like back then, but I know what it was *truly* like, and no words can ever express the heaven and hardship, nor the simplicity and severity, of those times. Beside the text is a reproduction of a family portrait from the seventeenth century. Peering closer at it, I stifle a gasp. My attention is caught by a young girl with fair complexion and milk-blond hair. She wears a bright blue bodice and petticoat –

'That's *me*!' I whisper in wonderment.

The shock at recognizing myself – so utterly different yet so undeniably me – sparks a shiver across my amber skin. For a brief moment I experience the bizarre sensation of being in two bodies at once . . . Then the feeling fades and I settle back into the present.

'Hey! What do you think you're doing?' exclaims an outraged voice.

Startled, I spin round to see a steward, grey-haired and indignant, standing in the doorway. He's glaring at Phoenix, who's managed to remove the stone and is now pulling out a dusty clay jar from the cavity behind.

'Put that back, you thief!' the steward snaps.

'I can't steal what's mine,' Phoenix argues, stuffing the jar into his backpack.

'*Yours?*' barks the steward as Phoenix gets to his feet.

'Yes, I left it here four hundred years ago,' he explains matter-of-factly.

The steward's wrinkled face creases even more in irate bafflement. Then his expression hardens. 'Give that back *now* . . . or I'll call the police!'

Through the window I notice a flurry of dark-blue uniforms crossing the lower bailey.

'Too late,' I say, with a glance at Phoenix in alarm. 'They're already here!'

22

'So my colleague was right about you two, then!' Smugly folding his arms, the steward waits by the door for the police.

As the unit of armed officers gather at the base of the gatehouse, I realize we don't have much time. 'Whatever you've read in the papers, Phoenix is *not* a terrorist and I've *not* been kidnapped,' I explain hurriedly. 'The truth is, we're being hunted. We need that jar in order to survive!'

The steward's stony expression tells me he's unmoved by my pleas. 'Tell that to the police, not me,' he says bluntly. 'In my eyes, you're common thieves.'

'Have it back, for all I care,' says Phoenix with a resigned sigh. Then, to my surprise and dismay, he pulls the Soul Jar from his backpack and tosses it to the steward. 'Here, catch!'

Taken off-guard, the steward fumbles with the antique clay pot . . . and drops it. 'No!' he cries as the jar shatters into a dozen pieces at his feet.

In the confusion, Phoenix grabs my hand and together we make a dash for the door. Pushing past the distracted steward, we rush down the spiral staircase to the floor below. But the clump of heavy boots is already rising to greet us.

'Not again!' Phoenix mutters, as a police officer in a bulletproof vest and riot helmet blocks our escape.

This no longer feels like déjà vu, rather a repeat of history. Without a sword this time to fend off the armoured officer, Phoenix kicks out at the man's chest. Hemmed in by the narrow spiral stairwell, the officer can't avoid the blow and tumbles backwards down the stairs, triggering a domino effect which knocks over all the other officers on the stairs behind. But now a second unit of armoured police is advancing along the narrow corridor from the main castle.

'Stay where you are!' orders the lead officer, a Taser gun in his hand.

Ignoring his command, we turn and sprint away in the opposite direction, towards a familiar heavy oak door that we both know leads on to the battlements. Just as we did some four hundred years ago, we make a desperate dash for the castle's keep.

The police are hot on our heels. But Phoenix doesn't stop to confront them like he did the Soul Hunters. Instead, we bound up the steep flight of stone steps, two at a time. Burdened by their riot gear, the officers struggle to keep up, and we reach the top far ahead of them and enter the keep through the portcullis gateway. Unfortunately the mechanism to lower the portcullis has been sealed off. I slam the inner door shut and tug the bolt across, but realize the rusted metal won't hold the police back for long.

'Where now?' I pant, looking round the circular inner courtyard, praying for another exit. The timber-framed living quarters from Civil War times are long gone, the square holes and stone supports in the walls the only evidence of their past existence. There's a large, bricked-up entrance to our right, but I recall that being blocked even in our previous life. A small, arched doorway to our left leads into the keep's tower, and above our heads a walkway encircles the battlements, offering us fine views of the surrounding countryside but no means of escape. The only option appears to be the steps in the centre of the empty courtyard – but I'm sure these just lead down to the keep's cellar and dungeon. Not the most promising way out of a fortified castle, I fear.

'Think, Genna. How did we escape last time?' asks Phoenix, appearing equally perplexed.

'My Glimmer didn't go that far,' I reply. 'Did we even escape? Perhaps we surrendered? Or did we maybe . . . *die*?'

Phoenix shakes his head. 'I don't remember, either. We need something to jolt our memories –' The clatter of footsteps approaches, and swiftly he grabs my hand and presses it against the cool flint of the keep's walls –

'We have to surrender, Captain,' rasps the guard of the gate as the dull boom of a battering ram sounds like a death knell.

I kneel beside William, my hand pressed against his side, a herbal poultice held to his wound. As I tend to his healing, I listen for the next ominous boom, praying it won't be followed by the crack of splintering wood. Tanas, impatient as ever, is determined to break down the portcullis and has been pounding the gate since dawn. So far the solid oak has withstood the onslaught, but for how much longer?

William looks sternly at the guard. 'No!' he declares. 'That isn't an option.'

'But, sir! Why do you insist upon holding out?' the young guard questions, his voice cracking in desperation. 'Our cause is lost. All our fellow Royalists, they're either dead or defeated.'

William looks at the guard fiercely, yet with pity; the man's sunken eyes and hollow cheeks are proof of the immense suffering and near-starvation he has endured since the siege began. 'Because, my man, more is at stake than the fate of our King.'

The guard stares at William in utter disbelief, clearly unable to grasp that anything could be more important than his revered King. 'But we have few weapons, sir . . . limited supplies . . . and no water,' he argues. 'We cannot hope t–'

'No water!' repeats William, suddenly standing up. 'Why didn't I think of that before!'

The sharp sound of wood splitting signals the first failure of our defences. I hurry to bandage William's wound again, but he brushes me off and grabs his rapier.

'No time for that, Anne,' he says, as a thud of the battering ram produces another bone-like crack of breaking wood. The portcullis won't hold them out any longer. 'We have to leave now!' cries William.

'But where are we going?' I ask. My mind races to think of ways of escape from the castle. I know there's a small *hidden exit tucked behind the northern tower of the main gate, but that's no good to anyone trapped in the keep. When it comes to a siege, the keep's impregnable strength is also its greatest weakness. I fear there is no other way out . . . or is there?*

Leaving the bemused guard behind, William takes my hand and leads me into the keep's well tower –

'The well!' I gasp, breaking out of the Glimmer. Despite the length of the vision, as with a dream, time is fluid: no more than a second has passed in my present life and the police have yet to storm the keep. But their voices are now worryingly close. I hear a whispered order, '*Hold here. We've got them. They're trapped.*'

But I know we're not.

23

This time it's me who takes Phoenix's hand as we duck through the doorway into the tower. The lower room leads straight to the keep's well. At the bottom of a short run of steps is a large stone-rimmed hole cordoned off behind a plastic barrier with a sign that reads, CLOSED FOR RENOVATION. On the wall an information panel declares the well to be over forty-five metres deep, and a domed iron safety grille has been placed over the top to keep visitors from falling in. But, for once, luck is on our side. Perhaps because of the renovation work the access hatch has been left open, the padlock hanging loose.

Phoenix peers into the well's dark depths. 'Did we *really* go down there?' he asks, evidently questioning his past incarnation's sanity.

I nod nervously. 'There was no water then, remember?'

He gives me an uneasy look. 'The question is . . . is there any water now?'

But we have no time to ponder this. There's a loud *CRACK* as the police batter down the wooden inner door of the keep and enter the courtyard. So, ignoring the safety barrier, we climb inside the iron dome and sit upon the lip of the well, our feet dangling over the black abyss. A safety rope has been left secured to the grille, its length dropping away and disappearing down into the darkness.

'D'you think that goes all the way to the bottom?' I ask.

Phoenix gives me a grim smile. 'Only one way to find out!'

Closing and locking the access hatch behind us, he grasps the rope with both hands, braces his feet against the stone wall and lowers himself into the well. I follow down after him, my hands gripping the rope for all I'm worth.

The stone is damp and slick, and my feet slide and slip down the inner wall as I move my hands one after the other down the rope. As much as my gymnast training helps me, the muscles in my arms are soon straining and my laboured breaths echo loud in the close confines of the well. Last time I recall, William lowered me down in a bucket, making my descent a whole lot easier and less treacherous. And, while Phoenix may be just beneath me now, I doubt he'll be able to stop me falling if I lose my grip.

As we descend further, a damp, mouldy smell of stagnant water wafts upwards and the air grows chill. It goes through my mind that the only reason we were able to evade capture during the siege in the English Civil War was because there was no water: the lake had been drained by the enemy forces. I start to regret my rashness; the Glimmer has made me foolhardy and reckless. If the well proves to be full, then our escape route will turn out to be also our grave!

The shaft is now so dark I can barely see my hands in front of my face. Below is all inky blackness, Phoenix no more than a shadow, just the soft scuff of his boots against the wall reassuring me of his presence. Above, the ever-diminishing circle of light is the only thing that indicates our descent. *But are we even halfway yet?*

I freeze as a gruff voice comes echoing down the shaft: 'Check the well!'

Above me, the silhouette of a face appears at the opening, partially blocking out the light. I hold my breath as the police officer peers down into the depths. I swear he can see us, suspended in the darkness . . . but after giving the padlock a firm tug, he walks away, satisfied the well is secure.

'Let's go!' hisses Phoenix.

With shaky arms I keep descending until I hear a splash. 'You OK?' I whisper, worried that Phoenix has fallen and plunged below the surface.

'All good,' comes his soft reply. 'The water's only waist deep.'

Cautiously I lower myself into the frigid water until my feet find a soft layer of mud. The sudden drop in temperature sends an involuntary shudder through me and a wave of goosebumps ripples across my skin. There's a putrid stench in the air that triggers an unwelcome flashback to the dead and decomposing rat that we found at the bottom of the well on our previous visit.

This time, however, I'm more worried we may encounter a *live* one.

Although my eyes have adjusted to the darkness, I can only discern dim shadows and the faintest of outlines. But it's enough by which to see Phoenix . . . and the black opening of a tunnel.

'It's still here!' I whisper in relief. In the back of my mind I'd been concerned that the secret passageway – the link between well and lake – might have been bricked up during the castle's renovation, or else we'd find its ceiling collapsed with age. But our escape route still appears to be accessible.

Angry voices echo down from above. 'They *must* be here somewhere. Use your torch and check that well again!'

Without waiting around any longer, we duck inside the tunnel. Forced by the low ceiling to hunch over, we follow the flooded passageway north under the keep, then beneath the motte and beyond the castle walls. The darkness seems to press in on all sides and my breathing becomes tight as my sense of claustrophobia mounts. I'm almost on the point of a panic attack when a faint halo of light appears up ahead. The brightness grows with every step and my anxiety subsides, and eventually we come to an opening with a stone archway and rusted iron gate. Beyond stretches a sun-dappled lake and . . . freedom!

I push at the gate . . . then grab the bars and shake them furiously before turning to Phoenix in dismay. 'It won't open. We're trapped!'

But Phoenix merely smiles. Reaching above the arch's lintel, his fingers prise out from a tiny space between two stones an old, rusty key. 'Seems like I expected us to return one day!' he says with a grin. He unlocks the gate and we wade out through a clump of bulrushes, then climb the bank and collapse.

I sigh with exhaustion and relief as we lie in the sun to recover and dry out, listening to the chirps of the crickets in the grass and honks of the geese on the lake. Our narrow escape has left me drained and disheartened.

'Well, that was all a waste of time!' I mutter, annoyed at the risk we've taken, and all for nothing.

Phoenix looks at me, his eyebrows furrowed. 'Why do you say that?' he asks.

'Because you destroyed the Soul Jar!' I reply through gritted teeth, glaring back at him.

'True,' he admits with an indifferent shrug, 'but maybe the jar wasn't what we came for.'

'It wasn't?' I question.

'No,' he replies, and with a satisfied grin he holds up a brown leather pouch.

I immediately recognize it. It's the pouch from my Glimmer, and I'm about to return his smile when a shadow falls across us.

24

'Rats should never use the same bolthole twice in two lifetimes!' sneers a callous voice. 'Their escape routes become predictable.'

Silhouetted against the sun, Damien looms over us. His lean, hungry face and jet-black eyes glare down at me like a bird of prey about to swoop.

I scramble to my feet with Phoenix, who stands in front of me. Damien is flanked by his gang of four Soul Hunters. Their silent presence is as sinister and unsettling as that first night in the park. Despite the daylight now, their faces remain cloaked in shadow. But I catch a glimpse of a tattoo of a small black widow spider on the neck of one of the girls, and a tuft of wiry blond hair sticking out from the hood of the shorter of the boys.

Fanning out in a semicircle, the Soul Hunters trap us on the bank and, with the lake to our backs, we've nowhere to run.

'How did you know we were in Arundel?' growls Phoenix.

Damien offers a thin sliver of a smile. 'Our Watchers are *everywhere*.' His deathless gaze sweeps the rippling lake and surrounding trees. 'Rather peaceful here, isn't it?' he comments, before laughing scornfully. 'I much preferred it during the Civil War, when there was killing and chaos. I miss the thunder of cannon and the clash of swords. Don't you?'

We don't humour him with a reply, just stand silent and defiant in his presence.

Damien's eyes glint wickedly. 'It was better back then, when you could kill a man without any reprisal, especially if they were Royalists! In fact, I recall executing a guard on this very spot. Chopped off his scrawny head for holding out on where you two had gone.' He scowls in annoyance. 'If it hadn't been for him, we would've captured you that day and sacrificed you all those centuries ago –'

'You soulless monster!' I yell, unable to hold my tongue any longer. After four hundred years I've discovered that poor guard from the keep had remained loyal to me and William, despite our side's crushing defeat. Even with the passing of so many years, my heart grieves for the young man and rages at my enemy's brutality.

Damien fixes me with his pitiless stare. 'Oh Genna, how wrong you are! I *have* a soul . . . one that will outlive yours.'

'Not if I have anything to do with it,' declares Phoenix fiercely. I feel his body tensing, coiling up like a spring.

Damien smirks at Phoenix's bravado. 'Always the valiant protector, aren't you? But just as Arundel Castle fell, so will you.' He looks Phoenix up and down with contempt. 'What are you doing back here anyway? You lost this battle.'

'Getting *this*!' Phoenix yells, and makes a sudden lunge at him. From the leather pouch, Phoenix has drawn a glassy shard of coal-black rock and now thrusts its sharpened tip straight towards Damien's heart.

But the Soul Hunters react with frightening speed. One has whipped out a bike chain and in an instant has wrapped it round Phoenix's wrist, yanking his attack off-target. Another kicks my Protéctor in the gut, doubling him over. A third knocks him to the ground, before trampling on his wrist and forcing him to let go of the bladed rock.

Throughout the attack Damien remains unfazed, not even bothering to move to avoid Phoenix's initial thrust. Peering down at my Protector with disdain, he sneers, 'Tut-tut. You're making a habit of losing battles here. But don't worry, that's the last battle *you*'ll ever fight!'

He nods at his silent minions to finish the job. But Phoenix, like his former incarnation William four hundred years ago, refuses to go down without a fight. Lashing out with his foot, he hobbles the tattooed Hunter with a well-aimed kick to the kneecap. She howls in pain and crumples to the ground. Then Phoenix heaves on the bike chain, pulling the thug on the other end close enough to elbow him in the face. I hear a sickening crunch as his bandaged nose is broken again. Screaming, the Hunter lets go of the chain and Phoenix leaps back to his feet. As he goes to tackle the blond-haired Hunter, the fourth and final hoodie enters the fray. I recognize her at once. She's the tall girl who'd taken Phoenix down with the steel pipe at the park. This time though she's wielding a pair of knuckledusters made to look like rings. She strikes so fast – with the speed of a rattlesnake – that her fist is a blur of glinting metal. Phoenix tries to dodge the punch, but the hard edge of her knuckleduster catches him across the chin. The bone-jarring impact almost knocks him out cold.

As he reels from the blow, Phoenix glances woozily in my direction. 'Genna . . . *RUN!*' he yells, blood spraying from his split lip. All four Hunters pounce on him and he disappears beneath a barrage of kicks and punches.

With Damien distracted and delighting in Phoenix's brutal beating, my first instinct is to flee for my life. To do as my Soul Protector commands, like before, at the park . . .

But this time I don't. As terrified and unprepared as I am, I refuse to leave him to fight on alone.

Snatching up a large stick from the ground, I rush forward and smash it across the back of the blond-haired Hunter's head. There's a thud as he collapses face first into the grass. I swing the stick again, this time at the girl who's pounding Phoenix mercilessly with her knuckledusters. But she blocks my attack with her forearm and the branch snaps in two. Dropping the now-useless weapon, I hurl a flurry of punches and kicks at her. But I may as well have been fighting an armoured tiger for all the effect I have. Fending off my feeble efforts, she seizes me by the throat and *lifts* me off my feet. Shocked by her strength, I hang helpless in the air, choking for breath, as Phoenix is subdued by the other three Hunters. The girl then drops me, gasping, to the ground beside his battered form.

Casually and calmly Damien picks up the discarded shard of black rock and weighs it in his hand. 'So *this* is what you sought. Hmm . . . obsidian rock. How did you ever come across such a thing in seventeenth-century England?'

Phoenix remains tight-lipped as he struggles in the Hunters' grip. Clasping the obsidian blade in his hand,

Damien stands astride him. 'I guess it'll be poetic justice to kill you with this, won't it?'

He kneels down, one leg on either side of Phoenix's chest, and begins to murmur an incantation. *'Rura, rkumaa, raar ard ruhrd . . .'*

I immediately recognize the ancient ritual chant. 'NO!' I plead. 'Please, don't!'

But Damien presses on, raising the blade-like shard above his head with both hands. Powerless to stop him, Phoenix looks over to me in soul-broken despair and, in that moment, as our eyes meet, I know he won't come back from this sacrificial death. Not ever. Not in this life . . . or the next.

'I'm sorry . . .' Phoenix splutters through bloodied lips. 'I've failed you . . .'

His eyes begin to lose focus and I let out an anguished sob, reaching out to him in desperation. But knuckleduster girl grabs my hair and wrenches me away.

'No! You *haven't* failed me!' I cry as I fight off the Hunter's vicious tugs. 'You've *never* failed me –'

'Qard ur rou ra datsrq, Ra-Ka!'

Damien's voice rises to a frenzy above mine and the Soul Hunters finally break their silence to take up the hypnotic and haunting chant.

'RA – KA! RA – KA! RA – KA!'

A black cloud passes across the sun, plunging us into shadow. As the temperature drops a degree, the rippling of the lake seems to fade away, the geese cease their honking and the crickets fall silent. It's as if the world itself has stopped breathing. Only the insistent rhythmic chanting and Damien's fervent voice go on:

'*Uur ra uhrdar bourkad . . .*'

'*RA – KA! RA – KA! RA – KA!*'

Through tear-filled eyes I watch Phoenix's body go limp as he falls under the demonic trance. Damien raises the blade higher, preparing to drive the shard through Phoenix's heart . . .

'DROP YOUR WEAPON!' a stern voice commands, as armed police officers suddenly surround us.

But Damien only grips the obsidian knife tighter, clearly determined to ignore the order.

25

The police van rocks gently as it heads north up the road from Arundel in the direction of London. I sit handcuffed with the other prisoners on the hard plastic bench in the back. Little more than a cage on wheels, the van's interior is all grey metal and rigid plastic, the toughened glass of the windows covered in a wire mesh. Stationed by the rear doors and separated from us by a metal grille is a stony-faced police officer armed with a Taser. I gaze dejectedly through the window where outside dusk is falling and the sky is turning a bruised purple.

After all that's happened, I can't believe I've been arrested. Surely I'm the victim in this situation, yet the police are treating me like a criminal, holding me on charges of attempted theft, obstruction and resisting arrest. Even though I know I'm innocent, I can't help but feel ashamed. That somehow I've let my parents down. I'm dreading the look on their faces when they see me shackled and in custody.

I'm also scared.

Damien and his Soul Hunters sit directly opposite me on the other bench, all handcuffed and hooded. However, while the gang's heads are bowed, Damien remains ramrod straight, staring directly at me. The air around him seems as cold and dead as his fathomless eyes, and his close presence makes me nauseous, as if I'm slowly succumbing to radiation poisoning.

'You're quite beautiful, you know?' he says out of the blue, having stayed dead silent for the past half hour.

I shift uncomfortably on the bench, avoiding his wolfish gaze.

He leans closer, until I can smell the sweet, sharp scent of his skin. 'That's one quality you seem to retain from one life to the next,' he remarks with apparent sincerity. A most beguiling smile graces his lips, and for a brief second I catch a glimpse of the handsome boy he could be . . . if it weren't for the pure evil emanating from his very soul.

'How very nice of you to notice,' I reply sarcastically.

Damien cocks his head to one side. 'I wonder if it has anything to do with the Light you carry within you? It'll almost be a shame to extinguish it –'

'Shut your mouth!' spits Phoenix through gritted teeth. 'Or I'll get that officer to Taser you again.'

Handcuffed beside me, Phoenix is suddenly alert and as vigilant as a guard dog. Up until that moment I thought he was still passed out, either from the effects of the ritual's trance or else the pain from his beating. One of his eyes is almost as purple as the sky, his lower lip is split and he sits awkwardly, the shotgun wounds on his back having opened up during the fight . . . But he's *alive*! That's more than I could ever have hoped for a few hours back. If it wasn't for the quick trigger finger of the police officer,

Phoenix would have been dead, the lethal shard of obsidian rock driven through his heart, his soul permanently destroyed. Fortunately the Taser darts struck Damien a moment before he landed the blow, and the high-voltage electric charge totally overwhelmed his system, locking up his body and incapacitating his limbs. The only downside is that he wasn't *permanently* immobilized by the Taser.

'Ooh, getting jealous, are we?' Damien teases Phoenix in a sing-song voice. He sits back in his seat and smirks. 'You've always been touchy that way. I don't blame you for fancying her though. Who wouldn't? You remember when I –'

Phoenix makes a lunge for Damien's throat but is stopped short by his handcuffs and seat restraint.

'Settle down!' barks the officer.

Reluctantly Phoenix lowers his hands but continues to glare at Damien, who smirks back at him, cocky and self-assured.

'I don't know why you're smiling,' I tell him. 'You've been arrested too.'

'So?' Damien scoffs. 'I'm still with you, and that's what counts.'

'Not for long,' I reply. 'As a convicted terrorist you'll be sent to a maximum-security jail for the rest of this life. Whether I'm imprisoned or not, you won't be able to get anywhere near me.'

Damien raises an eyebrow. '*Really?* Oh, *Genna*, you hold too much faith in this country's justice system. No prison will hold me. And no cell will protect you. The Incarnates have infiltrated all levels of society. You've met

DI Katherine Shaw, I believe? She's part of the criminal investigation team and, if I'm not mistaken, tends to *see* things my way, if you get my drift.'

I swallow nervously. The cuffs round my wrists suddenly feel a little tighter as I realize the police van isn't taking Phoenix and me to safety . . . but to our deaths.

'Don't believe him,' says Phoenix. 'Not everyone's an Incarnate. Tanas doesn't exert the influence he imagines he does. The Light is still strong enough to keep the Darkness at bay.'

Damien snorts. 'You reckon? But for how much longer?' He gives Phoenix a dismissive sneer, then turns his attention back to me. 'I bet this charlatan's told you that he's your Soul Protector, the *only* one who can save you, the *only* one you can trust . . .'

I narrow my eyes, wondering what Damien is getting at.

'But you shouldn't trust everything he says,' he warns.

'What do you mean?' I ask.

Damien leans towards me, conspiratorially. 'Let's just say, in some lives, he's not been your *best* ally –'

'Don't listen to him!' Phoenix interrupts.

'Why ever not?' says Damien with a smirk. 'Afraid she might learn an uncomfortable truth about you, perhaps?'

I glance uncertainly between him and Phoenix. 'What uncomfortable truth?'

Damien gives me a pitying look. 'Genna,' he says, his voice full of mock concern, 'it's only fair that you should know that young Phoenix here doesn't *always* protect you. Sometimes he –'

All of a sudden a deafening *BANG!* reverberates through the van. We veer violently across the road and, before we can recover, we're hit hard a second time. The van flips on to its side. I'm hurled backwards in my seat and my skull cracks against the wire-mesh window. My head rings and my vision blurs. A piercing *screech* of metal drowns out our screams as we slide out of control along the tarmac. Phoenix instinctively leans across me, bracing himself for another impact . . .

But mercifully none comes. The van skids to a shuddering halt. Its diesel engine splutters, then dies, leaving only the hiss of a burst radiator and the ominous reek of leaking fuel. As the chaos of the crash subsides, the injured and shocked groans of those caught inside fill the air. The gang of Soul Hunters all now hang limp from what has become the van's ceiling, their seatbelts pulled too tight for them to release the buckles. Damien is out cold, suspended from his seat like an upside-down marionette. The police officer has been knocked unconscious too. The metal grille separating the secure compartment from the doors is twisted and buckled, offering us a means of escape.

'You OK?' asks Phoenix, brushing the hair from my face and inspecting a cut to my brow.

Still stunned from the impact, I manage a nod. Unclipping his seatbelt, he crawls over to the grille, reaches through it and unhooks the keys from the officer's belt. After removing his own handcuffs, he quickly rubs his bruised wrists, then frees me. On hands and knees we squeeze through the gap in the twisted grille. Our confiscated belongings lie on a storage shelf that is now the floor. Phoenix rifles through them for the leather pouch and the shard of obsidian, which he stuffs into his backpack. Amid the debris the gleam of a green blade catches my eye.

However, before I can claim the jade knife, there's a clump of heavy boots outside the van followed by the *shriek* of grinding metal as someone tears the handle off and wrenches the doors open. A heavyset man in jeans and a baseball cap appears in the doorway, a crowbar in his hand. Phoenix deftly snatches the Taser from the police officer's holster and fires it into the man's chest. Convulsing violently, the guy collapses to the ground.

Behind me I hear an ominous *click* of a seatbelt, followed by the heavy *WHUMP* of a body. Glancing over my shoulder, I see Damien on all fours shaking his head clear.

'What the –?' he groans, groggily coming round. 'The idiots were supposed to free us, not kill us!'

'Let's go!' urges Phoenix, tossing away the spent Taser. He grabs my arm before I can recover the jade knife.

In a flash Damien pounces on it as we clamber out of the back of the van on to the road. The tarmac is slick with diesel fuel and the air noxious with its fumes. A large truck with a steel roll bar is rammed into the side of the police van and blocking the road, its hazard lights blinking in the gloom of dusk. Two other Hunters are waiting beside getaway cars. They spot us emerging from the van and rush to stop us. Further heavy *thumps* of bodies dropping to the van's floor urge us to move fast –

Dashing across the road, we dive into the nearest field and disappear among the rows of head-high corn.

26

Running blind into the night, I feel like a hare being hunted by hounds. The tall stalks of ripened sweetcorn whip against my face, making it impossible to see the route ahead or who's following us behind. The only indications of our pursuers are Damien's barked commands, the crash of stalks, and the occasional glimpses of a high-powered torch beam.

In the darkness I stumble over a root and fall face first on to the stony ground. All the breath is knocked from my lungs. Phoenix stops and is turning back to help me when a voice close by shouts, 'They're over here!'

We crouch, still and silent, listening as the rustle of corn draws nearer and nearer. A beam of light sweeps the ground barely a few metres from us. My heart beats so loudly I swear it can be heard by the approaching Hunter –

I screw my eyes tight shut and huddle closer to my Protector's chest. He's promised no harm shall come to me. Though he may be a slave of the Roman Empire and new to our household, I believe him. I feel safe in his arms. But danger is close by. As we hide in the ditch, I hear the pad of sandalled feet drawing closer and closer. The breeze rustles through the wheat, shaking the ears like a rattlesnake's tail.

'SLAVE!' calls a gruff voice that makes me tremble. I recognize it as the centurion's – the hulking commander from the infamous Twelfth Legion with eyes like polished beads of onyx. A war hero, he'd come bearing the trophies of conquest as gifts to my father, the Senator Lucius Aurelius Clarus. But Custos, my Protector, warned it was all a trick to gain access to our villa . . . and to kill me!

'Hand back the girl now!' the centurion demands. 'Believe me, slave, crucifixion will be a blessed relief after what I'll do to you!'

I feel Custos's heart pound harder in his chest. But he doesn't move, only holds me tighter to him.

'You can't hide forever,' warns the centurion, pacing in our direction. 'I've a hundred men sweeping the fields for you and the precious little girl.'

Opening my eyes, I glimpse the onyx-eyed centurion through the stalks. He's now no more than a few yards from us. A couple more steps, and we'll be discovered –

I blink away the Glimmer just as a hooded figure emerges from amid the stalks. Phoenix leaps up and shoulder-barges him in the chest. Before the man can recover, we bolt from our hiding place and disappear into the shifting sea of corn.

But the other Hunters have been alerted to our presence. They converge from all sides, racing to cut us off. My hand clasped in his, Phoenix drags me on towards the edge of the field. My heart pounding and my lungs burning, I feel like I've been running all my life. And all my lives before, in an endless and unrelenting pursuit; a never-ending sequence of narrow escape after narrow escape. Each time, the Hunters get closer to their quarry, and their prey becomes weaker and more exhausted with each fraught flight . . .

By some miracle we reach the fence before them and frantically clamber over to a busy main road. Cars and trucks whizz by, their headlights bright and blinding. A driver blasts his horn as he almost runs us over in the darkness.

With an arm up against the glare, Phoenix puts out his thumb.

'Hitch-hiking? Don't bother,' I say, and glance fearfully in the direction of the field. The cloak of night has swallowed the Hunters, but I know they can't be very far behind. 'Hardly anyone picks up hitch-hikers, specially in the middle of the night!'

But, even as I'm saying it, a delivery truck slows and pulls up at the kerbside. The passenger door to the cab swings open and the driver, a chubby-cheeked man, beckons us. 'Hop in!' he calls cheerily.

Preferring our chances with this stranger than our pursuers, we hurriedly clamber aboard. As soon as Phoenix shuts the door, the truck pulls away. In the wing mirror I spot the Soul Hunters emerging from the field. They sprint after us, but the truck quickly gains speed and soon leaves them behind. Damien is the last to give up, his silhouette briefly picked out by the headlights of a passing car, before he too disappears into the night.

Panting heavily, I lean back against the headrest and sigh. 'That was lucky!'

'More like divine intervention,' Phoenix whispers out of the corner of his mouth.

The truck driver smiles warmly at us both. His face has a lived-in look, grey stubble bristling his double chin, and he's so large that his belly barely accommodates the steering wheel. He's like a great big grizzly bear, but there's a reassuring faint, star-like glimmer to his watery eyes. 'I'm Mitch!' he says heartily. 'So, where are you two kids headed?'

'Wherever you are!' Phoenix replies with a friendly grin.

Mitch chuckles. 'Are you sure? I've got a helluva lot of stops along this journey!'

'Are you going anywhere near Havenbury?' I ask hopefully.

He purses his lower lip. 'Can't say I've heard of the place.'

'It's in the Cotswolds.'

Mitch peers at his itinerary, then taps at the sat-nav. 'Mmm ... that's a bit far off my route, but if I make a small detour I can drop you on the outskirts of Swindon. Still about thirty miles to this Havenbury, though. Any good to you?'

Phoenix nods. 'Yup! Thanks. That's good enough for us.'

Mitch resets his sat-nav, then pulls out a can of Irn-Bru from a small cooler in the footwell. 'Help yourself,' he says. 'There's water and cola in there too, as well as a packet of chocolates on the dashboard, if you want. Also, ice for that eye of yours, young man!' He arches a bushy eyebrow at Phoenix, but doesn't press him for an explanation.

'That's very kind of you,' I say, fishing out a couple of drinks, along with a handful of ice. 'Thanks for picking us up, by the way. You saved our lives.'

'No problemo!' says Mitch with a grin. 'Got a daughter of my own. Wouldn't want her left stranded at the roadside on a dark night.'

I wait, my can halfway to my lips, expecting him to question us further, to ask us what we were doing in such a remote place so late in the day. But instead he flips on the radio and settles back into his seat to drive, his head bobbing to the beat of an old seventies track.

Phoenix clinks his can against mine. 'See? We're not entirely on our own,' he says quietly as I take a much-needed sip of cola. 'We've met a Soul Brother.'

At first I think Phoenix must be referring to the music on the radio before realizing he means something deeper than that. I turn to him and lower my voice. 'Are you saying he's an *Ascendant*?'

Phoenix gently shakes his head. 'No, he isn't a Protector, or Seer either – just a good soul,' he explains in a whisper. 'Most Soul Brothers and Sisters like him aren't aware of their nature, or even conscious of our battle against the Incarnates. But they intuitively help souls like us. Think of them as . . . as angels on Earth. Sometimes they turn up in just the right place at just the right time.'

As Phoenix leans back in his seat and holds the ice to his bruised eye, I study Mitch, our Soul Brother. Humming contentedly to himself, slurping from his can and chomping on a large chocolate bar, he's certainly not your typical winged angel!

But in my eyes he's heaven sent.

27

I'm jerked awake as the truck comes to a stop. I find my head is resting upon Phoenix's shoulder, his jacket laid across my lap as a blanket. The warmth of the cab's heater and the gentle motion of the lorry had lulled me into a deep sleep. Phoenix too, by the looks of it. He greets me with a drowsy smile as I yawn and stretch.

'Morning, sleepyheads!' says Mitch cheerfully, switching off the engine. 'Your stop: Swindon! Will all passengers disembark?'

I peer bleary-eyed out of the passenger window. We've pulled in at a rest area. There's a mobile cafe, picnic area and a small toilet block, but little else. *No cameras at least*, I think to myself. Then I shake my head in mild dismay at how observant – or rather paranoid – I've become in only a matter of days.

Before my encounter with Damien and his Soul Hunters, I'd have been complaining to my parents at the grim facilities on offer. Now I'm judging places on their surveillance level and am simply relieved to find a toilet, however dire and dirty it may be!

We clamber out of the cab and shake the feeling back into our legs. After using the facilities and freshening ourselves up, Phoenix buys us both a cup of tea and a bacon butty from the cafe. Mitch declines the offer of breakfast and excuses himself, explaining he has his schedule to keep, but Phoenix insists on getting him a takeaway coffee at the very least.

'You two take care,' says Mitch, climbing back into his cab.

We wave him farewell, then sit ourselves down at a picnic table to tuck into our bacon butties. It wouldn't be my usual choice of breakfast, but I'm ravenous: the constant running and adrenaline surges of fight-or-flight have taken their toll and I'm almost shaking with hunger. But the hot food quickly revives me and the cup of tea calms my frayed nerves.

As we finish off our breakfast, Phoenix delves into his pack for the roadmap. He hunches over it to plan our route. 'OK,' he says, thinking aloud. 'Havenbury is at least thirty-five miles from here via the back roads. That'll take us a couple of days of walking at a steady pace. We could do it in a day at a push, I guess, but unless you're used to long distances, you'll get blisters after ten miles or so.'

'Why don't we hitch-hike?' I suggest.

Phoenix gives a reluctant shake of his head. 'We might not be so lucky next time. Not every truck driver's a Soul Brother – they could be a Watcher or worse. It's best we rely on ourselves.'

As he puts the map away, I notice the shard of black obsidian stowed inside his backpack. Having risked so much to recover it from its Soul Jar in the castle, I'm intrigued to know its purpose. 'Tell me,' I say. 'What's so special about that hunk of rock? How does it help us against Tanas?'

Phoenix passes it to me. 'Tanas is vulnerable to obsidian,' he explains.

'A bit like Superman and kryptonite?' I say, half jokingly, as I turn the blade over in my hand. The rock is smooth, surprisingly light and the edge as sharp as a scalpel.

'Sort of, except that it needs to be *in* him to have any effect. You may recall from an early Glimmer I once knifed Tanas in the chest with just such a blade. A part of it sheared clean away as it glanced off his breastbone. When he pulled the blade out, a splinter was left in his heart. From life to life, incarnation to incarnation, he carries this wound.'

I examine the black shard, entranced by its glassy smoothness. 'You think this would kill him . . . I mean, kill his soul?'

Phoenix shrugs. 'I don't know. It certainly weakens him for the next life. If we had the original blade, then maybe it would. But that one's been lost to time. So we have to make do with what we've got.' Taking the rock from me again, he slides it into the loop of his belt, accessible and ready to use at a moment's notice.

'What else was in that Soul Jar?' I ask, my curiosity piqued.

Reaching into the backpack, Phoenix pulls out the leather pouch and empties its contents on to the picnic table. A small blue amulet on a gold chain and a folded piece of parchment tumble out. Phoenix looks at this second item and frowns. 'I don't remember putting that in there.'

He unfolds the parchment and his bemused expression deepens.

'What's it say?' I ask.

'No idea,' Phoenix replies, handing it to me.

Written in red ink is a bewildering mix of ancient script and hieroglyphics. I can't make head or tail of it either.

'Perhaps it's a code?' I suggest.

'Hmm, perhaps,' he says, but the frown remains. 'However it found its way into the Soul Jar, it must be important. Maybe Gabriel will be able to decipher it. Keep it safe.'

Carefully refolding the parchment, I slip the mysterious note deep inside the front left pocket of my jeans.

Phoenix has now picked up the amulet. 'This is for you,' he says, and places the amulet on its slender chain over my head.

The chain feels cool round my neck and the amulet's circular ring of blue gemstone rests lightly beside my heart.

'Well, it's certainly a lovely piece of jewellery,' I say, admiring the gemstone's gleam. The amulet is about the size of a watch face, its sky-blue hues veined with flashes of pure gold. What appear to be Egyptian symbols – a bird, an eye and a loop-headed cross – decorate the amulet's bail.

'It's more than that,' says Phoenix. 'It's a talisman. A Guardian Stone that should help protect you from Tanas.'

'How?'

'It's meant to strengthen your Light and ward off his dark arts,' Phoenix explains. 'I don't know what all the symbols mean, but the looped cross is the *ankh*, the

Egyptian symbol of life. On an amulet it provides divine protection.'

When I put my hand to the precious amulet, I feel an almost-imperceptible fluttering, as if clasping a delicate butterfly between my fingers. I slip the talisman inside my blouse, its gentle weight against my chest both familiar and reassuring.

'Thank you,' I say. 'I guess I need all the protection I can get.'

'Then let's get you somewhere even safer,' says Phoenix, draining his tea and standing up. I notice him wince as he puts on his backpack.

'We should change the bandages on your back,' I suggest.

Phoenix waves me off. 'Later.'

'But you need fresh dressings if you're to heal,' I insist.

'And *we* need to keep moving and out of sight,' he replies, stubbornly heading out of the picnic area. Reluctantly I let the matter drop and hurry after him.

As we leave the rest area, I dump our rubbish in the bin and notice a discarded newspaper lying on top. Its headline catches my eye:

HOW DID THEY LET THEM ESCAPE?

TEENAGE TERRORISTS ROAM THE COUNTRY!

I snatch up the paper and show Phoenix. There's a picture of the overturned police van on the front page and underneath a row of mugshots of the suspects; two of them are of Phoenix and me.

It seems I'm no longer considered a hostage . . . rather an accomplice!

What must my parents be thinking now? They must be worried sick. And I can't even begin to imagine how my friends are reacting to all this. Mei must be flipping out!

'I need to call my mum and dad,' I tell Phoenix. 'Explain to them what's *really* happening.'

'You can't,' insists Phoenix. 'It's too much of a risk. Now we're clear of Damien and his Hunters, this is our best chance of reaching Gabriel.'

'But maybe my parents can help us?' I suggest. 'Give us a lift to Havenbury.'

Phoenix humours me with a look. 'So you're going to call them and tell them what, exactly?'

'That I'm on the run from Hunters, of course. That they want to kill me for my soul and that you're my Soul Protector, and Gabriel has the means to help us . . . in this fight . . .'

My voice tails away. Saying it out loud, I realize how ridiculous it all sounds. *Who on earth would believe such tales of Hunters and Protectors? Of Ascendants and Incarnates? Of multiple past lives?* If I hadn't experienced the Glimmers for myself or witnessed first-hand Damien's unnerving transformation, *I* wouldn't believe me, either.

Phoenix lays a hand upon my shoulder and looks me in the eye. 'I know it's hard to accept. But at this time we're on our own in this battle. It's just you and me against the Incarnates.'

28

The morning sun is warm on our backs as we head north-west in the direction of Cirencester. Taking the first footpath we come to, we hike across several fields, then wend our way down a narrow country lane. With breaks, Phoenix hopes we'll reach the border of the Cotswolds by nightfall. But our plan to stick only to back roads, country lanes and footpaths means our route isn't direct, and consequently our progress is slow.

Our journey isn't helped by the fact that every time a car or person approaches, we're forced to take cover until they pass, ducking behind hedges, hiding behind trees and even doubling back at some points to avoid any risk of contact. As we're concealing ourselves in a bush from an elderly couple walking their dog, I question whether Phoenix is being somewhat *too* cautious. Surely not *everyone* can be a Watcher or a Hunter! *How much of a threat can that little old lady be?* I wonder. And when the dog pees against the bush we're in, even Phoenix appears to acknowledge how absurd our behaviour is, shaking his head wearily as his boots get splashed. But once they've gone, he's at pains to point out to me – again – that as long as we remain undetected, I'm safe.

But still, the constant hiding doesn't make me *feel* safe. In fact it just reminds me how precarious my situation is. We may have got ahead of Damien and his Hunters. The trail may have gone cold for them. But I'm acutely aware now that a single slip-up, one unlucky encounter or false move, and they could pick up the scent again and be on to us like a pack of hounds.

We soon work up a thirst as we tramp across yet another open field. Thankfully we stocked up on water and snacks at the roadside cafe and so we take a break in the shade of an old oak tree.

Phoenix swigs from his bottle. 'I wish I had my motorbike still,' he says with a sigh. 'We could be there in under an hour.'

Sitting down on the ground, I ease off my trainers and inspect my left heel. A small blister is already forming, and we've only gone a few miles. Noticing my discomfort, Phoenix shrugs off his backpack, takes out the first-aid kit and hands me a plaster.

'Has it always been like this?' I ask as I cover the blister with the adhesive strip. 'Running and hiding, I mean?'

'No,' replies Phoenix, squatting beside me in the sun. 'There have been some lives when we were lucky. Where Tanas either hasn't reincarnated during that lifetime, or else hasn't found you.' He gazes off into the far distance and smiles wistfully. 'I recall one life, not sure what century it was, but we were both born on the same island in the Pacific. Somewhere off Fiji. I remember the waters being crystal clear, the sand as soft and golden as the sunrise, and the palm trees so heavy with coconuts that the tops bowed under their weight.' He glances sideways at me and his smile deepens in his reverie. 'You were the most lovely girl on the island. The daughter of the chief. We spent many an evening on Sunset Rock. I remember we had to wade out to it, but from there you got the most glorious views of the sun setting over the ocean, and the stars would burst to life across the velvet-black sky like a million angels . . .'

A long-forgotten memory stirs in me. Like a pebble dropped into a pond, thoughts, feelings and images ripple across time –

A warm breeze on my skin, the crisp scent of sea salt in my nostrils, the gentle wash of the waves, the touch of his hand in mine . . .

I ask shyly, 'Were we . . . *together*?'

Phoenix gives an awkward laugh. 'I'm your Protector, Genna.' He says it by way of answer, though the tender look in his eyes hints at a different story. 'Besides, your father had plans for you to marry the son of the chief of the next village. But I do recall that during our time together we enjoyed a most happy and peaceful life.'

Then his smile fades. 'To be honest, though, most lives have been a battle, a cat-and-mouse game. Depends on when you were found and by whom. Sometimes I could hide you. Other times we outran the Soul Hunters. Occasionally we'd even defeat them.'

'Have we ever . . . *lost*?' I ask hesitantly.

Phoenix stuffs the first-aid kit back into his pack. 'You wouldn't be here if we had,' he replies in a grave tone.

I bite my lower lip thoughtfully, unsure whether to bring up the next question. 'Then . . . what did Damien mean when he said you haven't *always* protected me?'

Phoenix's jaw stiffens. 'Nothing. Forget it.' He suddenly rises to his feet, ready to go. His curt response surprises me.

'But I don't understand why he'd say you aren't my best ally. That I shouldn't trust everything you say. What does he mean?'

With a laboured sigh, Phoenix shoulders his backpack. 'He was trying to manipulate you. Turn you against me.' Then he says more briskly, 'Just forget it. Now come on, we've still got a long walk ahead.'

I watch him stride off, not sure if he's angry or simply impatient to get moving. As I consider his reaction to my questions, it occurs to me that Damien's ploy to undermine my trust in Phoenix has worked. Like a weed planted in a flowerbed, he's sown a seed of doubt that I've allowed to take root. I have no reason *not* to trust my Soul Protector. In fact, it would be an insult to him – Phoenix has every right to act offended. He's kept me safe and alive despite the multiple attempts by Damien and his Hunters to kidnap and kill me. It'd be foolish of me to believe my tormentor over my Protector!

Hurriedly slipping on my trainers, I follow him across the fields, leaving any doubts I had behind under the oak tree.

29

'Should we really be doing this?' I whisper, glancing nervously around.

'You want to sleep in a barn again?' asks Phoenix as he inserts the blade of his penknife between the door jamb and the lock of a holiday cottage, the sign at the end of the drive promising cosy accommodation and a real fireplace.

I shake my head. Dusk has fallen in the fields and we've trekked some twenty miles or more. I'm exhausted beyond words. The muscles in my legs are aching and my feet sore and blistered. Although we took several breaks, the sparse lunch we had at midday was barely enough to sustain us on such a long walk.

As Phoenix tries to jimmy open the lock, I keep a lookout. The cottage appears deserted and is in a remote location, surrounded by fields, a single-track road leading up to its gravel driveway. In one pasture a herd of cows graze lazily, another has been left fallow, and in a third a trio of horses are paddocked. They trot up to the fence to see who the new arrivals are. However, apart from these three inquisitive horses, there's no one else taking any interest in us.

Giving the penknife a twist, Phoenix pops the lock and the door swings open.

'Wait here,' he whispers, then disappears inside.

I stand on the threshold, listening to his movements as he checks and secures each room in turn. I'm ready to run at a moment's notice – although how far I'd get in my shattered state is another question. I don't know how Phoenix can stay so sharp. He must be as tired as I am . . . plus he's injured, and still recovering from his beating by the Soul Hunters. Yet he continues to put me and my safety first. I can't help but admire him for his devotion.

Phoenix reappears in the doorway. 'All clear,' he says. 'Doesn't look like anyone's been here for a while.'

I step inside the cottage and start to explore. It's a small affair, with a cosy lounge and fireplace as promised, an old-fashioned-looking kitchen, and a single bedroom with an en-suite shower. The bed is made up, a pink, floral quilt laid on top, but there are no other signs that any guests will be arriving any time soon. For the first time in days I begin to relax. Kicking off my trainers, I collapse on the sofa.

Still on a mission, Phoenix raids the cupboards in the kitchen. He finds some salt, a jar of strawberry jam, a packet of dried pasta and a tin of chicken noodle soup. 'What do you want for dinner?' he asks. 'Jammy pasta or soup?'

Laughing at the idea of jam and pasta, I reply, 'Soup please.'

Phoenix pulls out a saucepan and turns on the hob. 'Why don't you take a shower while I heat this up?' he suggests.

Peeling myself off the sofa, I go into the bedroom, find some towels in a wardrobe and head to the bathroom. The steaming hot water in the shower is pure bliss. I wash three days of grime from my hair, scrub my face and body, and let the jets of water massage my aching muscles. As the tension eases from my limbs, I suddenly and unexpectedly burst into tears. Like a floodgate opening, all the stress, strain and struggles of the past week pour out, threatening to engulf me. I sink to my knees and hug myself. My tears mix with the water and my sobs are drowned in the gush of the shower.

I just want to be home, safe in my bedroom, comforted in Mum and Dad's arms. But I know that is now impossible. My whole world has been turned upside down. I'm no longer Genna, the girl who only has to worry about exams, what to wear and whether so-and-so likes me or not. I'm a First Ascendant with innumerable past lives. A sacred soul who supposedly carries the Light of Humanity and is being hunted by a sinister clan of Incarnates. Oh, and if that wasn't enough, I'm also a terrorist suspect on the run from the police. How can I ever return to school and my former life now I know there are Watchers and Hunters after me? Now that Tanas, the Lord and Master of the Incarnates, stalks my every step? *Will I be on the run for the rest of my life?* I wonder, my tears easing a little as I harden myself to the situation. *A fugitive from both the law and a supernatural cult?* Once we reach this Soul Seer in Havenbury, what then? Do we hide? Fight? *Disappear? Mum and Dad won't ever know what's happened to me!* I start crying again as I think of them, left heartbroken and grieving for the rest of their lives.

I can only pray that this Gabriel has some answers.

Gradually my sobbing subsides. Purged of emotion, I feel drained and spent. Slowly I rise back to my feet. Warmed and cleansed by the water, my strength returns and I pull myself together. My situation may be desperate but I realize it isn't without hope. Not as long as I have Phoenix by my side. I remind myself that *together* we have outrun and outwitted Tanas and his Hunters before. And we can surely do so again.

By the time I emerge from the shower, glistening and warmed through, I feel almost reborn.

Once dressed in my old clothes again, I come out of the bedroom, drying my hair, and discover Phoenix has laid the kitchen table. Two bowls of chicken noodle soup await us, and he appears to have found a packet of bourbon biscuits for dessert. The room is now dark, the curtains closed, and a single candle illuminates the table, its soft, flickering glow like a halo over our food.

I raise an eyebrow. 'Very romantic,' I remark.

For a moment Phoenix looks confused, then twigs. 'Ah, the candle! That's so no one knows we're here. I didn't want to switch on the main light, even with the curtains closed.'

'You're a true Romeo!' I laugh as he invites me to sit opposite him at the table.

Both famished from our long walk, we hungrily tuck into the soup.

'Feel better after a shower?' asks Phoenix, slurping from his spoon.

I nod and put on a smile. 'Much better, thanks . . .' Then, after a moment's hesitation, I say, 'There's something I want to ask you. When did you know you were my Soul Protector? In this life, I mean.'

Phoenix glances up from his soup. 'I've always known.'

'From birth, then?'

'I guess so.' He shrugs. 'My earliest memories were of past lives. In fact, they sometimes felt more real to me than my present-day life. Countless Glimmers of searching for you . . . of protecting you . . . of fighting off Tanas and his Hunters . . . It was a lot to take in as a child.' Phoenix stops to gaze pensively at the candle's flickering flame, then continues.

'My birth mother had a hard time understanding it too, from what I've been told. As soon as I could talk, I was telling her of my other lives . . . even saying she wasn't my mother . . . that I had a *different* mother before her –' His sapphire-blue eyes begin to glisten with tears – 'Now, I realize she *was* my mother in this life.' He sighs heavily and glumly stirs his soup. 'I just wish I could've told her that before she died.'

'I'm sorry, I'm so, so sorry,' I softly whisper, feeling his grief and pain. 'The police told me she died in a car crash.'

'That's true enough. They *say* it was a drunk driver –' he stares at me, his tear-filled eyes hardening like diamonds – 'but I don't believe them. I suspect it was an Incarnate.'

'An *Incarnate*?' I gasp.

Phoenix nods. 'Yeah. I was there. I know I was only three, but I swear the driver had black eyes. Must've been trying to terminate me, before I grew old enough to find and protect you. But I survived the crash.' His fist clenches round the spoon. 'Which means *I'm* the reason my mother died.'

'Don't say that!' I chide. 'You were three years old! It can't possibly be your fault.'

'Well, all I know is, if I wasn't a Soul Protector, she'd be alive today,' he replies bitterly. 'Yet her death gave me all the more reason to find you and stop these demonic Incarnates.'

I give him a questioning look. 'But if it was an Incarnate, why didn't they come back and finish the job when you were young and helpless?'

'They couldn't trace me,' he explains. 'Following the crash, I was put into foster care, my details changed and kept confidential. Then, because of my supposed "issues", I was constantly bumped from foster home to foster home.'

I reach out and tenderly clasp his hand. 'That must have been tough.'

Phoenix snorts a humourless laugh. 'Let's just say I haven't had an easy childhood,' he admits. Then he suddenly smiles warmly at me, his face golden in the glow of the candlelight. 'But I always knew my life had a greater purpose. And being with you now, seeing you with my own eyes, knowing that I was right all along, makes all those struggles worthwhile.'

I think of my own personal struggles in recent days, the battle to reconcile myself with being a First Ascendant, and I ask, 'So how did you come to terms with being a Soul Protector?'

'I just accepted it as the truth,' Phoenix replies matter-of-factly. 'This was what I was born for. Simple as that. It was my numerous therapists and foster parents who had difficulty accepting it. Every one of them tried to convince me you were just a fantasy, that it was all a delusion.' He leans towards me, his face intense in the candlelight. 'But that didn't explain why I possessed skills and knowledge that no other child my age did. And the older I got, the more Glimmers I had and the more skills I acquired. All for one purpose . . . to find and protect you.'

He grips my hand tighter. 'And now that you've become aware of your true nature, you too will gain more knowledge and skills to help you survive and evade Tanas.'

His words bring me comfort. Smiling, I take another spoonful of steaming soup, which, despite coming out of a tin, is possibly the best I've ever tasted, both nourishing my body and lifting my spirits. 'I guess it's true what they say about chicken noodle soup,' I say, clearing my bowl.

'What's that?' asks Phoenix.

'It's good for the soul.'

30

After dinner, Phoenix grabs a shower while I wash up and ensure we leave no trace of our presence in the cottage. When he finally emerges from the bedroom, I insist on rebandaging his back. When he takes off his T-shirt I have to hide my shock. Along with the peppering of shotgun wounds, his torso is now covered in a tapestry of bruises.

A surge of anger rises up in me. 'Those Hunters really gave you a good kicking, didn't they!' I say bitterly.

'Yeah, but I broke one of their noses,' he replies with a lopsided grin. 'And you –' he glances over his shoulder at me – 'you gave one a serious headache.'

With a shy smile, I reply, 'I couldn't stop that other Hunter, though. Sorry . . . but I'm not much of a fighter.'

'*What?*' Phoenix exclaims with a genuine look of astonishment. 'You were once a fearsome samurai warrior. I hardly had any need to protect you in that life. I remember you fighting *five* ninja with your bare hands once. You took them apart like they were rag dolls!'

I think of myself earlier in the shower, curled up in a ball and sobbing my heart out. 'Really? That doesn't sound much like me.'

Phoenix looks me in the eye. 'Believe me, Genna, you have a warrior spirit.'

'Maybe in that life I did,' I reply, dismissing the suggestion with a shrug.

Opening up the first-aid kit, I busy myself tending to his wounds. The idea of my being a fighter, and a *samurai* at that, seems so far removed from the person I am today – or anyone I may have been in the past, for that matter. I can imagine myself as a nurse . . . a farmer . . . a sailor . . . an explorer even. *But as a lethal warrior?*

I finish applying the bandages to Phoenix's back and am about to tell him he can put his shirt on again when I notice a thick dark line just below his shoulder blade. 'What's this?' I ask, gently tracing the line with my finger.

'A birthmark,' he replies.

I examine it more closely in the candlelight. 'Looks more like a scar.'

He nods. 'It's that too. Sometimes a traumatic death in a past life can have physical aftershocks in future lives. I got that from a poisoned arrow.'

A brief Glimmer of Necalli collapsing in the river flashes before my eyes –

. . . *his tattooed body floating lifeless in the water, the arrow piercing his back like a harpoon, as my canoe races safely away from the erupting volcano and the frenzied tribe of Tletl warriors . . .*

Even now, as I run my finger along the ghost of Necalli's scar, I can feel the anguish and grief that I experienced as Zianya. Painful and raw, like it had taken place only yesterday.

Then, lower down on Phoenix's left-hand side, I spot another birthmark, round like the entry wound of a bullet. *Was that from when he was Hiamovi and got shot by the white-hatted sheriff?* I wonder.

Tenderly my fingers brush over the mottling of bruises on his skin and across the fresh dressings covering his back. My heart breaks at the sight of so many injuries, and I can't help but shed a tear at all the pain and trauma my Soul Protector has endured from life to life and in death to death. 'You've suffered so much for me,' I murmur.

Phoenix turns to me. 'Nothing's too much for you,' he replies, wiping away the tear from my cheek.

On an impulse I wrap my arms round his waist and draw myself to his bare chest. I want to comfort him, to take away his pain, to ease his suffering on my behalf. Phoenix responds by enveloping me in his arms, and I feel the warmth of his skin, the tenderness of his touch and the strength in his battered body. I lose myself in the moment, never wanting to let him go again. In his arms I'm safe, secure and –

All of a sudden Phoenix tenses as a loud whinnying comes from the paddock. Breaking from our embrace, he blows out the candle, dashes over to the window and peers through the gap in the curtains.

'Anyone there?' I ask, hardly daring to breathe.

Phoenix stares deeper into the night. 'No, just the horses.'

But my unease doesn't subside. I'm conscious that, the next time, we might not be so lucky. 'Tanas will eventually find us, won't he?' I say, a note of despair in my voice.

'Probably.' Phoenix turns to me, his expression grim in the darkness. 'You'd best get some sleep while you can. I'll keep watch.'

I hesitate, wondering if I should go over to him and rekindle our embrace ... but I realize the moment has passed. His guard is back up. He's once more my Soul Protector, his mind focused again on the job in hand.

As he begins checking each window in turn, I make my way to bed, my body feeling bone-tired. Slipping under the quilt, I settle my head on the pillow, its softness like a cloud, and within moments I'm asleep, safe in the knowledge that Phoenix is watching over me.

31

'Wake up! Wake up, little girl!' hisses a low but insistent voice.

Roughly shaken by the shoulder, I open my eyes to be greeted by the slave's sun-weathered face. His cheeks are hollow, his eyes dark and sunken, his scrawny body now even more emaciated. Custos has survived on only a few berries and very little sleep since our escape from the villa three days before. My Protector has given me the lion's share of what he's managed to forage from the forest, and always stood watch over me while I slept, but his sacrifices are starting to take their toll on him.

'Morning . . .' I yawn. 'Wh–'

He clamps his hand over my mouth and puts a finger to his lips. I'm instantly alert, listening to the sounds of the forest. The birds are singing their dawn chorus. A soft breeze rustles the leaves. And nearby a brook babbles lightly over the rocks. There's nothing unusual –

Then I hear the sharp snap of a twig.

Someone is close by.

Peering through a gap in the bushes, I spy the red-pleated tunic of a Roman soldier. Sinewy and battle-

hardened, he wields a long, pointed spear. With every few steps, he makes random stabs into the undergrowth. As he approaches our hiding place, we stay still and silent as wild deer. I hardly dare breathe. A thrust of the spear pierces the leaves right beside my head, but Custos shields me and the iron point slices across his bare arm. Gritting his teeth against the pain, he hurriedly wipes the spear tip clean of his blood with a large leaf as the soldier retracts the weapon. His quick thinking saves us – the soldier moves on, unaware of just how close he was to finding us.

Only once he is out of view does my Protector scoop me up in his arms and bear me away in the opposite direction. I cling to him, watchful and afraid. He treads lightly, but it isn't long before his tracks are discovered, the drips of blood from his injured arm giving us away.

Soon I can hear the sound of hunting dogs barking in the distance. More red tunics appear, sweeping their way in a line through the forest. The soldiers are closing in on us. But Custos is fast and strong, like a horse. He carries me in his arms, darting between the trees. His breathing sounds harsh and ragged in my ears as we burst out of the forest . . . and come to an abrupt halt.

We're at the edge of a narrow gorge. Far below lie the jagged rocks of a dry riverbed. My Protector frantically searches for a safe way down, but everywhere the cliff face is sheer and treacherous. Cradling me in his arms, he turns back towards the treeline only to be confronted by the onyx-eyed centurion. Armoured in sculpted bronze, a blood-red cloak draped from his broad shoulders and a straight, double-edged blade clasped in his hand, the commander appears as formidable and fearsome as the statue of the god of war himself in the Temple of Mars at Rome.

As his soldiers surround us in an unbroken arc of shields and spears, the centurion demands, 'Hand over the kidnapped child to me, slave!'

I look to my Protector, confused and scared. I haven't been kidnapped – I've been rescued . . . haven't I?

Eyeing the ranks of armed soldiers, Custos seems to understand that resistance would be futile and carefully lowers me to the stony ground.

'Come to me, Aurelia,' beckons the centurion. 'Your father is waiting.'

I hesitate, unsure of what I should do. Custos says the centurion intends me harm, yet my father has apparently put his faith in this revered army commander. Who should I believe? A lowly slave, or a distinguished soldier of Rome?

Custos kneels down beside me. 'Do you trust me?' he asks.

I nod my head and then he does a wholly unexpected thing. He pushes me hard in the chest. Shrieking in terror, I fall backwards off the cliff and plunge to the rocks below –

I wake with a jolt, sweating, my heart palpitating. A piercing headache grips me like my skull's been cracked open. My body throbs as if every bone is broken.

As the agonizing sensations gradually fade away, I ask myself, *Was that a nightmare . . . or a Glimmer?*

Sitting up in bed, I try to shake my head clear of the disturbing vision. There's a chance I could have imagined it, of course. Perhaps the seed of distrust that Damien planted in my mind has spread and invaded my dreams, poisoned my thoughts . . . Yet deep down I *know* that that was a Glimmer.

The slave, Custos – or, rather, Phoenix as I know him now – pushed me off a cliff. *Killed* me with his own hands. *Murdered* me!

The very idea sends a chill straight through my heart. *What kind of Protector kills the very person they're meant to protect?*

Silently I slip out of bed and peek into the lounge. The candle has burned itself out. But in the darkness I can just about see Phoenix slumped in an armchair by the window, exhaustion having finally overcome him. *Am I right to trust this boy with my life?* I wonder. *A stranger I've known for little more than a week?* My mind still reels from the implications of the Glimmer. Rather than protecting me, has Phoenix now in fact *kidnapped* me? Like he did when I was a little girl in Rome. Maybe he intends to kill me again. Has he something to gain by my death, just as Tanas has?

It occurs to me that I've only got Phoenix's word that he's my Soul Protector. Yes, I know he's saved me from Damien and his Hunters in this life. And previous Glimmers may well show his former incarnations rescuing me too. But what of all the countless Glimmers I've yet to see? The ones where I die by his hands.

If he can push me off a cliff as Custos in one life, then Phoenix surely could kill me in this . . . any time he chooses.

All of a sudden I'm frightened to be with him. Mistrustful of his intentions, suspicious of his actions. In light of this most recent Glimmer, it seems I'd be safer back with my family and friends than here with this killer.

Picking up my trainers, I sneak across the lounge and head for the front door. My hands trembling, I ease the handle open and step barefoot out into the night. My breath mists in the chill air. Praying that Phoenix stays sound asleep, I quietly close the door behind me and creep down the driveway, clenching my teeth as my feet crunch painfully in the gravel.

Once I'm at the end of the drive, I slip on my trainers and run. The horses in the paddock give a startled snort as I pass. With only a faint gleam from the crescent moon to light the way, I dash along the single-track road in near-total darkness. I've no idea where I'm heading – only that it needs to be as far away from Phoenix as possible.

32

A hazy neon glow in the distance guides me to a main road and a service station. But it's still the early hours of the morning and everything is closed. With the building dark and deserted, there's only the low hum of the forecourt's strip lights and the green glare from the signboard at the roadside to keep me company.

In the corner of the forecourt I discover a public internet phone, the kind that no one ever seems to use, with a silvery metal keyboard, rollerball mouse and chunky, square display. Fumbling in my pocket for the single pound coin I still have, I go to call my parents – then think twice. If my home line *really* is tapped, as Phoenix believes, I don't want to risk alerting any Hunters. So I drop in the coin and go online instead. I've read somewhere that with certain messaging services the messages are encrypted end-to-end. Logging into my social network, I find Mei's profile and video call her, hoping her mobile is on at this time of night.

The phone rings for what seems an age. Then, just as the call is about to automatically disconnect, a bleary-eyed Mei answers.

'Genna?' she mumbles, peering at her screen. 'Is that *you*?'

I move closer to the webcam so she can see me in the gloom. 'Yes. Sorry for waking you, but I didn't know who else to call.'

Switching on her bedside light, Mei hurriedly sits up and rubs the sleep from her eyes. 'No, I'm glad you have. I've been so worried about you. Everyone here has been going *ballistic* since you disappeared! Are you OK?'

'I'm . . . I'm fine,' I reply, forcing a smile, before adding, 'at least not hurt or anything.'

My friend lets out a sigh. 'Thank goodness! Your parents will be so relieved to hear that. Have you spoken to them yet?'

I shake my head. 'You're the first person I've called. How are they?'

Mei grimaces. 'Not good, if you want the truth. The press are camped outside your door twenty-four seven. The police visit daily. Your mum's looking real pale and thin, while your dad is . . . well, he seems to be in a permanent daze. They don't seem to know what to think any more. To be honest, nor do I.' She fixes me with a questioning look. 'You've seen the news reports about you, I take it?'

I nod numbly as I'm racked with guilt at the strain my parents have been put under. 'At least enough of them to know it isn't good news,' I reply.

'No, it isn't!' agrees Mei. 'First you're abducted from a police car by a suspected terrorist. Then you're arrested at Arundel Castle for theft, before breaking out of custody and going on the run with this Phoenix of yours! To begin with, the press were sympathetic, but now they're accusing you of being involved in that Clapham Market terrorist attack. Oh, Genna, is any of it true?'

'What do you think?' I reply sharply, hurt that my best friend can doubt me like this.

For a brief second Mei appears conflicted, then she replies softly. 'No, I don't believe any of it, but some people at school – you know what they're like – they're saying you must be in love with Phoenix.'

'*In love?*' I protest.

'Yeah, but not that you mean to be. Stockholm syndrome, I think it's called.'

I wrinkle my brow. 'What's that?'

'It's when a hostage feels affection or trust towards their kidnapper, sympathizes with their cause . . . even *joins* them.'

I consider my growing attachment to Phoenix and wonder if Mei may be right. Maybe I *have* lost my sense of judgement. Maybe Phoenix *has* manipulated me with the threat of these Soul Hunters. *Perhaps my friendship with him is just my way to cope with it all . . . My way to survive?*

Mei lowers her voice and peers closer at her screen. 'Is *he* with you now?'

'No, I ran away,' I reply. 'I had a Glimmer that Phoenix killed me in a past life.'

'Oh my –' Mei gasps, her hand going to her mouth. For a moment I think my friend is shocked at the revelation of my past murder, but then she brings me back down to earth. 'Genna, you're not still wrapped up in this reincarnation fantasy stuff, are you? Look, I'm saying this as your friend: you need help. You should call the police. Turn yourself in.'

I think of my unsettling encounter with Detective Inspector Shaw, and shake my head firmly. Whatever is happening to me, I know *that* was real. The Hunters are a true threat.

'I can't trust the police,' I tell her. 'In fact, I can't trust anyone any more,' and I shoot her an accusing look.

'You can trust *me*, Genna,' Mei insists, a touch of desperation in her voice. 'I'm your best friend. At least tell me where you are.'

I hesitate, not sure of anything any more. But I know I need to trust someone. 'Ermm, I'm not really sure where I am –' I say, glancing round the forecourt, but then I spot the name of the service station on the petrol sign – 'Oh, hang on . . . I'm at Notchcutt Services, in Gloucestershire.'

'*Gloucestershire?*' Mei exclaims. 'What are you doing *there?*'

I sigh. 'We were heading to a village called Havenbury to meet some spiritual guide called Gabriel. But none of that matters now. I just want to get back to London, back home. Somewhere safe.'

'Of course,' Mei says, nodding. 'Listen, I'll send my brother to come and get you. He has a car. A white Ford Fiesta. Whatever you do, *stay there*!'

33

Shivering, I stand in the shadows at the rear of the service station. From my hiding place, I have a clear view of the forecourt but can keep out of sight of any passers-by. I don't want to risk being spotted: not by Phoenix, nor the police, nor a member of the public. And especially not by any Soul Hunters. My nerves are on a razor edge, my paranoia peaking with thoughts that I may be experiencing Stockholm syndrome.

The surrounding area remains quiet, though, only an occasional car zooming past on the main road. My hopes of rescue brighten at the approach of each set of headlights ... then fade along with the red glow of their tail lights into the early-morning gloom.

One hour ticks by. Then two. I wonder how long it'll take for Lee to drive from Clapham to Notchcutt. Do I need to start worrying yet? Is he actually coming at all? Or is he just delayed? Maybe his parents found out and stopped him.

Before my money ran out on the internet phone, I insisted that Mei tell no one else my location or that I'd even been in contact – not until I was safely back with her in London. Mei said I can trust her, and deep down I know that's true, but would her promise extend to her brother? She mentioned Lee was in trouble: their parents had discovered the jade knife was missing from their collection and suspected one of his friends. I'd told Mei that Damien had stolen it and intended to use the lethal relic for my ritual sacrifice. I'm not sure whether she believed this last part, although she certainly believed I was in grave danger. But what if Lee had gone straight to his parents and told them of the knife's whereabouts?

Then a darker, more disturbing thought strikes me: *What if Lee has been intercepted by Hunters? And what if my video call wasn't encrypted?*

Shuddering at the possibility, I hug myself for warmth and huddle closer against the wall, out of the wind. Dawn can't be that far off now, but the sky remains ominously dark, not a single star shining, the moon shrouded in a veil of black clouds. The weather seems to be taking a turn for the worse. I just hope I'm picked up before it starts to rain.

I check the time: coming up for four thirty. Phoenix is bound to wake soon. I wonder how he'll react when he discovers I'm gone. *Will he be worried? Angry? Violent?* I'd put nothing past him now. I already suspected that I was riding with a killer – I just didn't realize that *I* might be his victim.

From up the road I hear the low rumble of a car engine approaching. A pair of headlights on full beam cuts a path through the darkness, growing brighter and ever closer. This time the vehicle doesn't pass by. Slowing, it turns into the forecourt, its headlights sweeping the shadows aside as the driver pulls up at the far petrol pump.

I retreat further behind the corner of the station, peering warily out at the car.

The engine is still running and the headlights remain on full beam. My eyes having become accustomed to the night, I have to squint against the glare. It's *definitely* a white Ford Fiesta. But I can't make out the driver, who remains seated inside behind the wheel.

From a distance it appears to be Lee. *Who else would be stopping at this closed garage in the middle of the night?* But still I err on the side of caution. *Why doesn't he get out and look for me?*

Then I realize that maybe Lee is being careful too. If Mei has told him about the Soul Hunters, then obviously he won't want to risk his life any more than he's doing by coming to get me.

A full minute goes by.

Then another . . . and I start to worry that if I don't show myself soon, Lee will assume that I'm no longer around, or that the call to Mei was a hoax, and will simply drive off. Taking a deep breath, I steel myself to step out from the shadows. But, as I'm about to leave the cover of my hiding place, a hand grabs me from behind, another clamps over my mouth, and I'm dragged back behind the station. Kicking and flailing, I struggle to escape my captor's grip. Lee's car is barely fifteen metres from me. If I can just break free and reach the forecourt I'll –

'*It's me! Phoenix!*' hisses my captor.

Panicking, I fight even harder. Somehow my kidnapper has tracked me down!

'*Stop!*' snarls Phoenix, his grip tightening round my chest and mouth.

I bite down hard on his hand, tasting blood, but he refuses to let go. Struggling for breath, I'm eventually forced to surrender. I fall limp and compliant in his arms.

'Do *not* scream. Do *not* move. Do *not* run,' Phoenix orders harshly. 'Your life depends upon it. Do you understand?'

I nod mutely, terrified out of my wits. He relaxes his grip ever so slightly.

'Who are you meeting here?' he asks, his face remaining in shadow.

'L-Lee,' I whisper, my voice quavering. 'My best friend's brother.'

'You called him?'

Nodding again, I reply timidly, 'I spoke to Mei. She sent him.'

'Who else did you call?' demands Phoenix.

'No one,' I say, as the driver of the Ford Fiesta cuts the engine and switches off the headlights. He steps out of the vehicle and looks around.

'*GENNA?*' he yells.

Phoenix keeps a firm hold on me, his hand ready to smother my mouth at the first sign of a scream. 'Is that Lee?' he asks quietly, as the driver calls out my name again.

I peer at the figure standing in the forecourt. My heart tightens in my chest. Dressed in a black Adidas hoodie and ripped jeans, and with a designer haircut, the driver *could* be a Hunter . . . Then he turns in my direction and I see his face clearly: slim with defined cheekbones, and the same piercing brown eyes as his sister.

'*Yes, that's him!*' I gasp, as a spark of hope ignites in me. I tense myself, ready to make a break for freedom – but Phoenix's steel-like grip keeps me pinned and powerless.

'*Wait!*' he orders.

A car zooms past the service station, its lights briefly illuminating the far kerbside. Several dark hooded figures stand silhouetted against the skyline before melting back into the darkness.

Sensing but no longer seeing their presence, an icy dread invades my limbs. *Soul Hunters!*

My resistance to Phoenix crumbles, along with any hopes I had of rescue. I watch in despair as an infuriated Lee climbs back into his car and drives off.

34

'What the hell did you think you were doing?' Phoenix demands, after sneaking me away from the service station and frogmarching me back to the holiday cottage. We'd walked in silence the whole way, Phoenix too angry to speak, I too scared. 'Why did you call your friend? I told you the Hunters would be tapping the phone lines!'

He bangs the kitchen table with his fist and I flinch at his fury.

'I-I-I didn't call Mei's phone,' I reply nervously, glad to have the table between me and him. 'I went online and used a messaging service to contact her. I thought those things were encrypted!'

'Yes, but there are ways to get round encryption,' Phoenix says fiercely. He shakes his head in dismay. 'Then again the Incarnates probably just had a Watcher staking out your friend's house. Lee driving off in the middle of the night would've rung alarm bells. All they needed to do was follow him. Now the Hunters are on our trail again!'

Seething, he paces over to the window. As he stares out into the feeble light of dawn, I manage to muster up some courage. In a dead-cold tone, I declare, 'You killed me.'

Phoenix stiffens. Then slowly he turns to me, his brow furrowed, acting as if he's confused. 'What are you talking about?' he says.

Glaring hard, I stab an accusing finger at him. 'When you were a slave in Ancient Rome and I was just a little girl, barely eight years old, you told me you were my Protector. I *trusted* you with my life . . . and you pushed me off a cliff!'

Phoenix's face goes slack and he swallows hard. As if deflated from within, he walks over and slumps down at the kitchen table and cradles his head in his hands. For several long seconds he is silent, then he mumbles, 'I'd hoped you'd never relive that Glimmer.'

'So it *is* true,' I say with a fierceness that burns like fire. 'You *murdered* me.' Inside of me something breaks – I'm not sure whether it's my trust in him, or our souls' deep connection . . . or my heart.

Phoenix looks up, his eyes red and welling with tears. 'Believe me, Genna,' he pleads, 'that moment haunts my every life since.'

'And now mine,' I shoot back harshly.

'Killing you goes against the very grain of my heart!' he implores, reaching across the table for my hand.

I recoil from him, and it's clear by the wounded look on his face that my outright rejection has cut him to the bone.

'Genna, I'm here to protect your *soul*,' he insists. 'To defend the very essence of you, the element that carries the Light of Humanity.'

'Then why kill me?' I question.

Phoenix hangs his head in shame and lets out a heavy sigh. 'I had no choice,' he says finally. 'The only way to save you in that life – to prevent Tanas performing the ritual sacrifice and obliterating your soul forever – was to kill you by my own hand before *he* got his hands on you.'

'Then why don't you just kill me now?' I demand, unable to keep the resentment out of my voice. 'Reset the clock. Hide me again in death.'

'Because it's bad karma,' he explains. 'A violent or wrongful death not only leaves physical scars from one life to the next, it damages the soul, weakens the Light . . . as well as the bond between us. You *must* believe me when I say that killing you is the very *last* resort. Not only does it play into Tanas's hands, but the pain and guilt I cause my own soul are immeasurable.'

Raising his head, Phoenix offers me such a heartbroken and sincere look that my fury suddenly falters. I recall the hundred Roman soldiers encircling us at the top of the gorge, our hopeless situation in the face of an impenetrable wall of shields and spears. I see again the smirk of triumph on the centurion's face when Tanas realized he finally had us trapped – and the look of anguish in Custos's eyes as he's forced to make his most agonizing decision . . .

Phoenix meets my softening gaze, the blue starlight glimmer in his eyes fractured by a prism of tears. 'Genna, I'll do *anything* to save your soul. I've laid down my life for you again and again, and will do so for eternity if it means you live.'

He reaches out once more across the kitchen table. This time I don't flinch away. But I still hesitate to take his hand.

My implicit trust in his intentions has been broken and it'll take more than mere words to rebuild the bond between us. Yet his apparent devotion to protecting me with his life is convincing. And if the eyes are truly windows to the soul, then I can see how desperate Phoenix is to re-establish our connection.

Despite my doubts, I feel my resistance to him wavering just as there's a loud *crunch* on the gravel outside.

35

Phoenix springs to his feet and races over to the window. Peeking through the curtains, he whispers, '*There's a car!*'

A surge of adrenaline sends my pulse racing. 'Hunters?' I ask.

'Not sure,' he replies, rushing back to the table and grabbing his backpack. 'Whoever they are, we need to go.'

I follow him over to the front door. 'Why didn't we hear them drive up the track?'

'It's an electric car, that's why!' he mutters. 'You ready to make a run for it?'

I nod, steeling myself for another frantic escape. As Phoenix inches open the door, we're met by a smartly dressed woman in a cream jacket and blue pleated trousers.

'Who the hell are you?' she demands, her eyes widening in alarm.

'Hi. We're just leaving,' replies Phoenix, attempting to disarm her with his most charming smile. 'Thank you for a lovely stay.'

The woman puts up no resistance as we brush past. 'B-b-but I didn't have any bookings this w–' She abruptly stops and stares at me, her initial bewildered look of alarm hardening into one of fierce recognition. 'Wǒ rènshí nǐ,' she blurts in fluent Chinese.

Shocked not only by the woman's sudden change in demeanour, but also by the fact that I can understand her, I gape in horror as her eyes darken like thunderclouds –

'I know you,' says the round-faced official, stepping into my path and barring me from exiting the northern gate of Pingyao city. Robed in purple with a black winged hat and a thin drooping moustache, the whiskery man looks like a hungry cat who's just pounced upon a long-awaited mouse.

Hemmed in by two muscle-bound guards of the gate, I try to keep my expression calm and fixed, even as the official leans in closer to inspect my own bearded face.

'What's your name and birth town?' the official demands, his breath reeking of old fish and garlic.

My voice hoarse and deep, I answer, 'Hua Shanbo from Hebei province.'

The official's eyes narrow like a cat's and he grins to reveal a row of yellow teeth. 'Wouldn't a girl's name suit you better?' he suggests slyly.

With a stiff smile, I reply, 'Oh, I don't think so . . .' and I stroke my beard for effect. The two guards snort with amusement but their hands remain firmly upon their iron-studded clubs.

Glowering at me, the official wags a bony finger in my face. 'Oh, I believe you go by many names . . . don't you, Lihua?' Then without warning he tugs hard at my beard and rips off the false hair from my chin –

I gasp in pain, my cheek stinging as if I've been slapped. For a second, I can see the official's whiskery moustache superimposed on the cottage-owner's face, her past life momentarily overlapping with this one. Then the double-vision fades and I stagger away with Phoenix. As we hurry down the gravel drive, I hear the woman shouting into her mobile phone: 'Summerfield Cottage. *Xiànzài!* I mean . . . Now!' she barks, muddling up her languages.

'Just our luck – a Watcher!' remarks Phoenix, picking up the pace.

At first the woman doesn't give chase, just observes us fleeing down the track. Then she stalks towards her car, her unhurried manner more unsettling than if she'd run. Her behaviour suggests she's convinced our capture is a foregone conclusion – and she may well be right. Before we've got even halfway down the track, the roar of motorbike engines can be heard heading in our direction. Moments later five black-helmeted bikers appear at the top of the country lane, cutting off our escape. The lead biker flips up his visor and fixes us with his oil-black eyes –

Damien! I feel as if I've been punched in the gut. My tormentor has found me once again and it's all *my* fault! If I hadn't called Mei, we could have stayed hidden. Remained off the grid. Had a chance of reaching Gabriel. But now we're in the Hunters' sights once more.

'Back towards the cottage!' orders Phoenix.

As we turn on our heels, the bikers rev their engines. Like a pack of baying dogs, they power down the dirt track in deadly pursuit. My heart pounding in my chest, we make a desperate dash for freedom, but I can hear the Hunters closing in fast.

'We'll never outrun them!' I cry.

Phoenix skids to an abrupt stop. The woman, now in her car, is accelerating towards us from the other direction. We're caught in a pincer movement between bonnet and bikes. With nowhere else to go, we're forced to dive over the fence into the paddock.

'The horses!' says Phoenix, scrambling to his feet. 'They're our only chance.'

We rush across the grassy paddock. The three horses are skittish, but they tolerate our approach. I make for a sleek palomino mare, Phoenix for a dark bay gelding. Without breaking my stride, I reach up, seize my horse's mane and vault in one smooth motion on to her back. I barely register the astounding acrobatic feat, but now my riding skills seem as instinctive as breathing since my Glimmer as a Cheyenne.

Phoenix mounts his horse with equal ease. 'Head for the wood,' he orders.

I look beyond the fenced paddock and a stretch of open fields bounded by drystone walls to a broad expanse of trees in the distance. Their cover should offer us a slim chance of escape.

Digging my heels into the mare's flanks, I gallop with Phoenix across the paddock and towards the fence line. The motorbikes, riding parallel to us along the single-track lane, buzz like angry wasps in pursuit. As we approach the high fence, my horse shakes her head and snorts. Sensing she's spooked, I rest my hand upon her neck and whisper some words of Cheyenne into her ear. Immediately she calms and lowers her head to judge the jump, then in a single, graceful bound we leap over and land smoothly on the other side. Phoenix's gelding clears it too, and he keeps pace with my mare as we ride hell for leather for the wood.

However, zooming through an open gateway, Damien and his bikers fan out like a posse of bounty hunters. They thunder across the open field towards us.

'Ride like the wind!' shouts Phoenix, echoing his former incarnation as Hiamovi.

I urge my horse on, riding with the courage and swiftness of a true Cheyenne, while the horde of 500cc motorbikes bears down on us, closing the distance with unnerving speed.

Hooves thudding in the earth, my mare gallops towards the drystone wall and hurdles it effortlessly, as if leading the Grand National. Behind us, though, Damien and his Hunters, unable to make the jump on their bikes, are forced to veer away until they find a collapsed section of the wall further up and zip through.

Phoenix and I ride hard, trying to lengthen our lead, aware that for the Hunters each stone boundary is a potential barrier, while for us each one is a step closer to the sanctuary of the wood. But this field is far larger than the last and the motorbikes rapidly gain ground.

Pulling ahead of the pack, a black-helmeted Hunter comes up alongside me. Phoenix spots the threat and lashes out with his foot. His boot smashes him in the face, cracking his visor and sending him tumbling off his bike.

Without missing a beat, a second Hunter is quick to replace the first. She makes a grab for my leg and catches hold of my jeans. With no saddle or reins, I can only hold on more tightly to my horse's mane as she tries to unseat me.

'*Phoenix!*' I cry, feeling myself slip further and further with each sharp tug.

But Phoenix's horse is forced away by another biker.

Desperately I try to shake the Hunter off, but she refuses to let go. So determined is she to unseat me that she fails to notice the next stone wall coming up fast. Only at the last second does she spot the danger, releasing my leg in order to brake ... but too late! Her bike collides head-on with the wall. The Hunter flips over into the next field, her bike landing in a mangled heap beside her.

My trusty mare clears the wall at the same time. I cling on to her neck for dear life, my leg hooked over her back as she avoids the crash and gallops on. The stony ground rushes past, inches from my face. Trembling with the effort, I haul myself upright on my horse.

'Are you OK?' asks Phoenix, riding up alongside me. He too has managed to shake off his pursuer.

I nod, then glance back over my shoulder. Damien and the two remaining Hunters have been forced to take the long route once again, skirting the field boundary until they find the gate. With an angry roar of engines, they thunder after us, racing to make up lost ground.

But, with only two walls to go, the wood is now within striking distance.

Pulling ahead of Phoenix, I take the lead. 'We're gonna beat them!' I cry. *Surely our horses' ability to jump gives us the edge over the motorbikes' speed?*

Then the *zing* of a bullet zips past my ear. Gunshots echo across the open fields and I duck as more rounds whizz by. Damien, wielding a pistol while riding one-handed, fires again. Just like the white-hatted marshal on the Great Plains, he's intent on shooting us from our mounts. But the uneven ground and the speed of the chase hinder his aim and his shots go wild . . . except for one.

As we jump the next stone wall, Phoenix's gelding is struck in the flank. Whinnying in pain, the horse lands awkwardly and tumbles over.

'NO!' I yell as Phoenix is flung from the gelding's back. He crashes to the hard ground, rolling over and over.

My horse rides on and I have to squeeze my thighs hard to break off from the gallop. Turning round, I see that despite the heavy fall and his injured flank, the gelding has managed to struggle back up and hobbles away. But, to my dismay, Phoenix remains on the ground. A second ticks by, then another, and from this distance I don't know whether he's dead or merely dazed. Then, to my immense relief, I see him twitch and return to life. Groggily shaking his head, Phoenix looks up and sees me.

'*No, Genna! Ride on!*' he shouts.

I hesitate. If I go now, I can reach the trees before the Hunters are through the next gate. But, just like my former incarnation Waynoka, I won't leave my Protector behind to die. Spurring on my mare, I ride back for him. As he struggles to his feet, again the sound of gunshots punctuates the air. However, these bullets aren't aimed at Phoenix or at me. Damien is blasting the padlock off an old gate, before roaring through it and hurtling towards Phoenix, intent on mowing him down.

I urge my horse on, a life-or-death race to reach Phoenix playing out between Damien and me. If I'm to save him, I know I'll need every ounce of riding skill I now possess . . . and maybe even more.

'Phoenix! Your hand!' I shout, leaning over as I gallop towards him.

But Damien is almost on top of him too, his bike wheels chewing up the dirt and snapping at Phoenix's heels as he limps towards me. With barely a second to spare, I grab Phoenix's outstretched hand and I swing him up on to the back of my horse. Damien roars past in frustrated fury.

'That, I gotta say,' pants Phoenix, 'is some neat pony trick. Thanks!'

My Protector's arms wrapped round my waist, I turn sharply and race for the wood. The final drystone wall is in view and there's no gate in sight for the bikes. If we can reach the boundary, then we're in the clear!

Damien must realize this too. Opening up the throttle to the max, he powers his bike on ahead, risking all in a mad dash to get to the wall before us. With two riders to carry, my mare hasn't a hope of overtaking him. Her nostrils flaring, she's already tiring from her exertions.

Damien reaches the boundary moments before us and skids to a sharp stop, forming a barrier between us and the wood. A final deadly hurdle. But I don't slow my mare down, nor do I steer her away. Not with the remaining Hunters on our backs, hounding us.

'She won't make the jump!' yells Phoenix, his arms tightening round my waist.

'Yes, she will,' I yell back.

Sensing she's a horse of great spirit – a noble steed worthy of any Cheyenne – I again whisper into her ear.

Instantly, her head lifts and from somewhere she seems to find a well of hidden strength, because she puts on an extra spurt and gallops at full speed towards the final wall. Damien hastily draws his gun. Undaunted, my mare doesn't falter. She leaps high into the air. Despite the weight of two riders, she manages to clear both wall and biker . . .

Well, almost . . . Her rear hoof clips Damien's helmet, knocking him and his gun to the ground.

36

'Good girl,' I say, patting the palomino on her sweaty neck. She snorts softly, but I can tell she's exhausted, the long, fraught ride enough to tire even the best-trained race horse. 'You need to rest, don't you, girl?'

'We aren't far from Havenbury now,' Phoenix says. 'It's just over that hill.'

Ahead of us in the distance, a grassy slope rises to what looks to be a stone circle, like the one near Andover, at the crown of the hill. The sky above is leaden, a steel-grey cladding of storm clouds heavy with the threat of rain. As a chill breeze rustles the leaves of the trees around us, a shiver runs through me and I hear the growl of an engine passing along a lane nearby. Despite narrowly escaping Damien and his Soul Hunters, their motorbikes still criss-cross the countryside in a continuous and ever-tightening net, their guttural roar a constant and harrowing reminder that they're still on the hunt for us.

But the mare is on her last legs, barely able to put one hoof in front of the other.

'At least let her stop and have a drink,' I suggest as we come to a stream beside the bridleway.

Reluctantly agreeing, Phoenix dismounts and almost collapses to the ground himself.

'Are you all right?' I ask, jumping down to help him.

He grimaces in pain. 'I think I hurt my leg in that fall,' he replies, easing himself on to a patch of grass and shrugging off his backpack. 'I'll be fine once we get to Gabriel's. He should be able to fix me.'

Examining his injured leg, I ask, 'Are Soul Seers doctors too?'

'No,' he says, through gritted teeth, wincing as I touch his swollen knee. 'But they're powerful healers.'

Satisfied his leg isn't broken, I am however concerned about his knee. But he insists it's nothing to worry about, so I settle down next to him on the grass as we wait for my horse to drink her fill from the stream.

'I could do with some healing myself,' I say, stretching out and hearing my neck crick. My muscles are stiff and my legs rubbed sore from the ride. Whatever skills have transferred from my incarnation as a Cheyenne, my body in this life simply isn't used to the demands of bareback riding. 'I'm sorry I alerted the Hunters and put them back on our trail,' I say.

'Don't be,' Phoenix replies. 'It was only a matter of time before they tracked us down anyway.'

'Well, I'm really sorry for doubting your loyalty, for thinking you wanted to kill me.' Convinced by his actions during the chase, I know now that he *truly* is my Protector.

Phoenix turns to me, his eyes a mixture of remorse and forgiveness. 'No, you were right to doubt me,' he admits.

'I doubt myself at times.' He sighs heavily. 'The decisions I've made. The sacrifices I've sometimes forced you to endure. The people I've hurt – or had to kill – in order to protect you. To be honest, I sometimes wonder if any of it's worth it.'

He picks up a pebble from the path and tosses it into the stream, the splash causing our mare to flinch. As the ripples in the water fade, Phoenix studies my face with an intense devotion. 'But then I look into your eyes, and I see your soul, your Light,' he murmurs. 'And I realize that I must do *whatever* it takes to keep you safe. For without you, the world will become a very dark place.'

As he says this, the sunlight around us dims, the temperature drops by a degree or two, and the crisp scent of rain fills the air.

'So what is it, this Light that I carry?' I ask, shrugging off a shiver. 'What happens if it's extinguished?'

Phoenix lets out a long breath. 'Gabriel will be able to explain it far better than I can. He's the one who should tell you. Just know that the Light is very precious and must be protected.' He holds my gaze. 'So I'm glad you ran, after that Roman Glimmer. You have to be on your guard at all times. Remember: you can't trust *anyone* – at least not until you've seen their soul.'

'I've seen *yours* and I trust you,' I reply softly, once more feeling that irresistible magnetism pulling me towards him.

The first drops of rain begin to fall, pattering upon the leaves and path. I barely notice their cool touch upon my bare skin, so entranced am I by the starlight sparkle playing in my Soul Protector's gaze.

'We ... maybe we should get going,' Phoenix says, breaking away to study the thundercloud over our heads. He rises awkwardly to his feet, putting most of his weight on his right leg.

Coming back to my senses, I stand and help to support him. All of a sudden a streak of lightning flashes across the sky and a thunderclap shakes the heavens. Startled by the booming noise, our skittish mare bolts, racing off down the bridleway.

'Damn it!' snarls Phoenix as we watch her disappear back into the wood.

I'm saddened to see her go, yet secretly glad she's now out of danger. After all she's done for us, I wouldn't want Damien to shoot her in a chase.

Now the rain is falling in earnest and we're forced to tramp along the bridleway on foot. Phoenix struggles with every step, so I find a stout branch for him to lean on and shoulder the backpack. This quickens our pace, and we soon come to a country lane where a road sign points towards Havenbury one mile away.

'We're almost there!' I say, eagerly heading off down the lane.

But Phoenix stops me. 'The quickest route will be to cut over the hill,' he says, indicating a wayside footpath sign that shows the village to be less than half a mile's trek across the fields.

'But what about your knee?' I ask, shivering in the downpour. 'Wouldn't it be easier to follow the road?'

Phoenix nods. 'Sure it would. But we can't risk bumping into any Hunters.'

So, clambering over the stile, we make a slow yet steady ascent of the hill. The grass is slick and wet and we have to be careful to keep our footing. Exposed to the worst of the weather, we're soon soaked through – but at least the exertion of the climb staves off the chill from the storm.

We're halfway up when I hear the rumble of a motorbike engine and, turning, spot a black-helmeted rider dismount by the stile. He peers through the rain in our direction.

'They've found us!' I cry in dismay, as more bikes zoom along the lane to join him.

Leaving their motorcycles at the roadside, the Soul Hunters vault the stile and charge up the hill after us.

'Go! Go! GO!' Phoenix urges, gritting his teeth against the pain as he limps as fast as his injured leg will carry him.

With rain lashing in our faces, we climb the muddy footpath. Battling our way against the storm, I take Phoenix's hand, helping him over the uneven ground. Behind us, the Hunters are scaling the slippery slope with frightening speed. We're almost at the brow of the hill, the promise of Havenbury just down on the other side, when Phoenix's foot slides from under him and we both go crashing to the muddy earth. As he lets out an agonized cry, another flash of lightning strobes the sky. I glance back in alarm to see Damien bounding up the path, his coal-black eyes glinting in the brief blaze of light.

'Leave me,' groans Phoenix, leaning heavily on his makeshift walking stick as he tries to rise. 'Get to Gabriel!'

'No,' I reply, discarding the backpack and pulling his arm over my shoulder. 'We can make it. *Together.*'

Pulling him to his feet, I take his weight and we stagger on. Panting hard, I half carry, half drag him up the rest of the slope. As we crest the hill, the limestone boulders of the stone circle come into view. Havenbury is nestled in a shallow vale below, its church tower silhouetted against the thunderous skyline. The promise of sanctuary is so close . . . yet still a field too far away.

By now, Damien is almost breathing down our necks. Faster, fitter and fiercer, he and his Hunters are closing in for the kill and I realize with despair that we'll never reach the village. With Phoenix delirious with pain, our hopes of survival fade with our each and every lurching step. Stumbling under his weight, I'm almost on the point of collapse myself.

The sky flashes again, starkly illuminating the stone circle, and in that moment I remember what Phoenix told me in Andover: *Incarnates can't enter a sacred stone circle protected by the Light.* Praying he is right, I throw us both over the boundary ditch and into the centre of the circle.

Only a few paces behind, Damien comes to a sudden stop at the edge of the ditch. His Hunters join him and, together, they start pacing the boundary in frustration. Hooded and hungry for blood, they glare at us through the rain.

Feeling a familiar thrum in my bones, I allow myself a faint smile of triumph. 'You can't get us in here!' I call to Damien. 'This circle's protected by the Light.'

His jaw clenches at my boast, making him look even more like a ravenous wolf – one that has been denied its kill. Fuming, he glances at the ring of sacred stones. Then a sly malicious grin slides across his lips.

'Oh, but that's where you're wrong, Genna,' he says, before taking a bold step into the circle.

37

The rain falls in a torrent, running in rivulets down the eroded sides of the standing stones and flooding the henge's ditch. Wind whips the barren hill and lightning flares in a bruised sky, the sun all but banished by the dark and oppressive thunderclouds. Damien slowly advances on me and Phoenix, his skin glistening in the rain, his hollow eyes unnaturally large and cruelly cold.

'B-b-but how?' I stutter as we scramble away from him over the muddy grass of the circle's enclosure.

Damien, his body twitching strangely, nods towards a gap in the Neolithic monument. 'The circle is broken,' he points out with vindictive glee. 'Its head stone is missing, meaning its power's diminished.'

Deep down I know this to be true. The tingling of energy in my limbs is distinct, yet nowhere near as strong as at the circle in Andover. Still, its remnant power appears to be enough to give Damien the shakes and keep the other Hunters at bay. They continue to prowl the boundary like hyenas waiting for the lion to make its kill.

A kill that's only moments away.

Looming over us, Damien draws his gun and with a trembling hand aims the barrel at Phoenix's head. Exhausted and crippled with pain, Phoenix hasn't the strength to put up a fight. The rain drips down his battered face as he glares up at his rival in a final show of defiance.

'You won't win,' Phoenix spits. 'You'll *never* win.'

'Well, from where I'm standing our victory is assured!' sneers Damien, and he stamps on Phoenix's swollen knee and grinds his boot in.

As Phoenix lets out a tortured howl, Damien glances sidelong at me. 'Let's put this injured puppy out of its misery, shall we?'

'NO!' I cry, hurling myself at him and seizing hold of the gun.

I'm surprised to see that Damien's face screws up with effort as he struggles to resist me. I can feel an abnormal tremor in his arms and at the same time I notice a strange heat in my own.

It seems the Light that debilitates Damien ... empowers me!

As we wrestle for control of the gun, I'm starting to believe I may *truly* have the strength to beat him, when there's an ear-splitting *BANG!* –

I'm plunged into a muffled chaos. Phoenix flinches from the gunshot, but the bullet misses him and clips a standing stone instead. Fragments of rock fly off in all directions, the bullet ricocheting, forcing the other Hunters to take cover. In my dazed and deafened state, Damien angrily kicks me away then, again, takes aim at Phoenix. I try to rise but my head's reeling.

'Let him live,' I beg. 'It's me you want, not him. Show mercy, please.'

Damien frowns at me. 'But, Genna, I *am* showing mercy,' he says, his voice distant as if coming from the other end of a long tunnel. 'I *could* let him live to see your death. I *could* ritually destroy his soul for eternity. Instead, your precious Phoenix will die now so that he sees life *after* you're dead and your soul's long gone!'

He squeezes the trigger . . . but there's just the dull click of an empty chamber. Damien rechambers the gun and fires again. Still nothing.

'Out of bullets?' laughs Phoenix, his last-second reprieve seeming to revive him. With a bellow of fury, he smashes the stick across Damien's legs and sweeps him off his feet. Damien splashes down into the mud, his empty gun slipping from his hand. Phoenix, pumped with adrenaline, then launches himself at his rival. I'm knocked aside as the two grapple in the mud.

Pacing the edge of the circle, the Soul Hunters bay like hounds, urging their leader on. Phoenix, though, gets the upper hand and puts Damien in a chokehold. Damien's black eyes bulge, and I think it's all over when I catch a glimpse of jade stone.

'*Knife!*' I yell.

But my warning comes too late. Damien drives the jade knife deep into Phoenix's thigh. Screaming, Phoenix is forced to let go and, as he clasps his bleeding leg, Damien rises to finish him off.

In desperation I rush headlong at Damien. But he sees me coming and elbows me hard in the face. Stars burst before my eyes . . . my knees go weak . . . and I drop to the ground, stunned into submission.

My efforts, though, have given Phoenix enough time to roll away and scramble to his feet. He draws the shard of obsidian from his belt to confront Damien.

The two of them circle one another like a pair of caged tigers, their green and black blades glinting in the storm.

'The Light hurts, doesn't it?' taunts Phoenix, limping, his breathing laboured. 'You're weak inside this circle.'

Damien spits blood. 'But you're weaker!'

In my dazed state I watch powerless as Damien lunges forward, slashing with the jade knife. Its razor-like edge slices across Phoenix's chest, carving out a thin line of blood. Smarting from the pain, Phoenix retaliates with a thrust of his own blade. Damien deftly dodges the attack and stabs viciously back with the speed of a scorpion strike. I gasp in horror as the tip heads straight for Phoenix's heart – but with a last-second twist of his body Phoenix evades the lethal jab. He seizes Damien's outstretched arm and puts him into an armlock. Wrenching upwards, he forces him to drop the jade knife before kicking the ancient weapon into the flooded ditch.

'Now for a true mercy killing!' declares Phoenix, raising his obsidian blade to strike.

But Damien isn't beaten so easily. He shoulder-barges Phoenix hard, pushing him into a standing stone, winding him, then he stamp-kicks Phoenix's injured leg, causing him to collapse in agony beside the flooded ditch. With another brutal kick, Damien disarms Phoenix, the shard of obsidian spinning away into the mud; before Phoenix has a chance to rise, Damien drops a knee on to his back and shoves his face into the ditch. Phoenix struggles and writhes to escape the murky water, but Damien has his full weight upon him, his hand clamped to the back of Phoenix's head.

On the boundary of the circle, the Soul Hunters whoop their approval and beat their chests in rhythm. With their hoods over their heads, they look like a brethren of demonic monks as they take up the familiar chant:

'RA – KA! RA – KA! RA – KA!'

Still stunned from the blow, the rhythmic chanting somehow sapping me of the Light, I sit frightened and feeble in the centre of the circle as Damien drowns Phoenix right before my eyes. I cry out in despair. Phoenix told me I had a warrior spirit. *But if I do, then where on earth is it?*

My Glimmers seem to offer no help. Phoenix said I'd been a fearsome samurai in a past life, but what use is that when I've no such Glimmer to draw on and, while I may have acquired the riding skills of a Cheyenne, I can't recall any of Waynoka's *fighting* ability. My attempt to stop Damien just proved that. The glimpse of my life in the Second World War gifted me the nursing knowledge I need to patch someone up – but not to *beat* them up! And my time during the English Civil War as the daughter of a Royalist commander may have taught me to play the lute and sew a tapestry, but I learned none of my father's military skills. Even my most recent flashback to the city gate in Ancient China was far too brief to show me anything more than a questionable talent for disguise.

But then I remember my incarnation as Zianya, the young girl of the Omitl warrior clan. The spirit I showed when Necalli was in trouble. The risks I took to save him. Calling upon Zianya's courage – if not her fighting skills – I scrabble through the mud and rain, my fingers frantically searching for the dropped obsidian blade. Unfortunately the black rock proves impossible to spot against the dark wet earth.

With every passing second, Phoenix's struggles grow weaker, his spluttering less insistent. The Soul Hunters' chant becomes ever more frenzied as Damien continues to force my Protector's head beneath the surface of the water.

Then my fingers brush over something hard and smooth. Fumbling for the shard of rock, I clasp its crudely chiselled handle and, uttering an ancient Omitl battle cry, I charge at Damien. I am Zianya and I am Genna, and I summon every ounce of my strength to plunge the blade into his back.

Damien grunts in shock and pain. His grip loosens on Phoenix, and he slumps face first to the sodden earth.

Phoenix, choking and spewing up water, weakly lifts himself out of the ditch. I drag him away from Damien's body and the knot of Hunters, who have abruptly ceased chanting and fallen silent. Their heads bowed, they stand as still as the stones that form the sacred circle.

'I stabbed him with your obsidian blade!' I tell Phoenix, my hands trembling uncontrollably. 'I think . . . I think . . . I've killed him!'

Spewing up the last of the muddy water, Phoenix manages a weak smile of relief. 'See?' he says. 'I knew you had a warrior spirit.'

Although I've saved Phoenix, I don't feel much like celebrating. As I gaze vacantly at Damien's lifeless body, I feel a deep chill invade my heart. The shock of actually *killing* someone numbs me to my core, the murderous act going against my very nature.

'Come on – let's go,' urges Phoenix, recognizing that I'm in shock. 'While his Hunters are still mourning him.'

My body still shaking, I help Phoenix up, retrieve his makeshift walking stick, and take his arm over my shoulder. But, just as we're about to leave the circle, the Hunters start to softly and ominously chant again: '*Ra-Ka! Ra-Ka! Ra-Ka!*'

Turning slowly round, I feel the blood drain from me. There, as if risen from the dead, Damien is back on his feet. Silhouetted against the dark thunderous sky, he reaches over and pulls the sharpened rock from his back, an inky gleam of blood dripping from the tip of its blade.

'Tut-tut . . . Did you honestly think that would work on *me*?' says Damien scathingly. 'An obsidian blade?'

38

All of a sudden the rain stops, the wind dies away and the thunder recedes. Lightning plays in the clouds along the horizon and I realize we've entered the eye of the storm.

'That *hurt*, Genna,' says Damien, as if I've somehow offended his feelings rather than plunged a knife in his back. 'But not as much as I'm going to *hurt* you!'

I stare aghast at the seemingly invincible Incarnate. *If obsidian won't kill him, then what will?*

'You'll have to get past me first,' Phoenix declares. Despite his injured leg, he stands valiantly as my shield, his stick raised in defence. Ever my Soul Protector.

Yet as strong as my faith in him is, my belief in our chances of survival dwindles fast. The Soul Hunters slowly and slyly skirt the circle boundary, sealing off our escape route.

'Don't you ever get tired of protecting her?' snorts Damien, advancing on Phoenix with the obsidian blade in his hand. 'How many times have I run you through now? Driven a blade into your flesh? Broken your bones? Taken your life?'

'Clearly not enough!' Phoenix shoots back. 'I'm still standing and Genna's soul lives on.'

'But not for much longer!' Damien growls, and rushes at us.

Phoenix swings his stick in a bone-crushing arc. Damien ducks beneath it, at the same time thrusting with the blade. Hampered by his wounded knee, Phoenix is unable to move out of the way fast enough.

'Here, have your knife back!' Damien snarls, driving the black spike of rock into Phoenix's belly.

I watch in horror as the shard of obsidian sinks deep into him. Phoenix crumples to his knees with an agonized groan. Letting go of the stick, he clasps his stomach, the blood flowing freely between his fingers. With a desperate and final look up at me, he gasps, *Remember Gabriel! Go!* Then the glimmer in his eyes fades and he topples forward into the mud.

Damien smirks. 'I told you, didn't I? And now you've seen for yourself. He doesn't *always* protect you.'

The sight of Phoenix lying at my feet, his blood seeping into the earth, opens up a vast abyss in me. It's as if my heart has been wrenched from my body, my soul split in two. An excruciating grief crushes me from within and I drop down beside my fallen Phoenix. Bowing my head, I sob, the tears rolling down my cheeks like rain.

'Why are you crying?' says Damien derisively. 'His soul isn't dead. He'll be reborn – although, granted, that will be far too late to save your sacred soul.'

He seizes my arm and is starting to drag me out of the circle when the hairs on my neck begin to rise. The air crackles, then a light – brighter and hotter than the sun – scorches my vision and an ear-rending *boom* detonates so close that I'm flung backwards into a standing stone . . .

The soft persistent patter of rain upon my face revives me. My head pounds and my body aches to the bone. A sharp tang of ozone fills my nostrils, along with the acrid smell of burned flesh. Zapped of all energy, I can barely sit up.

The stone circle is littered with the bodies of Damien and his Soul Hunters. One of them lies beside a portal stone, the rock now cleaved in two, an ominous wreath of smoke drifting up from his charred remains. As the sky flares and thunder rumbles overhead, it quickly dawns on me that a bolt of lightning must have struck the stone circle. The ground current will have shocked us all off our feet. The Hunter closest to the split stone must have been hit by a side flash and killed outright.

Fighting my fatigue, I crawl over to Phoenix and gently shake him by the shoulder. '*Phoenix?*' I whisper, but I get no response. I cling to him, my grief still raw. Even though I know he'll be reborn, the loss of him in this life feels as sharp as any death. Without him, I feel totally alone.

Nearby, Damien's body twitches and he utters a pained groan. The other Hunters are slowly coming round too.

Remember Gabriel! Go!

Phoenix's last words echo in my head, his final act of protection stirring the survival instinct in me. Tenderly kissing his cold damp cheek, I murmur a heartbroken farewell into his ear, then stagger to the edge of the circle, pass beyond the ring of sacred stones and leap the flooded ditch.

Then I run. Run for my life . . . and for all my future lives.

Slipping and sliding down the hillside, I make for Havenbury. My legs are rubbery under me and I tumble several times, but gravity seems to carry me down more than my own strength. Mud and grass smear my clothes and hands. I reach the bottom of the slope and stumble on, across the field, until I come to a country lane leading into the village itself.

Havenbury is small, little more than a cluster of pale-yellow limestone cottages centred round a duck pond. The main street is narrow and deserted, the storm having driven everyone inside. I spot the dim glow of candlelight behind the drawn curtains of one of the cottages and hurry over. Banging on the squat wooden door, I stand dripping and shivering under its oak-roofed porch.

At first there's no answer so I knock again. Then the door creaks open and an old woman peers cautiously out. Through the gap between the door and frame I spy a tiny front room, with a sofa covered in a white, crocheted blanket, and an old TV set. A ginger cat is curled up on a rug by the fire, its flickering warmth so inviting.

The old woman's welcome, however, is cold. 'Yes?' she snaps.

'I'm looking for Gabriel,' I explain. 'Do you know where he lives?'

She casts her grey eyes over me. For several, long seconds she says nothing. I'm conscious that my bedraggled and mud-splattered appearance is enough to make anyone wary. Then a flicker of recognition passes across her wrinkled face. For a moment I'm worried she may be a Watcher . . . before my hopes briefly rise that she could be a Soul Sister . . . but no Glimmer comes, nor any smile.

Instead she slams the door in my face.

'*Please!*' I cry, hammering on the door. 'I need your help.'

'Go away or I'll call the police!' she shrieks. I hear the lock click and a bolt rattle across. I guess she's seen my face on the news. After what's happened to Phoenix in the stone circle, I wonder if calling the police would actually be the best thing for me or anyone to do now. Then I remind myself of my encounter with DI Shaw and it quashes the idea. The police can't be trusted to be on my side.

My only real hope is to find Gabriel, the Soul Seer.

Phoenix said he was the local priest, which means my best chance now lies with the church.

The cottage's curtains twitch, the old woman watching me, as I step back into the rain and head off down the street. Several times I glance back over my shoulder, half expecting to see Damien and his Hunters bearing down on me. But the road remains empty, only a pair of ducks waddling across to the pond. Yet I know it would be foolish of me to think they've given up the chase.

The old Norman church of Havenbury sits at the end of the road, hunched beneath its heavy square tower of Cotswold stone. Its long walls punctuated by narrow stained-glass windows, the building seems rather imposing for such a small village. I pass through an iron kissing gate, its hinges squeaking loudly, and make my way into the churchyard.

Lichen-covered gravestones thrust up from the ground in haphazard rows, the grass surrounding them long and untended. To one side of the path an old, twisted yew tree hunches over, casting a long, skeletal shadow over the ancient stones; in the far corner sits a large pile of rotting leaves, the smell of decay strong in the air as if some poor animal has long since crawled inside to die.

A lone black crow caws eerily from its perch atop the yew tree and a shiver creeps down my spine. I experience an unsettling sense of déjà vu, but I don't ever recall being here before and no Glimmer is forthcoming. It's the unnerving feeling that's familiar.

Quickening my pace through the graveyard, I approach the church's porched entrance. As I step inside, out of the corner of my eye I glimpse movement back along the road. A hooded figure is standing at the very far end of the village. My heart thudding in my chest, I conceal myself within the porch and watch as he's joined by the others. I don't know if I've been spotted, but I know it won't take them long to search this village.

Taking hold of the latch's cold, iron ring, I pray the church isn't locked. With a slow creak, the heavy oak door opens and I hurriedly slip inside, close the door behind me, then pull over a chair and wedge that against it. I realize my barricade won't stand up to much battering, but it may give me a few seconds' grace to escape.

Inside, the church is cold and dark, a musty smell permeating the air. A stone font stands near the entrance, along with a wooden collection box and a bookcase of dusty leather-bound hymnals. Several rows of pews lead up to the raised chancel at the eastern end of the church, where a large, stained-glass arched window depicts the crucifixion of Christ. There are no lights on and at first it seems that I'm alone. Then in the gloom I notice a spindly figure in a black cassock and white clerical collar tending to the altar.

'*Gabriel?*' I whisper, my hopeful voice echoing round the empty church.

The priest turns. His face is lined and pale like parchment, his cheeks hollow, and his thinning black hair parted and neatly combed over. He's wearing a pair of dark, wrap-around glasses, which immediately puts me on my guard, but his smile is gentle and welcoming.

'Yes, child?' he says softly.

I slowly and cautiously approach the altar. 'Are you . . . the Soul Seer?' I ask.

'And who might you be?' enquires the priest.

'I'm Genna, a First Ascendant,' I reply. 'Phoenix sent me.'

39

Stepping down from the altar, Gabriel eagerly reaches out a bony white hand to greet me. I clasp it in an awkward handshake. His skin is leathery to the touch; his grip cool yet firm. In fact, he grasps my hand so tightly that for a moment I fear he won't ever let me go, so pleased is he at my arrival.

'You're chilled to the bone!' Gabriel exclaims, then he feels the sleeve of my jacket. 'And soaking wet!'

Feeling his way along the choir stalls, he finds a frayed blanket and holds it out to me.

'Thank you,' I say, wrapping it round my shivering shoulders. 'But we have far more urgent matters to deal with.'

'Of course we do. Why else would you be seeking me?' says Gabriel as he picks up a thin white cane from beside the pulpit. He slides the tip across the floor until he locates the edge of the chancel's steps.

'You're blind?' I query, the reason for the glasses now obvious.

He turns sharply to me. 'Yes. Is that a problem?'

'No . . . of course not,' I reply, ashamed at my insensitivity. 'Just that . . . how can you be a Soul Seer if you're blind?'

Gabriel gives me a sage smile. 'One doesn't need eyes to see,' he explains. 'Many people in today's world have excellent vision yet still see nothing!' He grunts in mild amusement, then seems to stare directly at me. Even though he can't see, it feels like he's looking into my eyes . . . *into* my very soul. 'But *you* now see clearly, don't you, Genna?' he observes. 'Have you had a Glimmer?'

'Yes, several,' I reply.

Gabriel nods as if satisfied. 'Still, you have but touched the surface of your soul's history. Your past is deeper than any ocean. More layered than any book. The many lives you have lived are as countless as the stars, every one of them adding to your Light.' His blind gaze seems to assess some invisible aura around me. 'For you are surely the brightest Ascendant I've yet encountered!'

'There are others?' I ask. *Then I'm not alone!* My hope kindles at the thought of there being other Ascendants in this world.

'Not as many as there once were,' he replies sombrely. Stepping down from the chancel, he shuffles along the aisle, his cane sweeping the floor.

'Well, there's going to be one less –' I cry out, my words stopping him in his tracks – 'unless you can help me . . .'

Even as I say it, I'm wondering how this Soul Seer can possibly protect me from Damien and his Soul Hunters.

Gabriel turns back to me. 'You're being hunted,' he rasps, more as a statement than a question.

'Yes,' I reply hurriedly. 'They're searching the village for me as we speak.'

Gabriel's brow furrows. 'Where's your Soul Protector?' he demands.

'Phoenix –' I have to choke back a sob at the mere mention of his name – 'he died. Protecting me.'

Hanging his head, Gabriel makes the sign of the cross and murmurs, '*Mors tantum initium est.*'

Once again the Latin is clear in my mind: *Death is only the beginning.*

'We need to get out of here,' I insist. 'We don't have much time –'

'This church is the safest place for you right now,' Gabriel assures me. 'No Incarnate can enter hallowed ground without jeopardizing their blackened soul.'

A squeal of rusty hinges immediately counters his claim. 'Are you certain of that?' I say, as the kissing gate squeaks again . . . and again . . . and again.

The Soul Seer lifts his head as if sniffing the air. 'Who *exactly* is hunting you?'

'Damien,' I reply. 'Or at least that's what he calls himself in this life.'

His shoulders slumping, Gabriel sighs heavily. 'That makes sense. The brightest light attracts the darkest Incarnate.'

I swallow hard. 'You mean . . . Tanas,' I say, the mere mention of his name chilling my soul. 'Then you need to know he was able to enter the stone circle on the hill. One of the stones was missing, but I presume that ground was sacred too, not just the stone boundary.'

'Then we have a serious problem,' Gabriel concedes. Thrusting his hand into his pocket, he sifts through a set of keys and heads towards the door. I rush after him, panic welling up in me at his urgency.

The latch is turning even as we get there and I throw myself against the door. Gabriel goes to lock it, but, unaware of the chair I used as a barricade, he stumbles into one of the legs and drops the keys. The latch rattles and there's a rapping upon the door.

'Little pig! Little pig! Let me come in!' taunts Damien.

'Never!' I cry as the latch lifts free and the door is forced open a fraction. Jamming my foot against the bookcase, I use all my strength to hold the Hunters back, as Gabriel gropes for the keys on the floor. 'To your left!' I hiss. 'A little further . . .'

'Then I'll huff, and I'll puff, and I'll blow your house down!' snarls Damien. The door shudders in its frame as he shoulder-barges it from the other side. The bookcase shifts and the door gives another inch. I grit my teeth and fight to close it again. But only me against a strong Incarnate is a losing battle.

Gabriel's bony fingers finally touch upon the keys. Snatching them up, he throws his own weight behind the door too. It slams shut just long enough for him to insert the key and lock the Hunters out. They pound their fists on the other side, but the door is solid oak and no amount of hammering is going to break it down.

Then suddenly all is quiet. The silence more ominous than the banging.

'We need to put more protection in place,' hisses Gabriel, picking up his cane and striding back down the nave. I follow him to the pulpit, where there's a small box containing pens and several stumps of white chalk. His fingers forage for a piece of chalk, then he returns to the centre of the church where the transept and nave intersect. Getting down on his knees, he begins to mark out strange symbols on the stone-flagged floor while uttering phrases in Latin: '*Dum mors erit, desperatio* . . .'

I peer over his shoulder. He may have lost his sight, but his movements are precise and with purpose. Still, I can't make head or tail of what he's drawing. 'Er . . . I was thinking more of barricades,' I suggest tentatively.

'By all means block the entrances,' mutters Gabriel, preoccupied with his task. 'But they'll only keep these Incarnates at bay for so long. We require a far more powerful defence than mere physical barriers.'

Leaving Gabriel to his sorcery, I race down to the church's large double doors on the west face. They're locked, but nonetheless I drag across a heavy pew. Then I also wedge the porch entrance shut with the bookcase for good measure.

'What else can I do?' I ask, unable to spot any other doors that need barricading.

'Light some candles,' Gabriel replies as he continues to draw with feverish intensity. 'Chase away the darkness.'

Looking around, I spy a small metal rack containing the blackened stumps of several votive candles. I manage to find a few slim white ones tucked away in a drawer, along with a half-filled box of matches. I light all three, before noticing two larger candles in brass holders upon the altar. Entering the chancel, I go over and set their wicks alight too.

As their flames take hold, their flickering glow illuminates the wooden crucifix over the altar. It's then I notice that the crucifix is *upside down*!

Convinced we need all the help we can get, I go to right the crucifix when the stained-glass window above me shatters. Shrieking in shock, I shield my face as shards of glass cascade down and a brick clatters across the floor. A moment later a small door that was hidden behind a screen in the north transept bangs open and Damien strides in.

'Hope I'm not late for the service,' he smirks, 'but it took me a while to find *this*!' The jade knife, glistening and wet from the flooded ditch, is clasped in his hand.

'Gabriel! Watch out!' I shout as Damien heads directly for the kneeling Soul Seer. 'It's Tanas!'

Gabriel rises to confront him. But, before striking the priest with his knife, Damien stops and turns his dead, black eyes towards me and laughs, his unholy cackle reverberating through the church. 'My precious Genna, you're very much mistaken . . . *I'm* not Tanas.'

I stare at him, confused. He *must* be Tanas. This black-eyed boy before me has been present in all my Glimmers. His soul is like a stain on my past lives. Then I'm drawn deeper into his gaze and catch a horrifying glimpse into the darkest recesses of his soul. Unbidden, a streak of faces flash before my eyes: *the bounty hunter shot from his horse by Hiamovi's arrow ... the Roman soldier in the red tunic searching the forest with his spear ... the Roundhead who'd pierced William's side with his double-ended halberd ... the Tletl acolyte with the elongated skull who'd tried to complete the ritual sacrifice until a lump of molten rock had burned a hole in his head ...*

Only now do I see who Damien *really* is and has been in my past lives. Not the US marshal, not the Roman centurion, not the Roundhead with the broadsword, not even the High Priest ... No, none of those: rather, always, the Incarnate leader's right-hand man. No wonder the obsidian blade didn't kill him.

'Then ... w-who's Tanas?' I stutter, a creeping dread entering my veins. For only now do I notice how odd everything looks in the church. The flowers are all dead. The votive candle stubs in the rack are of blackened wax. The Latin quote upon the pulpit reads: '*Where God has a church, the devil will have his chapel.*' And most telling of all ... the upside-down crucifix over the altar ... This church is not only abandoned, it's been *deconsecrated*. It's no longer hallowed ground. No wonder the Soul Hunters could enter unharmed.

It's then that a horrifying realization dawns on me: *the priest didn't lock the doors to keep these Hunters out ...*

As my gaze falls upon the chalk symbols on the floor – a large inverted pentagram surrounded by occult symbols and sinister depictions of scorpions and scarab beetles – Damien smiles cruelly. 'Oh, Genna, how you've been deceived,' he says. 'I'm not Tanas ... I *serve* Tanas.'

And, bowing, he turns and presents the jade knife to Gabriel.

'*NO!*' I cry, falling back against the altar in horror. Clinging on for support, I feel as if the ground beneath my feet has given way. 'This *can't* be true . . . You're the Soul Seer . . .'

But the priest gladly receives the jade knife from Damien. Then he discards the glasses and reveals to me his true face. A scream wells up in my throat as his serpent-shaped eyes fill my vision – dark, swirling and fathomless. I drown in his eternal darkness.

40

'Rura, rkumaa, raar ard ruhrd . . .
Rura, rkumaa, raar ard ruhrd . . .
Rura, rkumaa, raar ard ruhrd . . .'

The hypnotic murmur of long-dead words drags me back to consciousness. My eyelids flutter open and a low, vaulted ceiling swims into view. Crumbling limestone pillars, engraved with grotesque faces, prop up the ceiling, while shadows warped and misshapen shift across the rough stone walls under the flickering light of a dozen black candles. The brick walls have been daubed with archaic symbols and inverted pentagrams just like on the floor of the deconsecrated church. And a thick, cloying scent from the candle wax taints the dank air, making me heady, and the chanting voices *thrum* in my ears.

Glancing nervously about, I appear to be in a medieval crypt. My body has been laid out upon the flat slab of a marble tomb, its smooth surface as cold and white as bleached bone. The Soul Hunters are congregated in a semicircle at the foot of the tomb, their heads bowed, their faces hidden by their hoods. They each carry a candle, the hot wax running over their fingers like black blood.

With them seemingly lost in their ritual, I seize the opportunity to look for a way to escape. However, as I turn my head, a pale, gaunt face with blank, white eyes confronts me and I suppress a horrified scream. The ashen face stares at me, sightless and silent. The skin is waxy, the lips drawn and grey, long white hair wreathing round the wrinkled ears. As my immediate shock subsides I realize the old man set upon the adjacent tomb is dead . . .

Then a grim horror seizes me as I notice his chest has been sliced open and his heart ripped out. This is the gruesome sacrifice that awaits *me*. The one that Phoenix warned me about. The one that will extinguish my soul forever.

I realize this mutilated body has to be all that's left of Gabriel the Soul Seer. Tanas having got to him first, the ritual was performed to ensure that the Seer could never be reborn.

The incantation stops suddenly and the Soul Hunters look at me with their coal-black eyes. My blood chills at their unholy stare. They're like corpses risen from the grave. One bears red fern-like lesions across his face and neck, and I recognize him as the thug who I thought had been killed by the lightning strike.

In turn, each of them pinches the wick of their candle, extinguishing the flame and dousing the crypt into deeper darkness.

'Time to snuff out *your* Light, Genna,' sneers Damien, leering at me as he kills the flame of his candle.

Jolted into action, I rise up from the slab, but my limbs are seized and pinned down by the Hunters. As I writhe in their grip, Tanas looms out of the darkness. He now wears a cowl, casting his lined face into heavy shadow. While he no longer possesses the same jutting cheekbones and bladed nose of the High Priest, his eyes remain as black and unforgiving as obsidian stone.

'I've waited an eternity for this moment,' Tanas rasps. A scythe-like smile cuts across his thin lips and I shudder at the presence of such evil. His breath reeks of the grave; sickly sweet and rotten, it makes me gag.

Leaving me to be held down by his Hunters, he heads over to a stone altar carved into the wall where a godhead with cat-like eyes and sharp, pointed fangs resides. Within its snarling, open mouth burns a black candle, the hot wax flowing down the god's tongue and dripping into a silver chalice. Kneeling before the altar, Tanas produces the jade knife and scores a deep line into his open palm. Then, squeezing his hand into a fist, he lets his blood drip into the chalice and mix with the melted wax as he recites a hex in an ancient tongue: '*Ruq haq maar farad ur rouhk ta obesesh!*'

I've no idea what the arcane words mean, but I sense their deeply destructive power. Fear tightens its icy grip on me and I struggle harder, kicking out at my captors. The Hunters are strong, though, and keep me pinned upon the marble tomb as Tanas picks up the chalice and carries it towards me. He seizes my jaw and forces open my mouth, then, putting the silver chalice to my lips, he pours the bitter liquid down my throat. I spit it out into his face.

Scowling, Tanas wipes away the waxy potion with the back of his bony hand. 'I'd drink this if I were you,' he snarls. 'The pain won't be quite so unbearable. And you'll live long enough to see your heart ripped out!'

He pours the remainder of the liquid into my mouth, then clamps a hand over my lips and pinches my nose. Against my will I swallow the acrid potion. Spluttering and coughing, I can feel it burn my throat and scald my stomach.

Tanas lets go of me. So do the other Soul Hunters.

I try to rise, to fight, to flee. But my limbs now feel heavy and cumbersome. My heart throbs and my hearing sings. My vision starts to blur, tracer lines of candlelight swirling before my eyes.

Tanas returns to the stone altar, sets down the poisoned chalice and picks up the jade knife. As I lie helpless upon the tomb, he presents the curved green blade to the godhead for its blessing before returning to my side. The Hunters bow their heads and take up the ritual chant of 'Ra-Ka! Ra-Ka! Ra-Ka!', their voices sounding like pounding drums in my delirious state.

Holding the sacrificial knife high over my chest, Tanas resumes the incantation he started all those millennia ago –

'Rura, rkumaa, raar ard ruhrd . . .'

His wicked words worm their way into my head. Like snake venom they seep into my ears and poison my very soul –

'Qmourar ruq rouhk ur darchraqq . . .'

Falling under his spell now, my body becomes heavier and heavier, my soul's attachment to it weaker and weaker –

'*Ghraruq urq kugr rour ararrurd . . .*'

As if a surgical blade is slicing through the connection between my body and soul, I feel myself drifting away. Anchorless . . . disorientated . . . and disembodied. My bond with life and all my previous lives seems to separate and disperse, disintegrating like dust in the wind –

'*Qard ur rou ra datsrq, Ra-Ka . . .*'

Untethered from my physical form, I see myself as if from above. A young girl with dark ringlets of hair and amber-brown skin laid out limp upon a stark, white marble slab. The five hooded Hunters now stand at each point of the inverted pentagram inscribed in chalk upon the stone floor. Tanas stands at its centre, the jade knife gleaming in his trembling hands as he recites the final line of the soul-splitting spell –

'*Uur ra uhrdar bourkad, RA-KA!*'

With a look of cold, wide-eyed desire, Tanas drives the blade downwards. A blinding blue-green flash blazes like an exploding star over my body and the deafening sound of a thousand panes of glass shattering reverberates through the crypt.

Then . . . silence . . . and darkness.

41

Am I dead?

I don't feel dead. Then again I have no idea what death feels like. *Or do I . . . ?*

Faint memories of the Upper Realms are slowly surfacing. Of the place between lives. The reality beyond our perceived reality. The eternal Truth where souls reside until they are reborn.

That bright, all-encompassing Light . . .

But if I am truly disembodied, then why can I still feel my body – sense the bruises and aches in my muscles, taste the bitter burning in my throat, hear the rasp of my breathing?

Perhaps these are the residues of my former life? Phantom sensations that will fade with time. If there is such a thing as 'time' here . . .

As my eyes grow accustomed to the darkness, I notice tiny embers in the firmament. Red like dying stars.

This Realm is colder than any I remember. Dank too.

I can hear pained groans. Smell the acrid taint of smoke. Feel hard stone pressing against my back. *Am I in Hell?*

Then a bright white light bursts before my eyes . . . and the devastated scene is revealed.

I'm still laid out upon the marble tomb. The glare comes from a mobile phone screen. The tiny embers are from blown-out candles, the groans from floored Hunters.

Tanas, a thin stream of blood dripping from his right nostril, has been thrown back against the altar and is slumped at its base. He holds a splinter of jade in his limp hand, the rest of the ritual knife shattered into several pieces across the floor.

What's happened? Did his ritual fail to destroy my soul?

Glancing down at my chest, I see that my blouse is ripped, but there's no blood nor any wound. Only the blue sheen of my amulet radiates through the tear in my top . . .

My Guardian Stone!

Even from the grave Phoenix has protected me.

Feeling both shock and relief, I clasp the precious, life-saving amulet in my hand. But I can no longer sense the fluttering within it and I notice a fracture in the gemstone's polished surface. Whatever divine power the amulet once held, it's spent now.

The beam from the phone's torch now jerks erratically as Damien pulls himself up to his feet with the help of a pillar. A set of steep stone steps is briefly illuminated in the far corner of the crypt. Fighting the potion's effects, I slide off the tomb and stagger towards the promised exit.

'Where do you think *you're* going?' growls Damien, lurching in front of me.

The other Hunters now slowly rise up around me to block my escape.

Terrified, I retreat until my back hits the cold stone of the rear wall. With only the light of Damien's phone, the darkness presses in upon me on all sides. In my hallucinating vision, the Soul Hunters with their hoods and hungry eyes look like distorted ninja hiding in the shadows –

'Ninja are your greatest and most deadly enemy, Miyoko-san,' explains my bald-headed sensei as he paces the darkened dojo, the night silent apart from the gentle trickle of a fountain in the Zen garden. 'Yet, while they may appear invisible, they aren't invincible.'

'But how do you fight an enemy you can't see?' I ask, kneeling upon the rice-straw tatami in the centre of the dojo. My hands rest lightly upon the silk of my ivory-white kimono, the reassuring weight of my samurai sword held firm against my hip by my obi.

'Eyes may be the windows to the soul, but they're not the sole means by which we see,' my teacher replies from a distant corner. His voice seems to float round the room as he explains, 'Your ears and hands must become your eyes at night ... Rely upon your other senses to guide you ... Listen out for the singing of a sword, the whistle of a shuriken, the flick of a fist ... Feel for your opponent's shift in balance, their sudden tensing of a muscle, or the slight adjustment of a foot ... Even smell the air for subtle scents of perfume or perspiration! To the trained warrior these warnings are as clear as day that an attack is imminent –'

The lightest swish *of air from behind prompts me to duck. My sensei's bokken passes within a hair's breadth of the top of my head, clipping my kanzashi pin. I let out a silent sigh of relief at my narrow escape. While the wooden blade wouldn't have beheaded me, it would certainly have knocked me senseless!*

'Good, Miyoko-san,' praises my sensei, suddenly close to me. I hear him sheathe his sword, and I relax my guard, glad to have passed his test.

But then the trickle of the fountain quietens behind me, as if the sound is in shadow. There's a gentle depression of a foot upon the tatami mat, followed by a soft wisp of cotton, and I'm kicked hard in the back. Flung forward, I tuck my head in, roll and spring to my feet. Even as I recover from the blow, I raise my hands into a defensive guard and peer into the darkness, searching for my elderly sensei. For an old man, he certainly kicks like a mule!

'Just because you evade one attack doesn't mean the fight is over, Miyoko-san!' he chides. I whirl around as his voice seems to echo from all directions in the dojo. 'Remember Zanshin – warrior awareness. After winning the battle, tighten your helmet!'

A fist flies unseen through the dark. Only the flutter of my sensei's gi jacket forewarns me of the oncoming attack. I twist to one side, feeling his bony knuckles graze my cheek but miss their intended target. I lash out with my own punch . . . yet connect with nothing but thin air.

'The battle does not end when you win,' taunts my sensei, jabbing me in the ribs with a spearhand strike. 'It only ends when you lose concentration!'

I whip my foot in the direction of his disembodied voice, but still fail to find him. Clenching my fists in frustration, I ready myself for the next unseen assault.

'But if ninja are invisible to me,' I say, 'how do I know where to punch and kick?'

My sensei whispers close into my ear, startling me. 'Strike with the soul, Miyoko-san, and you will never miss!'

42

I feel a hand grab my arm. Without thinking, I wrap my own arm round my attacker's and wrench it upwards until I hear a sharp *snap*. The unseen Hunter howls in agony. Guided by his cries, I front-kick him hard in the chest. The Hunter hurtles backwards into a pillar and slumps to the floor. I sense the other Hunters staring at me, stunned at the brutal efficiency with which I dispatched one of their number.

I too am in awe of my new-found abilities. Just as my incarnation as a Cheyenne gifted me with horse-riding skills, it seems my martial arts expertise as a samurai has migrated to my present life.

Phoenix was right . . . I do have a warrior spirit!

Strengthened by my Glimmer, I feel the sedative effects of the potion ease off a little, enough to be aware of a fist flying towards my face. Shifting to one side, I evade the punch and the Hunter's knuckles crumple against the brick wall instead. Bringing my knee up sharply, I strike her in the gut. Then, grabbing her hair, I fling her head first into the wall. She crumples to the ground in a shower of brick dust.

A third Hunter, the thug, judging by his size, puts me into a chokehold from behind. A few moments before I wouldn't have had a clue what to do. But now my samurai instincts tell me to flick my legs high into the air, twist my body and use my whole weight to execute *ura-maki-komi* . . . a sacrifice throw. As my legs come back down, the thug is flung over my shoulders. I land on top of him, knocking the air from his lungs. A well-aimed strike to his solar plexus ensures he stays down.

Scrambling to my feet, I'm then confronted by the fourth Hunter. As Damien tracks me with the light of his phone, I glimpse a gleam of steel in the darkness and realize this must be the girl with the knuckleduster rings and steel pipe, the one who's been the bane of both me and Phoenix. But no more. Undeterred by her speed and strength, I roundhouse-kick the girl in the ribs . . .

But she catches my leg and, with the end of the steel pipe, deadens my thigh. Gritting my teeth against the pain, I jump up and kick out with my other foot, hoping to catch her under the chin. But she's as quick as a viper, bending like a reed to avoid my blow.

I flip over and land awkwardly back on my feet, my deadened leg giving way under me. As I try to regain my balance, the girl rushes forward and pins me against a pillar. She drives her steel pipe up against my throat, lifting me off the ground and throttling me.

Despite my new skills, it seems I've met my match. Gasping for breath, I claw at her fingers, but it's no good – the steel pipe is like a locked bar. My head starts to pound and my lungs scream for air. Still, I'm not as helpless as I was at Arundel Castle. Remembering my samurai training, I spearhand the girl in the base of her own throat and she chokes. Released briefly from her vice-like grip, I follow up with a kick to her stomach that sends her stumbling backwards and the steel pipe clattering into the darkness. Swiftly I spin round and deliver a final hook kick to the head. There's a pained grunt as the girl slumps to the floor.

'That's for Phoenix!' I snarl . . . then I hear the sound of slow clapping.

'Impressive!' admits Damien, glancing round at the fallen Hunters. 'But you're not the only one to recall such fighting skills . . . Miyoko-san!'

Mobile phone in hand, Damien takes up a cat stance: knees bent, left leg forward, ball of foot lightly touching the floor, his hands held out like claws. I recognize the stance as *neko-ashi-dachi*, the favoured fighting guard of the infamous ninja –

'Tora Tsume!' I spit, as the assassin crouches before me like a panther primed to pounce. The rest of his killer clan lie broken and bleeding around the Dragon Temple's Zen garden, the full moon shimmering silver upon the raked ripples of gravel. Between two mountain rocks, the steel blade of my katana gleams . . . tantalizingly close, but out of reach.

'Miyoko-san,' taunts the ninja, 'you fight well . . . for a samurai!'

Panting heavily from fending off the deadly ambush, I reply, 'And you'll die well . . . for a ninja!'

I dive for my sword. But Tora Tsume leaps into my path. Swiping with a gloved hand, his shuko tiger claws rip across my face, scoring bloody lines into my cheek. He then lashes out with his other clawed hand, attempting to lacerate my throat. But I block the attack, seize his arm and throw him high over my shoulder. Gravel and dust fly as he hits the ground hard. Before he can recover from the impact, I snatch up my katana, turn, and raise the blade to end his pitiful life.

'Have mercy!' Tora Tsume cries, cowering and shielding his black-eyed face. 'I'm a mere servant of Tanas ... forced to do his bidding ... I beg you ... show me the way back to the Light!'

Seeing a weak and defenceless soul at my feet, I hesitate in my strike. I even begin to feel pity for him ...

More fool me! Having crushed a hidden eggshell in his hand, Tora Tsume blows its contents of metsubushi powder into my face. The eye-watering mix of ash, shell and sand momentarily blinds me –

Unable to see, I stagger backwards and hold my hands up to my face.

'You know what happened last time,' taunts Damien, continuing to shine his phone's torch directly into my eyes. 'Why not save yourself all that suffering and surrender to me now?'

As he advances on me, I'm determined not to let him trick me or beat me again. If anything, I've learned my lesson to never trust a ninja.

'I don't need to see to stop you!' I reply, lashing out with a crescent kick. My foot arcs through the air and I knock the mobile from his hand. It clatters across the floor, its torch going out and plunging the crypt into pitch darkness once more. My advantage, though, is short-lived.

'Nor do I!' says Damien with a cruel laugh, reminding me that his eyes favour the dark.

As I try to blink away the after-glare of the torch, I hear the scuff of feet against stone and the whisper of an attack. Instinctively I duck as an unseen fist skims overhead. But that was a feint to force me into an oncoming knee strike. Caught hard under the jaw, stars burst before my eyes and I reel from the blow.

Damien laughs in the darkness. 'I'm going to enjoy tearing you apart, *again*. I just wish I still had my shuko tiger claws!'

I shudder as I recall my fateful and bloody battle with Tora Tsume. It didn't end well. If I'm to survive this fight, I realize I'll need every ounce of Miyoko's fighting skill. Homing in on where Damien's voice came from, I lash out with a side kick . . . but my foot fails to find its target.

'Over here!' he taunts, and he retaliates with a brutal blow to my ribs.

I stagger backwards and hit a pillar, dust showering down on me from the ceiling. As I sense another assault, I raise my forearm and block his hook punch. Considering how strong Damien is, I'm surprised at the lack of force behind his strike. Then I remember his knife wound and immediately target his shoulder – he howls in pain and backs off.

Taking advantage of his weakness, I go on the attack, following the scrape of his feet as he retreats. But Damien, quick to recover, fends off my onslaught. Like the old adversaries that we are, we match each other blow for blow. I fuel all my fury and frustration, all my gall and grief, into the fight, each punch and kick a revenge blow for the murder of Phoenix.

Yet while I may possess the martial skills of my former incarnation, I don't have Miyoko-san's stamina in a battle. The fight is rapidly taking its toll on me. Breathing hard, my muscles tiring, I can't keep up with Damien, who's far stronger and fitter than me. As I lose my rhythm, he throws a low punch to my gut, followed by a surprise uppercut that catches my chin and floors me. Winded and weakened, I try to crawl away, my fingers clawing at the dust. But, grabbing my ankle, Damien pulls me back for more punishment.

I have little strength left and realize that, like my battle with Tora Tsume, the fight is all but over. So I curl up in a ball at his feet. '*Please* . . . no more . . . have mercy!' I beg, sounding just like the infamous ninja he once was.

Standing over me, Damien sneers, 'Disappointing . . . *You're* no Miyoko-san.' Then there's just the slightest *wisp* of fabric as he lowers his guard –

That's when I fling a handful of brick dust into his eyes!

Blinded by the stinging dust, he can't avoid my sweep kick and crashes to the floor with a pained exhalation of breath. I follow up with an axe kick to his chest. There's a sharp *crack* of ribs.

Not waiting for him to rise, I leap to my feet, dart round his fallen figure and feel my way along the wall until I reach the steps. Bounding up them two at a time, I escape the crypt and leave the Darkness and its disciples behind.

43

I stumble back into the light. The abandoned church is cold and empty, the rain drumming on the leaden roof and streaming in through the smashed stained-glass window. I stagger down the aisle, bumping into the pews. The stone walls appear to contract and expand as if the church itself is breathing, the floor beneath my feet shifting like the deck of a boat. Tanas's ritual potion must still be entering my bloodstream, its toxic effects washing through me in waves. I force myself to vomit, black bile spewing all over the limestone slabs. This seems to help clear my head a little.

I hurry over to the porch entrance and drag the bookcase away. However, in my stupefied state I've forgotten that Tanas locked the door and still possesses the key. The wind blows hard outside and I hear the faint rattle of a latch, and I remember the concealed door in the north transept. But, as I head back towards it, a sudden jingling sound causes me to falter . . .

'Is this what you're looking for?' taunts a snide voice from the pulpit. Tanas dangles a set of keys in his skeletal hand. The blood no longer streams from his narrow nose, but his ashen features are more sunken and skull-like than ever before. The failed ritual has taken a visible toll upon him.

Damien stands below his master in the chancel, his coal-black eyes still watering from the brick dust, a hand clasped to his busted ribs. There's a thunderous look on his pale face, clearly furious that I beat him with his own ninja blinding trick.

Tanas tosses the keys into the centre of the pentagram chalked on the stone-flagged floor. 'Here – they're yours if you want them,' he goads.

Like cheese for a mouse, I know the keys are bait. He's set a trap. The occult symbol is where his dark power most likely is strongest. *But what choice do I have?* I glance towards the north transept. *Is the door still open?* Grab the keys or run for the door . . . Either choice is a huge risk.

Cautiously I make my way back down the aisle, keeping my eyes upon both Tanas and Damien. Neither of them makes a move. Hands clasped in front, Damien stands on the steps of the chancel like a young groom waiting for his bride, the priest smiling as she walks up the aisle. Except this feels more like a funeral than a wedding.

As I near the point where the transept and nave cross, I notice Damien's muscles tense. I can see he's expecting me to bolt for the north exit. Tanas too moistens his thin lips in anticipation, a serpent poised to strike.

So I do as they both anticipate, and sprint towards the door. But, as soon as Damien commits to the north transept, I double back to the pentagram. Entering the five-pointed star, I reach down to grab the keys and . . .

suddenly feel weak. Like an inversion of the stone circle, the pentagram drains my strength away. It's as if I've left my samurai spirit behind in the crypt and I'm once more just an ordinary teenager, with no Glimmers to empower me.

Damien is on me in a matter of seconds, forcing my hands behind my back and wrapping an arm round my throat. Held within the confines of the energy-sapping symbol, I'm unable to resist as Tanas slowly descends from the pulpit and advances on me.

Stepping into the pentagram, he reaches out a talon-like hand towards my neck, the scrape of his fingernails making my skin crawl as if a corpse is caressing me. Then he snatches the amulet from round my neck, breaking the chain.

'So, *this* is what thwarted the ritual!' He glares in distaste at the fractured Guardian Stone. 'No matter,' he sneers, casting it aside. 'We *will* complete what we started.' In his other hand he grips the remaining splinter of jade, its tip sharp and needle-like. Without the amulet, I have nothing to protect me against the ritual.

'*Rura, rkumaa, raar ard ruhrd ...*' Tanas intones rapidly, his voice resounding through the church like some twisted prayer. On my other side I hear Damien muttering, '*Ra-Ka! Ra-Ka! Ra-Ka!*'

Everything starts to swim round me – pulpit, pews and altar revolving like an insane merry-go-round. The sudden wrenching of my soul from my body feels as if I'm dropping fast in an elevator, the separation swifter and more savage this time round. A wave of despair rolls through me. After all the running, fighting and sacrifice, Tanas is going to have his vile victory. He's going to extinguish my soul and its Light . . . *forever.*

In my distorted vision Tanas's fathomless eyes turn to whirling black holes and from the broken stained-glass window a shadowy figure rises like smoke. A winged angel of vengeance, it drops down upon the altar and, as the incantation reaches its climax, rushes towards me to take my soul –

Tanas screams . . . a truly demonic shriek . . . as a spike of obsidian pierces his chest. Blood spews from his twisted mouth and he sags to the floor. Damien's grip on me loosens and he too slumps down beside his dying master.

I stand, bewildered yet unharmed in the centre of the fatal pentagram. *Has the ritual failed again?* Then the winged angel grasps my hand and pulls me out of the star's evil influence.

'*Phoenix!*' I gasp, as my Soul Protector drops, exhausted, to his knees. Blood soaks his T-shirt and he looks half dead, but he's smiling and his eyes gleam like stars once more.

'Talk about cutting it close!' he manages to say with a pained laugh.

'You're alive!' I cry, kneeling down and embracing him. 'But *how*?'

'The stone circle saved me,' he wheezes. 'The power of the Light healed me, enough to –'

'*Curse you!*' Tanas spits, as he writhes within the pentagram in a spreading pool of his own blood. He weakly reaches for the splinter of jade. My strength returned, I kick it away from his grasp. He grabs my foot, his bony fingers wrapping round my ankle like a poisonous vine. 'Another turn of life's wheel . . .' he splutters, glowering at me, 'and I'll be back to claim your soul!'

Then his head slumps to the floor and his grip loosens.

I kick away his hand, but Tanas continues to fix me with his stone-cold stare.

'Is he . . . *dead*?' I whisper, unnerved by the dark, unblinking depths of his serpent-like eyes.

Phoenix gives an exhausted nod. 'As dead as he'll ever be in this life.'

I glance over at the other unconscious body in the pentagram. 'What about Damien? And the others?' I ask fearfully.

Phoenix leans back gratefully against the end of a pew. 'They're no longer a threat. When Tanas dies, so does his hold over his followers. It's likely Damien won't even recall his true nature any more.'

I turn to Phoenix in shock. 'You mean, he'll remember *nothing* of what he's done?'

'Oh, he'll remember for sure. Damien will have the darkest of nightmares,' Phoenix explains gravely. 'But the Soul Hunters will all now lie dormant . . . at least until Tanas reincarnates again.'

'And when will that happen?' I ask with dread.

'Not in this lifetime,' Phoenix reassures me. 'Maybe not even in the next. The obsidian blade will have greatly weakened Tanas's evil soul. He'll be licking his wounds for a very long time.'

I peer down at the worrying patch of blood staining Phoenix's T-shirt. 'But what about you?'

Phoenix smiles weakly as the wail of sirens sounds in the distance. 'Oh, don't worry about me . . . it's only *you* that matters.'

Wrapping his arms round my waist, he leans in closer and, for a moment, I think he may be about to kiss me. Then he rests his head upon my shoulder, closes his eyes as if ready for a deep sleep, and sinks slowly to the floor.

44

'Your daughter's safe now, Mrs Adams,' declares Detective Inspector Shaw. The police officer is sitting in our front room with a cup of tea in her hand. A row of stitches criss-cross the wound that's healing on her forehead and, while the area round her eyes is black from bruising, her irises once more look a benign grey behind her glasses.

I perch nervously next to my mother on the edge of the sofa, ready to run at the slightest change in DI Shaw's appearance or behaviour. A blond-haired police officer stands by the door and, as athletic as she appears, I don't much fancy her chances if DI Shaw 'turns' again.

The detective takes a polite sip of her tea before setting the cup aside. 'Having concluded our investigations, it would appear a religious cult was responsible for the Clapham Market attack as well as the abduction and attempted murder of your daughter. If it wasn't for that phone call the observant old lady in Havenbury made, we may well have been too late. But I can assure you, the ringleader – a heretic priest – is now dead and all his followers rounded up and arrested.'

I doubt that very much! I think to myself. For one thing, the detective inspector, herself until recently one of Tanas's followers, is sitting opposite me, in my lounge, at this very moment. But I hold my tongue, knowing that my 'ravings' about Soul Hunters won't be listened to. I've tried countless times to explain what *really* happened and not a single person has taken me seriously.

'What about the Phoenix boy?' enquires my father, who stands close behind me like some paranoid bodyguard. Dad hasn't been able to let me out of his sight ever since I came home.

'As soon as the hospital discharges him, he'll be deported back to the United States,' the detective informs us.

'What will happen to him then?' I ask. I clasp the fractured Guardian Stone tighter in the palm of my hand, its smooth, rounded feel reassuring to me and my sole keepsake from my Protector. I've been distraught ever since the police turned up at the church and separated the two of us. Phoenix was whisked away by ambulance under armed escort and I haven't seen him since. Despite my repeated requests, they won't let me visit him, and at one point I didn't even know if Phoenix had survived his injuries.

'That isn't for me to say,' DI Shaw replies crisply. 'On the basis of your own statements, he's already been charged and convicted of manslaughter on the grounds of self-defence. It's only because he's a juvenile, and in light of the exceptional circumstances, that the judge has spared him a prison sentence. But it'll be up to the US authorities to decide what happens to him when he gets home.'

'Phoenix *saved* my life!' I exclaim. 'Why are you treating him like a criminal?'

My mother rests her hand upon my knee and pats it gently. 'Because, darling, he kidnapped you and killed someone,' she explains in an infuriatingly patronizing tone, as if she was explaining the situation to a three-year-old.

'He was *saving* my life!' I argue. 'He's my Protector! Why won't anyone believe me?'

'Genna, we *do* understand how distressed you are,' Dad assures me, squeezing my shoulder. 'You've been through a hellish experience, but it's *our* job now, as your parents, to protect you.'

I shrug off his hand. 'I only need *one* Protector . . . and that's Phoenix!'

My father's jaw stiffens and Mum anxiously bites her lower lip at my outburst. An awkward silence descends over the room. The adults exchange knowing glances, as my parents offer an unsaid apology for my 'irrational' behaviour.

DI Shaw clears her throat. 'I can see you need time as a family to heal,' she says, rising to her feet with the help of a crutch. 'But please don't hesitate to call me if you require any further assistance.' She looks meaningfully at my father. 'We can recommend some *excellent* post-trauma counsellors.'

'Thank you, Inspector,' says Dad, shaking her hand. 'Thank you for everything you've done for Genna. We're just so sorry the other officer was killed in that car crash.'

I want to scream at him. To shout. To tell everyone that this so-called detective *murdered* her own officer! But I've no proof: the car crash covered up all evidence of her attack. Besides, following Tanas's death, DI Shaw seems to have no memory of her crime. So, despite giving the police a full account of my side of the story, many aspects of it have been dismissed as the delusions of a traumatized teenage girl.

'Thank you, Mr Adams,' says the detective. 'I'll pass your condolences on to his family. Sadly, though, it's one of the hazards of our occupation.'

My father nods sympathetically, then Mum rises to shake the detective's hand, before escorting the two officers out. At the door, DI Shaw turns back to me and offers me what she thinks is a consoling smile.

'Genna, I realize you're still in shock,' she says kindly, 'but take strength from the fact that you've survived this horrendous ordeal. Hopefully such strength will stand you in good stead in your life to come.'

I don't know if she's aware of how apt her words are, but I shudder as I watch the former Soul Hunter limp from the house and down the path.

45

'Do you think you'll ever see Phoenix again?' asks Mei as we sit on Clapham Common feeding the ducks by the pond. My dad is on a bench further along the path, doing his best to pretend he's reading the newspaper.

I shake my head sadly. 'My counsellor considers Phoenix to be a "negative influence" on me, and my parents have agreed with his assessment.'

Mei snorts in disbelief. 'But Phoenix is the reason you're still alive!'

'I know,' I reply, breaking off a bit of bread and tossing it among the flurry of ducks and pigeons. 'He's the reason I've survived all my past lives too.'

Mei raises an eyebrow, giving me a doubtful look, as if to say, *Seriously? You're not* still *fixated on that reincarnation fantasy, are you?*

Over the past couple of weeks my post-trauma counsellor has been attempting to rationalize my experiences, to explain the past-life visions as simply a 'coping mechanism of my fragile mind to deal with the stress and strain of being attacked, kidnapped and almost ritually murdered'. Which I guess makes some sense. But what about all the evidence to the contrary, such as how I knew about the escape route in the well at Arundel Castle, and how I suddenly acquired highly advanced skills in horse-riding and martial arts? This he's tried to justify as a 'fortunate tapping into innate abilities, forced to the surface by pure survival instinct', an argument that is less convincing to me. Whatever anyone says, an untrained person like me should have no chance in a fight against five fit young attackers – and yet I defeated them all. I *know* survival instinct alone can't account for that!

My counsellor has also diagnosed my 'attachment issues' to Phoenix as the direct consequence of Stockholm syndrome. While I have to admit that I do exhibit many of the symptoms – positive feelings towards my 'captor', a belief in the same values and core goals, a refusal to cooperate with the authorities against him – Phoenix *wasn't* my captor. He's my saviour and my friend. More than that, we have a *deep* connection, a bonding of souls. I feel the loss of Phoenix in my life like I'm missing a vital organ, like there's a huge hole in my heart.

Still, as a result of these professional assessments, and because of my parents' continued insistence on therapy, I've begun to keep my own counsel, so I no longer broach the subject of reincarnation or Phoenix if I can help it.

Except I sometimes let my guard drop and express my true feelings and beliefs when I'm with my best friend. Thankfully, in this instance, she doesn't pursue the contentious topic of past lives with me. Instead she asks, 'So when's Phoenix being deported back to the States?'

'Tomorrow, I think.' I fall silent and stare at the sunlight glinting off the ripples in the pond. My eyes blur with tears at the thought of never seeing my Soul Protector again. My breath hitching, I clasp a hand to my chest and feel the cool touch of the amulet against my skin. This reminder of Phoenix's absence and all the sacrifices he made to protect my life – my soul – only makes me cry more.

Mei reaches out and puts an arm round my shoulders. 'I know it's hard, but take heart that your guardian angel survived and is going home rather than to prison. Besides,' she says, 'you never know what the future may hold.'

I force a smile on to my face. Now I know the truth about reincarnation, I realize my future is an open book. One with a bittersweet ending in this case. I may have lost Phoenix, but I'm safe from Tanas and his Hunters. I can enjoy this life without his shadow hanging over me. Yet my current life is just one of many unwritten stories, each with the same relentless villain and brave hero in different guises. Each with an ending yet to be determined ... except I know there's one story that ends in ritual sacrifice which will finally end them all. That's the one I need to avoid at all costs.

'What about Damien?' Mei asks, shooing away a mangy-looking pigeon with her foot. 'What's happened to him?'

Despite the warmth of the sun on my back, a shiver runs down my spine at the mere mention of his name. 'As far as I know, he's been charged with abduction and attempted murder. His lawyer is pleading diminished responsibility.'

Mei frowns. 'What does that mean?'

I screw up the crust of bread in my hand and let the crumbs drop to the ground. 'That he supposedly wasn't of sound mind when he was under the control of a religious cult leader.' I glance sideways at her. '*Meaning*: he isn't wholly to blame for his actions.'

Mei looks shocked. 'But he'll still go to prison, right?'

'I guess so,' I reply with a shrug. 'A young offender institution probably.'

'Good,' says Mei firmly, throwing the last of her bread to the birds. 'As long as he's no longer a threat to you. And with that creepy Tanas guy dead too, you needn't worry about him either.'

No, I don't, I think. *Not in this life at least.*

46

'Come on – hurry up!' says Dad, urging me out of the back seat of his silver Volvo.

'What's the rush?' I ask, almost breathless as he hustles me across the underground car park towards the lifts. Having got me up early, he bundled me into the car and fought his way through the morning traffic, but wouldn't say where we were going, or why, and I was half-asleep most of the way so have no idea where we are.

'You'll see,' he replies, stabbing impatiently at the button to call the lift.

As soon as the doors open, he ushers me inside. I stand nervously next to him as we ascend to the second floor. He appears anxious, wringing his hands and swaying ever so slightly on the balls of his feet. There's a strained smile on his face whenever he glances at me, but he won't hold my questioning gaze. It's as if he's excited about something . . . but equally afraid. I wonder what on earth's going on.

The doors ping open and we're greeted by a bustling scene of excited travellers, tanned holidaymakers, weary business executives, smiling flight attendants and overloaded luggage trolleys. Queues of passengers wait impatiently at automated check-in desks, and huge screens display the international and domestic flights departing that morning from Heathrow Terminal 3.

I stare at my father, bemused and somewhat suspicious. 'What are we doing *here*?' I ask as he leads me through the crowd. 'Are we going on holiday?'

I feel a ripple of excitement. Aside from counselling sessions and seeing Mei a couple of times, I've been pretty much housebound for the past fortnight, not even being allowed to go to school.

Dad shakes his head. 'Sorry, not this time.'

'Then why are we here?'

He smiles broadly. But then his grin falters ever so slightly and once again I'm struck by how anxious he is.

'I'll admit . . . your mum wasn't in full agreement with me on this,' he explains, swallowing his unease. 'To be honest, I'm questioning the entire plan myself. Yet considering how upset you've been and how grateful we should be as parents, I decided you should at least have the chance.'

Dad comes to an abrupt halt at the departure security gate and steps aside. He nods to the police officer who guards a tall athletic boy in denim jeans, a white T-shirt and black leather jacket. The faintest signs of bruising colour his high cheekbones and a small scar marks his lower lip. He leans upon a crutch, but appears strong enough to stand without it. Happier and healthier than when I last saw him, his waves of chestnut-brown hair hang easily to his shoulders and his sapphire-blue eyes shimmer with traces of starlight.

I stare at Phoenix a full minute, unable to believe he's standing there right in front of me. I didn't think I'd ever see him again! I glance over at my father and mouth, *Thank you*, and his previously tense smile relaxes. Just my beaming expression is enough to tell him he's done the right thing.

Phoenix looks equally thrilled to see me, his eyes never leaving mine. Then my world flips and –

We're standing together on the platform of a busy train station. I'm in a nurse's white pinafore apron and dress, my blond hair tied up in a bun; he's in full khaki army uniform, his beret in hand, a canvas backpack slung over his shoulder. Steam billows around us and I can hear the tearful goodbyes of several other couples.

'Do you have to go?' I ask Harry, as he opens the door to the waiting carriage.

He nods gravely. 'You know I do. They're enlisting every soldier. Word is we're going for the Big Push!'

I grab his hand. 'I realize there's a war to be won,' I whisper under my breath, 'but what about our *war? What about the Incarnates?'*

'In some ways, with this world war, they're one and the same,' he replies, a weary look of resignation on his face. Then he puts on a smile and plants a kiss upon my cheek. 'But my duty is done here.'

I gaze at him, tears welling as the soft press of his lips fades from my skin. 'So we'll never see each other again?' I ask, my heart bruising at the thought.

The loud blast of a whistle interrupts his reply and the train prepares to depart. With a final embrace, Harry clambers aboard, before turning and throwing me a last kiss.

'Never say never,' he calls as the carriage pulls away in a cloud of steam –

The Glimmer vanishes like smoke before my eyes and I find myself back in the airport terminal with all its chaotic hustle and bustle as travellers dash for their flights. In the midst of this constant stream of passengers, I realize I'm standing like a startled deer, still staring at him.

'Phoenix!' I cry, and I run into his open arms.

He winces slightly at my embrace. 'Careful,' he wheezes. 'I'm still healing.'

I ease off from my hug but he continues to hold me close a little longer, his arms wrapped round me like a safety net. In his presence I'm aware of feeling *whole* again. Reunited with a key part of me. I pull back and gaze into his eyes, once more experiencing that strange yet familiar magnetism of souls.

'How are you doing?' I ask as he adjusts his weight on the crutch.

'Good,' he replies, his grin sincere but with a touch of bravado. 'The doctors tell me I was very lucky. My knee had a torn ligament but no fracture or break, and the stab wound to my stomach missed any vital organs. I should be fully fit within a few months, with the right rest and care.' He takes me by the hand. 'But, more importantly, how are *you* doing?'

With the Second World War Glimmer fresh in my mind – convincing me yet again that I *have* lived before – I reply, 'I'm OK . . . but no one believes me about my past lives or that you're my Soul Protector.'

Phoenix tenderly brushes a curl of hair from my face. 'Genna, it doesn't matter if they do or they don't. What matters is that you're no longer being hunted. You're safe in this life now.'

I nod, comforted by his words. 'But I still need you by my side. I feel lost without you,' I admit. 'Only *you* understand what I've been through.'

His eyes soften with a sad tenderness, beneath which is a bittersweet look of acceptance, an understanding that this moment has played out before and that he already knows the outcome. And deep down I know it too.

'The paths of our lives appear to separate at this time,' he says gently. He rests the palm of his hand upon my chest, exactly where the Guardian Stone lies. 'But I'll never be far from you.'

My heart melts at his words, yet aches at his imminent departure. 'How will I get in touch with you?' I say. 'Do you have a mobile number? Email?'

Phoenix sadly shakes his head. 'You know what I said about technology – I don't trust it.'

'So where are you going now?'

'Back home, I hope.' He glances over at the police officer. 'As long as the authorities allow me to.'

'And where is home exactly?' I press.

He frowns slightly. 'I've had many homes in this life, but I guess Flagstaff, Arizona, is home. That's where I was born. Or I might hang out at the beach in LA. The sun and surf will do me good.'

'You surf?' I ask, intrigued to gain some small insight into his life prior to finding me.

'A little,' he replies modestly.

'Did you learn in a past incarnation?'

Smiling, he shakes his head. 'No, in this one. Although I'm not sure how this particular skill will help me protect you in a future life, unless Tanas comes back as a shark, I guess!'

I laugh, free and easy, for the first time in a long while, and I realize how relaxed I am with Phoenix. How secure I feel in his presence, even when there's no longer any threat. We continue to talk like the old friends that we are, with me asking most of the questions, keen to find out as much as possible about him so I can picture him living in America when he's gone. But the short time we have together seems to tick by in a matter of seconds and the police officer is all too soon tugging on Phoenix's arm.

'Final boarding has been called,' the officer tells him.

'No!' I beg, not wanting to let my Soul Protector go. I look to Phoenix in desperation. 'Will I *ever* see you again?'

'Of course you will,' Phoenix replies, smiling as he's escorted away through the security gate. 'If not in this life, then in the next.'

DON'T MISS
GENNA AND PHOENIX'S
NEXT THRILLING
ADVENTURE

THE SOUL PROPHECY

2022

READ ON FOR A SNEAK PEEK...

1

Los Angeles, present day

Siren wailing, lights flashing, the ambulance threads its way between the traffic as the sun sets over Huntington Park. Pulling sharply up at the kerbside, the vehicle's doors fly open and two paramedics leap out. They push through the knot of onlookers surrounding the body on the sidewalk.

A well-built man in a crisp suit and dark glasses has his hand pressed firmly against the casualty's chest. 'Alex has been shot!' he explains to the paramedics, blood seeping through his fingers. 'Lost consciousness a minute or so before you arrived.'

The first medic, a young woman with copper-red hair tied into an efficient ponytail, kneels down and sets to work assessing the casualty. 'Single entry and exit wound . . . nine-millimetre calibre round, at my guess . . . significant blood loss . . . Let's get some pressure bandages and vented seals on fast . . .'

The other paramedic, an older man with a trimmed beard and bald head, immediately tears open a packet of sterile dressings and tends to the wounds. Releasing his hold on Alex's chest, the suited man moves aside to allow the medics to do their job.

'Alex, can you hear me?' asks the pony-tailed paramedic, but she gets no response. Opening the casualty's airway, she checks for vital signs, while her partner inserts an IV drip and runs in vital fluids. 'Victim's no longer breathing,' she observes, and immediately commences CPR.

With a renewed urgency, the male medic pulls out a portable defibrillator from his med-bag and attaches a pair of electrode pads to the victim's chest. As soon as the unit powers up, the ECG monitor bleeps a rapid and erratic rhythm, its digital graph going haywire.

'Heart's gone into cardiac arrest,' he diagnoses, then as a light flashes red he warns, 'Stand clear!'

The female medic takes her hands away as the defibrillator delivers an electric shock. Alex's body jolts slightly but the graph on the ECG monitor continues to spike out of control ... before flatlining entirely. The paramedic immediately resumes CPR, all the while the heart monitor sounding its ominous drone ...

Alex watches this life-or-death struggle from above with an almost indifferent attitude – as if it was happening to someone else. In fact, it's the man in the tailored blue suit and sunglasses who seems more concerned at the outcome. He's talking rapidly into his mobile phone, an intense and troubled expression on his rugged face. What's his name? Clive, is it? ... no, not Clive, Clint!

But, unlike Clint, Alex no longer feels any pain, worries or cares. After all the struggles and stresses of life, this sense of detached calm is blissful . . . welcome even. The connection between body and soul now little more than a fine silver thread in the growing darkness.

As Alex observes the two paramedics working frantically to resuscitate their casualty, a bright, warm light appears at the end of a long tunnel. Drawn towards the light, Alex leaves the body lying sprawled on the sidewalk and glides away down the tunnel, the silver thread connecting soul to body becoming thinner and thinner . . .

'Administer an adrenaline shot! It's our last hope,' orders the pony-tailed paramedic, and her partner dives into his med-bag looking for the syringe.

'Hurry, or we're going to lose this patient for good!' she urges, her chest compressions and rescue breaths yielding little result.

In the background the wail of police sirens closes in from all directions.

Pulling the cap off the syringe, the male medic locates a suitable vein and injects the stimulant to kickstart the heart. But the drug seems to have no effect whatsoever . . .

The fraught scene on the sidewalk fades, the colours and sounds muting, until the two paramedics and their patient are little more than a silent black-and-white movie flickering in the distance. Alex drifts further and further along the tunnel, the celestial white light growing brighter and more vibrant with each passing moment.

But, as the end of the tunnel approaches, a long, spindly shadow blocks the light.

Alex hesitates, not recognizing the soul that has suddenly appeared. Hello? Do I know you?

No! *comes the sharp reply.* But you will do!

Moving with frightening speed, the shadow rushes forward, devouring all light and suffocating Alex's soul with its cloying darkness . . .

Back on the street, the two paramedics are forced to abandon CPR and declare the patient dead at the scene. The suited man swears and throws his phone to the ground in a fit of rage and grief.

Then, just as the male medic is disconnecting the defibrillator, a faint bleep sounds on the monitor.

'Hang on, we've got a heartbeat . . .'

Acknowledgements

So begins a new chapter in my life and for my loyal readers a new adventure! First let me thank *you*, good reader, for following me across to this series from Young Samurai and Bodyguard; and a big welcome to those new readers who are joining for the first time. I hope you enjoy this action-packed journey through the ages and are ready for the second book of the Soul Prophecy next year!

I must also express my eternal gratitude to Mary, to whom this book is dedicated. It's so wonderful to meet you again, old friend. Thank you for proving to me that my ideas are sometimes more fact than fiction; and for all your care, kindness and healing.

To my agent Charlie Viney, I give thanks for your constant and unwavering support and belief in my writing. This is *the* book series we've been working steadily towards!

My editor Emma Jones for her superb editorial eye, ideas and enthusiasm for *The Soul Hunters* – it's so good to be on the same wavelength; Sarah Hall for her incredible job honing and polishing the manuscript; Marcus Fletcher for his ever-accurate eye on the proofread; and of course my constant guiding star at Puffin . . . Wendy Shakespeare (you're not ever allowed to leave!).

Camilla Kenyon for managing all my events and school visits with such efficiency and dedication.

With special thanks to Philippa Luscombe and Andy Hitt for their specialist editorial advice on horse-riding and medical procedures. Also Pippa Le Quesne for her early input into the proposal.

A Marcela, por ayudar a sanar mi alma y mi corazón. Solo te deseo felicidad en esta vida.

To my dear mum and dad for their love, support, guidance, feedback and faith in all I do.

For my two boys, Zach and Leo, I know you both chose to be with me in this life and for that I am truly blessed. You are two of the brightest souls to shine in my life and I love you dearly with all my heart. I am and will always be your Soul Protector.

And, finally, thank you and love to my dear departed Nan, whose own story inspired this story . . .

See you all in another life!
Chris

Any fans can keep in touch with me and the progress of the Soul Prophecy series on my Facebook page, Twitter @YoungSamurai or via the website at www.thesoulprophecy.co.uk

A Deep Look into
Chris Bradford's Soul

Where did the idea for *The Soul Hunters* come from?
My nan. I always remember her telling me a story about
when she visited an old stately home for the first time, yet
she *recognized* the place. She knew her way around the
house and that there was a water closet (toilet) hidden
behind one of the walls. My nan was a very sensible, logical-
minded person, and the strange experience really threw her.
She had been there before, but not in that life.

Do you believe in past lives?
I am very open-minded to such ideas. I often meet people
with whom I have an instant and deep connection, and I
do wonder if I've perhaps met them in a past life. Who
knows? Whatever the case may be, I certainly believe in
the soul and that it is the essence of our being.

Has it been easy to write this book?
Writing is never easy. It always takes hard work, commitment
and inspiration. But this series has proven far harder to
write than Young Samurai and Bodyguard. The multiple

timelines, huge array of diverse characters and the numerous cultures I've had to get to grips with has meant each book is like writing a hundred books in one!

Who was your favourite character to write?
Genna, of course! This is my first action series with a female lead. My books have always included powerful, aspirational female characters, like Akiko in Young Samurai; and I wrote *Bodyguard: Target* with Charley in the lead role (that was my test run to establish whether I could write convincingly as a female protagonist!). The Soul Prophecy trilogy, though, is my first to follow the epic journey of a young girl from innocent schoolgirl to experienced warrior to world saviour! At least, I hope she can defeat Tanas . . .

What research have you done for this series?
I'm known for being a 'method writer'. So, for Young Samurai, I trained in martial arts and samurai sword fighting. For Bodyguard, I qualified as a professional body-guard and flew to Switzerland for firearms training. For Soul Prophecy, if I were truly 'method writing' I would need to die and come back in another life . . . which isn't particularly convenient when writing to a deadline! So, instead, I travelled extensively to experience first-hand some of the cultures featured in *The Soul Hunters* – from living with the Shona people in Zimbabwe, to trekking the Inca trail, to meditating in a Buddhist temple amid the mountains of Japan.

What's next for Phoenix and Genna? Can you give us a hint?
As my loyal readers know, I always like to turn my stories

on their head, such as in *The Ring of Earth*, the fourth book of the Young Samurai series, when Jack goes from being a samurai to learning about ninja. This means that in the second Soul Prophecy book Genna will quickly need to acquire some more past life skills in order to survive, since she won't always have her Soul Protector by her side . . . and he might even need her help!

Finally, a few quickfire questions . . .

Favourite book? *IT* by Stephen King – terrifying, all about childhood fears!

Favourite film? *Aliens* – because of how tough Sigourney Weaver is.

Favourite food? Steak and chips – I need the energy.

Favourite sport? Martial arts – currently Muay Thai kickboxing to stay fit.

Favourite saying? 'Seven times down, eight times up' – in life you must never give up!

About the Author

As an author, Chris Bradford practises what he terms 'method writing'. For his award-winning Young Samurai series, he trained in samurai swordsmanship, karate, ninjutsu and earned his black belt in Zen Kyu Shin Taijutsu. For his Bodyguard series, he embarked on an intensive close-protection course to become a qualified professional bodyguard. And for the Soul Prophecy trilogy, Chris travelled extensively to experience first-hand the cultures featured in the story – from living with the Shona people in Zimbabwe, to trekking the Inca trail, to meditating in a Buddhist temple amid the mountains of Japan. His bestselling books are published in over twenty-five languages and have garnered more than thirty children's book awards and nominations. Chris lives in England with his two sons.

To discover more about Chris, go to
www.chrisbradford.co.uk